M

APR 11, 1998

THE
KARNAU
TAPES

MARCEL BEYER

THE
KARNAU
TAPES

Translated from the German by
John Brownjohn

HARCOURT BRACE & COMPANY
New York   San Diego   London

© Suhrkamp Verlag Frankfurt am Main 1995
English translation copyright © 1997 by John Brownjohn

This is a translation of *Flughunde*.

Library of Congress Cataloging-in-Publication Data
Beyer, Marcel, 1965–
[Flughunde. English]
The Karnau tapes/Marcel Beyer; translated from the German
by John Brownjohn.
p.   cm.
ISBN 0-15-100255-X
I. Brownjohn, John.   II. Title.
PT2662.E94F5813   1997
833'.914—dc21   97-24782

Text set in Spectrum
Designed by Lori McThomas Buley
Printed in the United States of America
First edition
A C E D B

*"I hear the sweet little voices that are
dearer to me than anything else in the world.
What a precious possession!
May God keep it safe for me!"*

THE
KARNAU
TAPES

CHAPTER

1

A voice punctures the dawn stillness: "For a start, get those signs up. Hammer the posts in good and deep, the ground's soft enough. Hard as you can, the signs mustn't sag."

The Scharführer's commands ring out across the stadium. He aims a finger at several boys in swastika armbands, who detach themselves from the rest and set to work. All have been freshly shorn down to ear level, to the point where the shiny skin of their clean-shaven necks begins. They look like puppy dogs with stubble. If they had ears and tails, they'd be docked for good measure. That's the way our youngsters are reared these days.

"Get cracking on those ramps for the wheelchair attendants—the boardwalks, so all the cripples can be wheeled into the front few rows. I don't want any of them getting stuck in the mud if the rain comes down any harder."

The rest of the Scharführer's minions stand stiffly at attention, not even shivering in the dank air. Weary, ghostly figures, they're alert to every gesture and word of command that emanates from their Hitler Youth troop leader in his sodden brown uniform.

"Six of you, take the line markers and lay down some parallel lines along the boardwalks for the guide dogs to follow. Distance between the lines, sixty centimeters precisely: the width of one man's shoulders plus dog."

This is a war of sound. The Scharführer's voice slices into the gloom, carries as far as the platform. The acoustics here are odd. Six microphones are required in front of the speaker's desk alone, four of them for the batteries of loudspeakers aimed at the stadium from all angles. The fifth, which serves to pick up special frequencies, will be adjusted throughout the speech to bring out certain vocal effects. The sixth is hooked up to a small loudspeaker beneath the desk and can be controlled by the orator himself.

Additional microphones are installed at a radius of one meter to create a suitably stereophonic effect. Positioning these is an art in itself. They're concealed inside the floral decorations and behind the flag, so the audience can't spot them from below. But they must also be invisible to the guard of honor and the Party bigwigs seated behind the speaker's back. Where are the stadium's blind spots, acoustically speaking? Where will the sound waves break on the listening ranks to best effect? Will any stray sounds be deflected and unexpectedly rebound on the speaker himself? No one really knows if our calculations are correct. There are numerous doubtful areas, but they're only vaguely indicated on the ground plan.

Of special importance to the general effect is a microphone mounted in the Party emblem suspended overhead. This precludes any loss of volume when the speaker projects his words at the sky. The night is over, but it's still dark out here. Raindrops are falling from the outsize swastika above me. One lands on my upturned face.

Down in the stadium the marshals are receiving their instructions. "All the amputees are to be wheeled in first. Double smartly across the field and keep to the lines, utmost care essential while pushing the wheelchairs. No collisions, so watch it!"

The leading wheelchair attendants come trotting in, barely visible through the pall of mist that enshrouds the stadium. They double across the field, each pushing an empty wheelchair ahead of him. The whole procedure will be rehearsed several times more before noon to ensure that the World War One cripples and other disabled veterans are paraded without a hitch. Chairs have been ranged along the boardwalks to represent the audience during rehearsals. One boy slips on the wet planks and crashes into this barrier, wheelchair and all. He earns himself an immediate tongue-lashing: "You useless blithering idiot! Do that this afternoon and you're in for it. One little goof and you'll be on punishment parade. All right, once more from the beginning. Back into the tunnels, all of you, then out across the field in double-quick time."

The way that Scharführer bullies his underlings... How can they meekly endure his strident bellowing so early in the day? Do they knuckle under and submit to such humiliation, do they grit their teeth and tolerate the sound of his domineering adolescent voice because it makes them feel they're part of a movement in which they themselves will grow up to be just as domineering? Is it their firm belief that a similar organ will implant itself in their youthful throats as time goes by?

My gaze lingers on the luckless bungler as he doubles off, surreptitiously rubbing his knee and elbow. I turn up my overcoat collar. The clammy material adheres to my Adam's apple and gives me gooseflesh. My fingers are cold, so cold and stiff they can hardly hold the cigarette I'm smoking. The men with the cable drums appear. They thread their way through the retreating youngsters and make for the platform. Someone must have a word with the man in charge of the design team before the cables are laid up here. That's because the oak leaf arrangement he's planning must be used to camouflage them. All the cables must be carefully taped aside and led beneath the platform through holes in the floor. The speaker will want to come down and mingle with his audience after addressing them, so nothing must get in his way.

They're already installing the lights. We sound engineers are running a little late. The Scharführer, too, is becoming edgy because the blind veterans' entrance has presented unforeseen problems and his boys are getting into a lather.

"Apply wheelchair brakes! Amputees to stay exactly where they are. After them will come the blind plus their guide dogs trained to follow the white lines. Canes to be carried under the arm. They're not to make contact with the ground until all the blind are in position."

A few blind men have actually been rounded up to help rehearse this procedure, but they keep blundering into their Alsatians. Many of them become entangled in the leads and nearly fall headlong in the mud. Young dogs stray off the boardwalk or stand there looking bewildered. The Scharführer rallies his youngsters with a note of panic in his voice: "Those white lines—thicken them up! Go over them again at once, two or three times. The brutes can't see a thing in this light."

One of the blind men pauses in the beam of a spotlight, warming himself in its glow. His dog tugs at the lead, but the man refuses to budge. The harsh glare is reflected in his dark glasses and bounces off the tinted lenses, straight into my eyes.

"All the dogs know their places. Procedure as follows: they're to park the blind and then turn, but not on the spot, not back the way they came. Around the front and then out, rear rank first, front rank last."

The blind veterans are to listen to the speaker in a relaxed pose, and their dogs would only spoil the picture. Besides, the press photographs must mitigate any impression of frailty in favor of strength and martial fervor. Everyone is more or less lined up at last. For the past week the blind have devoted one hour a day to practicing the correct execution of the Hitler salute. Now, however, as they raise their right hands, a horrific sight meets the eye: some arms are parallel to the ground, others point almost vertically at the sky, and one or two are extended so far to the side that they brush the faces of their owners' next-door neighbors. The Scharführer has recovered his voice, and words of command ring out in quick succession: "Up! Down! Up! Down!"

The Hitler Youth boys kneel to adjust the blind men's arms until they're neatly aligned. A technician reports the loudspeakers in position and the cables laid. The microphones can now be hooked up. Someone in the distance gives me a wave: the power is on. Who's going to try out the sound? Not me, definitely not. In any case, the Scharführer renders any sound test abortive: "Last of all, march in the deaf-mutes! The deaf-mutes won't be able to cheer the Führer, so they'll have to stand at the very back."

The Hitler Youth boys exchange uncertain glances. Two of them, I notice, are actually whispering. The deaf-mutes... Here they come, emerging from the tunnel. Or maybe they aren't deaf-mutes at all, those men crossing the running track with resolute steps. Has the Scharführer got it wrong? Aren't they simply guests of honor? No, this must indeed be the heralded arrival of the contingent of men unfit for military service. What a spectacle they make in the half-light of dawn, conversing in their esoteric sign language and attired in weird, absurdly starched and well-pressed uniforms beaded with raindrops—fancy-dress uniforms, given that none of those wearing them could ever serve in the armed forces.

What are we to do with them, we sound engineers? They won't be able to follow the text of this afternoon's speech, but the gigantic public address system will set up continuous vibrations in their bodies. Even if they can't grasp the meaning of the sounds, we can set their innards churning. We adjust the public address system accordingly: higher frequencies for the cranial bones, lower for the abdomen. The sounds must be made to penetrate the darkness deep inside them.

Some SS men are sighted in the stadium, come to check on the progress of preparations. The Hitler Youth boys seem intimidated by their black uniforms. The glances they exchange differ from the ones that preceded the entry of the deaf-mutes. Leather boots, waterproof capes—even the faces in the shadow of the peaked caps are only dimly visible against the pale, misty background. But now, as luck would have it, the Scharführer has his invalids neatly drawn up. All are in position, medals tinkling faintly. There follows a trial run-through. The Scharführer gives vent to a few words at the speaker's desk. He bellows them in emulation of his Führer's characteristic delivery, subjecting the public address system—and his voice—to maximal strain.

Isn't he aware that every shout, every utterance of such volume, leaves a minuscule scar on the vocal cords? Aren't they aware of this, the people who so brutally erode their voices and subject them to such reckless treatment? Every such outburst imprints itself on the overtaxed vocal cords, steadily building up scar tissue. Marks of that kind can never be erased; the voice retains them until silenced forever by death.

The stadium shakes. My body shrinks and contracts. Or does it? Hasn't it simply been compressed into a rigid mass by sound waves? Putting your hands over your ears is forbidden, not that it would do any good: the din is enough to drive the marrow from your bones. Air masses are churning around with undreamed-of force. Meantime, the little band of supernumeraries in the arena stands there spellbound.

As soon as the sonic pressure ceases the deaf-mutes raise their right arms and open their mouths like everyone else. This creates a homogeneous impression, but whereas a loud *"Sieg Heil!"* rings out from the first few ranks, all that can be heard at the rear is a chorus of faint, laborious croaks. Next, standing in for the speaker, an SS officer inspects the front rank. The veterans, whose outstretched arms and sightless eyes are directed at nothing, stare past him into space as he grasps one upraised hand and gives it an appreciative shake. Simultaneously, the band strikes up a march.

My job is done. On the way out I see a bunch of deaf-mutes loitering some distance from the parade. Wearily shuffling from foot to foot, they smoke and converse in sign language under the paling sky. Like bats, their hands flutter silently in the limbo between day and night.

One of them puts two fingers to his lips, then jabs his arm in the air. Does the vehemence of that gesture carry some special force? Is it the equivalent, in a deaf-mute, of speaking loudly? If so, what form does a quiet, diffident remark assume? That man with his head bowed—should the tremors that run through his limbs be construed as a message to the others? What if they themselves are trembling so much in the dank morning air that they don't even notice? Trembling alone may mean something, but it's no substitute for sound.

Deaf-mutes are unrecognizable, whereas amputees can be recognized at a glance. The blind, too, can be identified by their dark glasses, by their canes and hesitant gait, by the lifeless gaze or empty eye sockets revealed when they raise their glasses to scratch their noses or wipe the sweat from their eyelids. But deaf-mutes defy recognition. Even if a deaf-mute fails to react when addressed, you may mistake him for a naturally taciturn person or assume that he simply hasn't heard you.

All these men incapable of speech, what expelled the voice from their bodies before birth? What do they have inside them, these voiceless ones? What resonates within them if they can detect no sounds, if they cannot hear voices even in their imagination? Is it ever possible to fathom what goes on inside such people, or does a lifelong void prevail there? We know nothing about deaf-mutes, nor can we vocal creatures elicit anything about their world. Yet these men have plenty to say to each other as I, unnoticed, walk past them. One deaf-mute's gesticulations break in on another's, and their flying hands fail to keep up with the sheer urgency of their conversation.

As for me, I'm a person about whom there's nothing to tell. However hard I listen inwardly, I hear nothing, just the dull reverberation of nothingness, just the febrile rumbling of my guts, perhaps, from deep within the abdominal cavity. It isn't that I'm unreceptive to impressions, or apathetic, or inattentive to the sights and sounds around me. On the contrary, I'm overly alert—alert as my dog and constantly aware of the slightest changes in sound and lighting. Too alert, perhaps, for anything to lodge in my mind because my senses are already perceiving the next phenomenon. I'm like the colored leader affixed to the beginning of an audiotape: no matter how hard you listen, you can't hear a sound, however insignificant.

My dog is an example to me, not a mere companion. As soon as Coco hears me coming he gets excited, knows who will be entering the house when the gate is unlocked down below, recognizes the way my soles scuff the worn stairs, knows exactly how the banisters creak when I lean on them, thrusts his nose into the crack beneath the apartment door and inhales his master's scent, scrabbles at the handle with his paws, jumps up at me with his ears pricked when the door finally opens; then, and only then, does he hear me speak his name. That's what one has to learn to do in the acoustic hinterland: to listen to the state of the air an instant before the first word is uttered.

A belch. Someone sitting near me in the tram has belched, and the hairs on my neck bristle even before the nature of the sound sinks in. I scan the reflections in the window for the passenger in question—it has to be a man somewhat older than myself—and there, two seats behind me, I dimly make out a gargoyle of a face intent on an open newspaper as if nothing has happened, though the belch was so loud that all the other passengers must have heard. If it happens again I'll have to look for an empty seat up front. Many people seem determined to tyrannize their fellow creatures in this way. This is a war of sound, yes, but where are the war correspondents? Unprovoked assaults like these should be reported and repulsed.

I look upon myself as I might regard a deaf-mute: not a sound to be heard, and even my gestures are unintelligible. Pushing thirty, and I'm still a smooth, blank wax disc when others have long since been engraved with countless grooves, when their discs already hiss or crackle because they've been played so often. No discernible past and no events worth mentioning, nothing in my memory that could help to constitute a story. Nothing there save a few isolated images or, rather, specks of color. No, not even that: just a gray-and-black iridescence, a twilight zone, a brief moment sandwiched between night and day.

Once, when the whole class had turned out for compulsory physical training in the gloom of a winter's morning, we heard a strange sound coming from the gymnasium roof, and when the teacher turned on the lights we saw something black flitting around in the rafters. "A bat," said someone. It had probably strayed in not long before, desperately seeking a safe place in which to hibernate, and now it had been disturbed, first by a horde of noisy youngsters and then by the lights. While my classmates continued to horse around I stood stock-still, as though my solitary silence could drown the others' din and soothe the agitated creature. I even hoped that the class would be postponed and the bat left in peace until spring. But gym shoes were already being hurled at it, and one boy, who had brought along a ball, handed it to the best marksman in the class. He flung it with all his might and only just missed. The thud of the impact was drowned by warlike yells. He took aim and threw the ball again and again, and someone kept running to retrieve it for him while the bat fled to and fro. All that brought this scene to an end was a loud call to order from the gym teacher, who wanted to get on with the class.

The bat's trembling body and helplessly fluttering wings lingered in my mind's eye all morning. The black creature's after-image persisted, and I failed to fade it out and replace its hysterical gyrations with the freewheeling flight of flying foxes in the wild as illustrated in my album of cigarette cards. As soon as I got home I turned to the page I'd opened so often that it was dog-eared and grimy. I can still see it now, that African scene: a bare-branched tree starkly outlined against a red sunset with a cluster of black creatures hanging from it upside down, and, circling in the air overhead, a few flying foxes awakened by the approach of night, soon to fly off to their feeding tree, guided there by the scent of night-flowering plants. Nocturnal creatures. Night: the unfolding of a world in which there are no warlike cries, no gymnastics. Come, dark night, enshroud me in shadows.

I'm soaked to the skin and thoroughly hoarse, even though I exchanged barely half a dozen words with my colleagues at the stadium. I'm back on inside duties for the next few days— stupid little chores, for the most part, though the man whose office I share prefers them to working in the field. I can't think why he's a sound engineer at all, when he could be compiling endless lists of statistics for any number of firms. Who cares whether the public address system we installed this morning generates its exact quota of decibels, or whether it displays some minor deviations from the norm? But that's just the kind of donkey work that appeals to my officemate: ascertaining whether the values recorded in laboratory experiments precisely correspond to those attained in field trials. He's quite uninterested in the sounds themselves, in fact it seems to me that paperwork is his way of avoiding the world of sound with which he would come into contact, willy-nilly, in the field or the laboratory. I'm not going back to the office today. The parade doesn't take place till after lunch, so the relevant figures won't, in any case, be available till late this evening.

The morning mist has dispersed, but my room is still filled with lingering shadows. Birdsong and cold, soupy air drift through the small window and the balcony door, which are wide open. My desk is littered with papers, writing materials and books—dusty appurtenances all, since I seldom touch them. A space has been cleared in the midst of the clutter. This is where the gramophone resides, permanently within reach, so that I can put on a record without having to get up. It occupies the only dust-free area on the desktop, for dust is lethal: it kills every sound. Not that I can listen to any records at the moment. They've been lying untouched in their cardboard box and faded paper sleeves for quite a while. This is because the gramophone, dismantled into its separate components, has been consigned to the floor with its works spilling out. A fault in the drive mechanism. The driving band or the motor itself?

We all bear scars on our vocal cords. They take shape in the course of a lifetime, and every utterance, from the infant's first cry onwards, leaves its mark there. Every cough, every scream or hoarse croak disfigures the vocal cords with another nick, ridge, or seam. We're unaware of these scars because we never set eyes on them, unlike the furrows we notice in our tongues or the ominous areas of inflammation we see when peering deep into our throats. Yet everyone is familiar, if only from hearsay, with the symptoms of excessive vocal strain: the nodules, polyps and fistulas to which singers are prone. Our vocal cords deserve to be treated with extreme care. By rights, we should scarcely utter a word.

Very few voices are free from scars and simply coated with a soft, delicate network of veins. Small wonder that the impalpable something called the soul—the molded breath of life that constitutes the human being—is thought to reside in the human voice. So the scars on our vocal cords form a record of drastic occurrences and acoustic outbursts, but also of silence. If only we could explore them with our fingers, if only we could trace their routes, cessations and ramifications. There, hidden away in the darkness of the larynx, is the autobiography that you yourself can never read.

You merely sense, without knowing why, how it manifests itself: when your mouth goes dry from one moment to the next, when your throat becomes constricted, when breathlessness assails you for no apparent reason and all that issues from your lungs is nothing. Why, for instance, while I'm waiting to purchase a spare part for my gramophone, do shivers run down my spine when the electrical appliance shop is invaded by a young woman whom I can hear loudly talking to herself even before she comes in at the door? Her muddled monologue changes tack: she proceeds to harangue the dumbstruck customers in a hoarse voice, catches each eye in turn and complains of having to wait three weeks for her radio to be repaired. What do I detect in her voice that makes me recoil? Why do I even find my own voice repugnant—yes, mine above all? I've no idea. I stare at the demented woman, who, stung by our lack of response, speaks even louder: "I want to hear my beloved Heinz Rühmann again. They ought to broadcast his songs all day long, not victory fanfares and rubbish like that."

Then, to crown it all, she herself breaks into song, belts out a few bars from a popular hit. Her voice quavers and breaks. She starts again from the beginning, but no one protests. The other customers seem wholly unaware of how her dreadful voice is boring its way into every nerve cell. Am I the only one to perceive this bloodcurdling sound—a sound that hammers on the temporal bone and sets up vibrations throughout my skull? It's as if I'm the only one who's wide awake at dead of night when an air raid is imminent, when bombs are already raining down and there's no safe cellar within reach. Next, the woman buttonholes an elderly man and thrusts her face into his: "Guess what? I bumped into Santa Claus just now. We made a date for next Thursday. How often have *you* bumped into Santa Claus like that?"

The old man doesn't bat an eyelid. I couldn't do that. She's committing an assault, after all, like the man who belched in the tram this morning. Now her torrent of words hisses close by my ear: "Got to go home soon, my teddy bear's all alone, he needs his oats and his straw."

Quite suddenly, before you know it, you're in the aural front line. Just erase it. Erase it all.

I don't know the origin of my profound aversion to crude, overwrought vocal phenomena. Or the reason for my predilections. Why do I feel so infinitely serene when I sit down beside my gramophone of an evening—at dusk, the twilight hour when none of the lights in the apartment has yet been switched on—and hold one of those black shellac discs in my hands? On the central portion, just between the label and the innermost groove, each disc bears an inscription in an unknown hand: technical particulars such as a serial number and a note indicating which side is which, but also, in many cases, brief, anonymous messages secreted there by the recording engineer.

I put the first side on. The turntable begins to rotate, the gramophone is back in commission. The silence in the apartment would soon have become intolerable. I lower the tone arm, and at once I hear the hiss that precedes the recording itself. Then: a baritone voice. How it vibrates, how it ruffles the air! I shall always find it inexplicable that a recorded voice—just the fluttering of someone else's vocal cords—should have such power to stir the emotions. Coco sits down beside me and we listen together.

The needle leaves its trail across the shiny black shellac,

painfully probing and imperceptibly eating away the grooves with every revolution, as if its purpose were to delve deeper and draw nearer to the origin of the sounds. Every playing of the record erodes a little of its substance, an amalgam of resin, soot, and the waxy deposits of the lac insect. Living creatures made their contribution to the disc. Their secretions were compressed so that sound could become matter, just as the sounds engraved on the disc are themselves secretions and vital signs of human origin.

Black is an essential additive. Only with the aid of black, the color of night and burning, can sounds be captured. Unlike writing or painting, in which color is applied to a white ground without injuring it, the capturing of sound requires one to damage the surface, to incise the recording agent with a cutting stylus. It is as if the most transient, fragile phenomena demand the harshest treatment and can only be captured by means of a deleterious process.

And then the singing dies away, the song is at an end. The tone arm, having reached the end of the recording, is firmly lodged in the escape groove. It emits a loud click every time the needle jumps back and re-embarks on the same circular journey.

I look through some new, still unheard recordings. Not on sale anywhere, they're rare items from our sound archive. That's one of the few perquisites of my job: access to our collection of special recordings. I often trawl the card index for interesting material after office hours. Almost anything can be heard, strange sounds of almost every conceivable kind have been engraved on wax: bird calls, wind of every type and strength, rushing water and avalanches, passing cars and machinery in operation—even the noise made by a large building as it collapses. Discs of this kind were not cut for the listener's pleasure. They're used for experimental purposes when testing acoustic recording and playback equipment in the laboratory.

Most of these pressings are unique. I've brought home some recordings of speech, but also some unusual sounds of human origin. I'm even fonder of the voice alone than of singing with instrumental accompaniment. The quivering glottis and the operation of the tongue can be heard far more clearly when the organ lies naked and exposed to the ear. Purely on the strength of a voice, these records conjure up an entire person in the mind's eye. Like an archaeologist examining a potsherd, one can use a tiny fragment to form a picture of the whole. All one has to do is to listen closely, nothing more.

It's also exciting when, having first heard a voice on the telephone and mentally provided it with a body, we meet the owner in person and are able to compare the fruits of our imagination with reality. The result tends to be disappointing, however: people in the flesh are far less interesting than their voices lead one to suppose. I must study the subject more closely. I must develop an even keener ear and listen to every nuance if my mental image is ever to match a person's actual appearance.

I play a record of sneezing, throat-clearing and breathing. Meanwhile, Coco insists on being patted. He presses against me, rubs his soft, tremulous flank against my leg. Is it the sounds that prompt him to act this way? He jumps up on my lap, exuberantly licks my hands, refuses to be deterred by my feigned indifference. Finally I give in: I fondle him, tweak the fur between his ears. His moist nose thrusts itself into my palm. He can hear better than any human being with those furry ears of his. In daylight one can look deep inside them and follow their pink convolutions down into darkness. I tickle Coco's throat, and he instantly raises his head as far as possible to give my hand free rein. I palpate the hard canine larynx with my fingers. This is the spot from which sounds emanate; this is where the source of the voice resides, beneath that gristly protective shield.

I run my hand over Coco's skull. Where is his sense of hearing located? Where is the capacity for generating sounds rooted in his canine brain? The shape of the skull and its bumps and indentations enable one to infer the site of certain regions of the brain, so Professor Joseph Gall discovered at the end of the eighteenth century. To Gall, every head was a cerebral map. If deaf-mutes had their heads shaved, for example, he could diagnose the nature of their disability by sight, without having been told anything about them beforehand. Professor Gall's observations filled whole phrenological atlases.

Only by keeping a record could one guard against the intrusion of distorted sounds. The nature of the human voice is such, however, that this record would be no more than a few cursory sketches of vocality comprising a few jagged lines scrawled on paper so as to define the hearers' location. It would merely be the rudiments, perhaps, of a map on which the bottom left corner, at most, displays a few faint lines devoid of an established scale, together with a few equally faint dots that do little to assist one's orientation. Where is one, in any case? In what area, since the map lacks a key?

Coco has curled up on my lap and gone to sleep. The record comes to an end. Without getting up, I open the balcony door and continue to sit there for the time it takes to smoke a cigarette. A very clear, cold night. In air such as this, every external sound penetrates the innermost recesses of the ear: a horse-drawn cart, footsteps slowly receding. No, Coco isn't really asleep, or not deeply so. His ears always twitch an instant before I myself hear something.

I'm planning a map on which even the most insignificant human sounds must be recorded. For example, a practice common to many smokers: the violent expulsion of air between slack lips. A half-casual, half-voluptuous habit, it makes a disgusting sound that irritates me to death and provokes an involuntary urge to strangle the author of such repellently tuneless whistling. But I'd always be far too much of a coward to commit such an act, however justified. Too much of a coward even to rebuke the offender or to point out, very politely, that he's being a nuisance. I'm not equal to hand-to-hand combat—in fact I wouldn't even dare to clear my throat in an admonitory way. Those Hitler Youth boys this morning, perhaps *they* will be capable, when they grow up, of doing such things without turning a hair. Doubtless they will, if they can already bring themselves, as children, to get out of bed on a cold, dark morning for the sole purpose of sweating at their Scharführer's behest. It's lucky for someone like me that I grew up in the days before the Third Reich: no parades, no sojourns in camp, no physical training followed by the masculine stench and clamor of a steamy changing-room, no supervised wet dreams.

The born coward fears everything on principle, even immersion in a group of equally bashful youngsters compelled to bare everything to the gaze of others, their half-aroused penises included. He dreads standing naked in the vaporous heat of the communal showers, dares not even peer between the others' legs for signs of pubescent fuzz. If only it weren't for the coarsely suggestive tone that seems so manifestly proper to those masculine voices. It can prompt a person to cut himself off from the rest because he simply can't bear to listen to it, and because it's inseparable from another tone of voice: the imperious, unambiguous, front-line organ from which all color has been leached. It's so easy for someone who has mastered the first tone of voice to switch, quite instinctively, to the other. Are we all in danger, sooner or later, of adopting that barrack-square tone? It may be that none of us can rid himself of the temptation—none of us, of course, save deaf-mutes, who are immune to it because that particular tone of voice is incapable of penetrating their consciousness. Professor Gall was a lonely child like me. It won him few friends when he noticed at the age of nine that the more pop-eyed of his schoolmates were exceptionally good at learning things by heart. Still, Gall was always surrounded by his skulls. He did at least have his family of death's-heads.

Like Gall, anyone intending to compile a map of all the vocal nuances must not be put off by his fellow men. Nor, like that master of craniometry, can he afford to be thought a coward. He mustn't shrink from the most extreme human utterances; must be there on the spot when danger looms in order to record any sounds that result; must not be deterred by the fact that many vocalizations sound far from pleasant, both to the hearer and to those who utter them. The listener must regard his subjects as sources of sound, nothing more; just sound sources and not, for example, painracked men in urgent need of assistance. I mustn't allow myself to be distracted from a collectable voice by such things as the brutal way in which the Scharführer abused his underlings, or the squalid conduct of the boor in the tram, or the behavior of the demented woman who pestered the old man with questions about Santa Claus and allusions to her teddy bear's diet. I mustn't be so preoccupied with deaf-mutes' strange gestures, either, that I fail to notice when one of them gives vent to an inarticulate sound. Even if I fly at the throat of someone who noisily exhales tobacco smoke, the effort involved in throttling him with my bare hands must not divert my attention from the sound of his last, dying gasp.

My vocal map will not be compiled in accordance with familiar rules or confined within predictable boundaries. It will not merely survey familiar terrain from a novel viewpoint, but display an area extraneous to every human cartographic domain. Implementing such a plan will require infinite patience. To capture a specific type of whimper it may first be necessary to make comparative recordings, for only then will my atlas cover all the nuances of that plaintive sound. It may be years before a related utterance from the lips of another sound source fills the last gap—indeed, a single human life-span may be far too short to accomplish this. An animal has to follow beaten tracks. We, being optical creatures convinced that all phenomena should be regarded in the same way forever—as our lifelong habits dictate—must do no such thing. We must persevere until, quite suddenly, the heavens burst open and the world of sound breaks over us with elemental force, reducing all that is familiar to ruins in the same way as the belch that startled me even though my ears should have accepted it simply for what it was: an occasion for making another entry on my map, which is still almost blank.

CHAPTER

2

Now there are six of us. My dream isn't over yet, it's pitch dark, the middle of the night, let me go on sleeping, stop shaking me, let go of me. So we've got a little sister, Heide, she's just been born, but that's no reason for us to get up now, in the middle of the night, we'll go and see her in the morning, as soon as it's light. Leave me alone, it isn't time for school yet, and there's no air raid on, there really isn't.

All that shaking has woken me up. She's gone again, taken the others to the bathroom with her. What time is it? Do we have to go down to the shelter? I'm still dreaming. Who turned the light on? The bed's nice and warm, the pillow's all squashy. Someone whispered, "Quick, get yourselves washed and dressed." Who was it? The nursemaid. I can hear her in the bathroom, talking quietly to the others. "They're coming to collect you," she said.

Collect? Why? Where are we going? To visit Mama in the hospital and see Heide? They'll be asleep at this hour. Has something happened? Mama has been in the hospital a whole month, she wasn't well, she was waiting for the baby all that time, she was always so sad when we saw her. And now it's a girl after all, not another boy the way Papa wanted. When Mama was allowed to visit us at home one afternoon, she and Papa talked about having another little son.

I peep through the crack in the curtains: still pitch dark outside, not a light anywhere, everything blacked out. It's so quiet, too early for birds or people. Any wind? Don't know, can't see the trees. Yes, there, a branch waving around just outside the window, but it's bare. That's not leaves rustling, it's water running in the bathroom. I can't hear anything else. The nursemaid's calling me: "Helga, pick out some toys, will you? Only one each, mind, that's all you can take with you."

I'd like to ask her what's up, but I'm too sleepy to talk. We never need to take any toys with us when we go to stay at our house at Schwanenwerder. And what are those two suitcases doing here, full of warm things? We've got plenty of clothes in all our houses. It's warm in the bathroom, the tiles are so steamed up you can hardly see across the room. The nursemaid's standing at the basin with Holde, but Holde won't open her mouth to have her teeth brushed. What's the point of the suitcases and all those clothes?

"You're going to spend a few days with a friend of your parents', he's waiting for you downstairs. Your mother's still too weak, she's got enough on her hands with Heide for the moment, and your father doesn't have time to look after the five of you, what with working till all hours and spending the night at his office or at Lanke and being away so often. Hurry up, all of you. Stop dawdling."

The others aren't listening, they're far too sleepy. Helmut's standing there in his undershirt, waiting to be washed. Hedda's rooting around in the pile of clothes and Hilde's gone to sleep again, sitting on the toilet. Nobody says anything. Holde's scratching her leg, she's got goose pimples all over. The nurse-maid is doing her braids.

It's cold in the nursery. Hilde and I can take the new dolls Papa brought us from Paris. He doesn't have much time to spare, it's true. Paris last week, then straight on to Vienna, and back here only two days ago. I rummage in the drawer for Helmut's soldiers and Holde's farm animals. Hedda never plays with anything but her rag doll in any case, it's still over there in her crib, underneath the warm bedclothes. The suitcases are full now, but if we're going to be away overnight we'll need our cuddly toys as well. Who is this friend of Mama and Papa? Have we ever seen him before? I don't want to go out in the dark this early. I'm cold now, I ought to get dressed but I'd sooner keep my nice warm nightie on a bit longer, not put on those nasty cold things.

Where is Papa, anyway? Isn't he going to say goodbye to us? Is he still asleep, or is he at the hospital with Mama? Maybe he drove out to Lanke yesterday evening, after his birthday party, and spent the night there. The nursemaid calls to me across the dark landing: "Finished, Helga? Then comb your hair neatly and go down to the drawing room, the gentleman's waiting for you in there. Say how do you do and tell him the others will be down right away."

Papa's bound to be downstairs, waiting to say goodbye to us and chatting with his friend. I stop to listen on the stairs, but I can't hear any voices from the drawing room, only plates clattering in the kitchen. Perhaps they're speaking quietly.

It's very dark in the drawing room, only one light on, the one on the coffee table. I can see someone's head over the back of the armchair. It's in shadow, but Papa's head is smaller and his neck is thinner, it must be his friend. I pause in the doorway: he doesn't move, he hasn't heard me sneaking down the stairs. I'm just about to turn around and tiptoe off to the kitchen when he stands up and looks at me, so he must have heard me. He says how do you do and introduces himself. His name is Herr Karnau. I thought he'd be much older, this friend of our parents'. How will such a young man manage to look after the five of us? He's looking very tired, too. He smiles at me in the gloom and says, "You're Helga, the eldest, right?"

I just nod and shake hands, then I go to the kitchen. I've never seen the man before, and Mama and Papa have never mentioned having such a young friend. The others appear in the kitchen one by one, last of all the nursemaid with Hedda, who's all clean and tidy. There's cocoa and bread and jam, but none of us can eat anything as early as this. We don't finish our cocoa and leave half-eaten slices of bread on our plates. The nursemaid fetches Herr Karnau from the drawing room. He says hello to us all, but the others just stare at him and say nothing.

Now we're standing in the hall with our coats and scarves on. The nursemaid tells Herr Karnau a few things to look out for, like we're not allowed to play on the floor or sit in a draft because we catch cold so easily—if one of us gets it the others do too, she says. Herr Karnau looks at us all in turn, then picks up Hedda and walks on ahead, out into the street. Papa's chauffeur has already loaded the suitcases. It isn't anything like as cold as the nursemaid thought, but it's drizzling, the rain is almost like mist, it glistens in the beam of the masked headlights. Papa hasn't come to say goodbye, and I'd have liked to ask him about Herr Karnau. A few cars are already driving along Hermann Göring Strasse. The air smells funny, like autumn leaves rotting, like porridge when the milk boils over.

Papa's chauffeur opens the door for us. We fit in the back,

all five of us. Hedda and Holde share the fold-down seat, they lie there and go on sleeping under a big woollen rug. Holde's head is propped against the cold windowpane; her hair quivers whenever the car goes over a bump. Herr Karnau looks back at us from the passenger seat and talks to Hilde and me in a low voice. We're sitting on the back seat with Helmut between us, he's resting his head on my lap and dozing with his eyes open. The rain is pattering on the roof, the windshield wipers are squeaking. The chauffeur doesn't speak, he's staring straight ahead through the windshield, which keeps steaming up. Herr Karnau has a dog at home, he says it's looking forward to seeing us. How did Herr Karnau know that Hilde loves animals more than anything in the world? Did he ask Mama and Papa about us? Quietly, so as not to wake the two little ones, he says: "Coco has black fur, it's specially soft on his neck, that's where he loves being tickled."

Hilde's wide awake in a flash. "Coco?" She giggles. "That's not a dog's name. Have *you* ever heard of a dog called Coco, Helga? We've had a red setter since the summer, but he's out at Schwanenwerder, not in town. His name is Treff, that's a proper dog's name."

But Hilde says she's sure Coco is a darling in spite of his funny name. The car comes to a stop and the chauffeur toots his horn twice. We wait until a woman comes out of the house where Herr Karnau lives. She pulls on a raincoat, then opens an umbrella. She's his housekeeper, Herr Karnau says, and she'll be helping to look after us while we're here. He doesn't have a wife, I suppose. Papa's chauffeur comes inside just long enough to deposit the suitcases in the hall, then he has to drive home. Now we're all alone in a strange apartment.

Coco really does have black fur, he romps around and wags his tail, sniffing at everything: our shoes, our coats and my hands, which tickles. Herr Karnau shows us our bedroom. We're all going back to bed to finish our sleep.

I lie beside Hedda on the sofa bed. Herr Karnau mustn't have thought of getting a crib for her, I suppose. Are the others asleep already? The bedclothes smell different from the ones at home. The pillow crackles when I rest my head on it and the blanket we have to share is too small. Hedda grumbles and clamps one end of it under her arm. The light goes out. Was that Herr Karnau? I hear him whispering to his house-keeper outside, the door's ajar and a strip of light falls across our bed.

Footsteps are going down the stairs. Someone says good night in a low voice—Herr Karnau's voice. He locks the front door and goes into his bedroom. It's pitch dark now that the strip of light has disappeared.

BREATHING REGULARLY, ALMOST silently, in the darkness, that's how they're sleeping in the room across the passage, and each child has a respiratory rhythm of its own, five different rhythms in concert. They weren't really awake on the way here, their slumbers were scarcely interrupted by our drive through the night, and they all went back to sleep at once. Now the apartment is filled with a faint, nocturnal sound that won't subside before morning, not until the five of them wake up. I've never before heard children breathing in their sleep; the only breathing I know is my own, before I drop off. A patter of paws on the floorboards. The door to the living room, the children's makeshift dormitory, is ajar. Unable to sleep for curiosity, Coco gently nudges it open with his nose. He'll now be sniffing my guests, I suspect, and carefully sampling their unfamiliar scent.

How those children stared at me earlier on. The girls had

their hair so neatly parted that strips of scalp showed through it like scars, and they all wore plaits. Who's going to braid their hair when they wake up late tomorrow morning, tousled and homesick?

Coco reappears, but he pauses at the head of the bed and plants his forepaws in front of my face, sniffing the covers as if his master, too, is a stranger now that there are strangers in the house. His moist, warm breath fans my nose. At last he jumps up, gingerly picks his way across my body and curls up between my legs. He heaves a noisy sigh. Nothing more for a long time, just the five children next door, clearly audible again. One of them, probably Helmut, gives a sudden, nervous cough. The others, their deep sleep disturbed, change position in turn: bedclothes rustle, someone sighs in the throes of a dream. Then the dog's breathing predominates again.

I'm the first to wake up. Nothing stirring anywhere. A curious silence prevails for a moment every morning, just before the noise of the day erupts. I glance into the darkened living room. The children are still in the depths of their nocturnal world. Dry, stale air. Peering through the gloom, I see that all the beds are rumpled. The blanket has slipped off the sofa bed onto the floor, one corner of it tightly clutched in Helga's arms. Little Hedda is lying alongside with her nightie rucked up, and a bare leg is dangling from Helmut's camp bed near the window. I quietly close the door, go to the kitchen and draw the curtains: a gray day after yet another night of blackout.

The war has lasted a year already. It's Wednesday, 30 October. Seven thirty, and not really light yet. The pigeons across the street are just waking up. They poke their heads out and do a little preening. Then they fluff themselves up again and thrust their beaks back into their plumage. Their sleeping quarters, the ledge between the tailor's shop on the ground floor and the first-floor windows, are white with glutinous droppings. I put the kettle on for my first coffee of the day. Do the children like malt coffee too?

I try to imagine how it would have tasted to me as a child, on my child's tongue. What flavor first filled my mouth, even before I cleaned my teeth? What was it, every morning, that ended the drought afflicting my gums overnight? I run my tongue around my mouth. It was a drink made with water, not milk, as far as I recall. Camomile tea? No, children don't like camomile tea, it's something you're made to drink when you're ill. Sleepily, I put an imaginary cup to my lips. It's filled with . . . rose hip tea, that was it, with plenty of sugar. So hot, the first sip used to burn my tongue.

I light my first cigarette. Unnoticed on their ledge, the pigeons are watching some passers-by on the pavement below them. They crane their necks to follow the progress of two dawdling schoolchildren. A woman, probably late for work, overtakes them in a hurry. So the children will have some hot, diluted fruit juice. But what about Hedda, the youngest? Perhaps she's used to hot milk? The five of them will be waking up in a stranger's home, so the least I can do is offer them their usual breakfast drink without having to ask them first. They may easily take fright unless I do, because the vague sense of menace inspired by my unfamiliar apartment—and, no doubt, by my unfamiliar person—will haunt them until they leave. I wonder if they like bread as early in the day as this?

My own favorite breakfast as a child was apple flan with a sugary glaze on top, straight from the baking tin, before daybreak, in a dimly lit kitchen, the teaspoon cold in my hand as I huddled there in my nightshirt. How long I always took to eat a slice of flan. So little of it would be gone by the time my parents were washed and dressed and standing there, ready to leave, that I had to take big bites and wolf them down. Either that, or it was wrapped up and put in the bread bin, and the rest would be waiting for me at supper that evening. And then, instead of a teaspoon, I'd find myself holding my father's hand, or my mother's, as I was towed along the dark street to kindergarten.

The way those children got up in the dark last night, at this time of year. Not a murmur from any of them. Are they already so inured to discipline? Helga and Hilde are hardly out of the nest and Helmut must be far too young for the Hitler Youth. Or are they irresistibly attracted, as I was at their age, to the early hours of the morning?

Eight o'clock will soon have come and gone, but I can still detect, in this dim light, a little of the sensation I used to have of being part of a night in whose clear air every footstep, every whispered word, re-echoed before vanishing without trace into the darkness. Every sound held some special significance: a bird chirping once or twice in its sleep; a sudden rustle of leaves as mice or hedgehogs foraged by the roadside, unaware that they would soon be overtaken by daylight and humankind. It was as if noises were created anew each morning; as if voices had first to be born in travail and refashioned at daybreak; as if night were entirely devoid of harsh cries, loud voices hailing each other across the street, and the peremptory tone of which so many people are capable—all acoustic impressions calculated to strike terror into a child; as if shouting had died away and even idle chatter could originate only in the light of the sun, after that brief respite during which my breath evaporated like warm mist in the chill of the night. That's how it was while the street was still deserted except for the few muffled figures I saw every morning, known to me only as sleepy silhouettes and not as the noisy, wide-awake people they doubtless became as the day wore on.

It wasn't within my power to prolong the darkness and make those strangers' voices sleep on while a parental hand continued to tow me through the residue of the night that would inevitably, menacingly, transmute itself into the world of imperious voices, of clamor and commotion. On I went, so firmly yanked along by that grown-up hand that I almost had to run to keep up with the adult beside me. It was as if I had to traverse that region as quickly as possible, as if passive surrender to light and noise—to the diurnal transformation of all those ghostly morning figures into figures with voices— were the only course open to me. Only the flying foxes in my album were exempt from this. They never flew in sunlight, only in the darkness that lent still further intensity to those black bodies, as if their wings had swallowed the last of the light. They alone could have preserved me from the day, enshrouding me in their soft wings and immersing me in lightlessness. Such was my morning world, so far divorced from the world of daylight that I could never have finished off my half-eaten slice of apple flan during the day. That could only be done in the evening, long after the return of darkness.

The row of pigeons comes to life at last. Another bird, which probably spent the night on this side of the street, lands on their ledge. Startled, they proceed to strut to and fro. One nearly tumbles off. It spreads its wings as it falls, flutters in my direction, and disappears from view overhead. Will it have occurred to my housekeeper to bring the children some pastries? I'm sure I gave her plenty of coupons. Children get special allocations, full cream milk for Hedda, genuine honey, butter too. Rationing has now been in force for over a year, but I still haven't grasped the various categories and entitlements. Where have my tobacco coupons gone again? Did she take them with her by mistake?

I pour boiling water on the coffee. Will we fit around the table, all six of us? Can Hedda feed herself yet, or will the housekeeper need a place too? One thing's for sure: she's so little she'll have to have a cushion on her chair or she won't be able to see across the table. The first of the pigeons glides down to the pavement. There goes another. They peck around in the gutter and waddle out into the roadway, undisturbed. Still no traffic at this hour.

I sit down at the table with my coffee and light another cigarette. Coco emerges from the bedroom. The invariable morning routine: first he briefly rests his head on my lap and asks to be fondled, as if to reassure himself that we still belong together after the intervening night. Then he trots around the kitchen and sniffs every corner: yes, it's still the same room as it was last night. Finally he watches the pigeons outside. They're now perched everywhere, on window sills, roofs, gutters. Everywhere except the ledge across the street, which is now deserted. Coco whimpers in frustration as the first flock circles above the rooftops before flying off. I can hear the children talking quietly in the room next door. Eight thirty already. I must get dressed, Coco wants his morning walk. It'll never get really light today, I can tell.

HILDE AND HOLDE must have woken me up, they're whispering in bed. Why are we all sleeping in the same room? Hedda's tossing and turning beside me, Hilde and Holde are giggling. I remember now: we're in a strange house—we're staying with that friend of Mama and Papa, Herr Karnau, and all because we've got a new sister. We didn't have to go away the other times, the nursemaid looked after us while Mama was in the hospital. Now there are six of us. Mama did have another baby, but that one doesn't count, nobody ever saw it. The little ones don't even know that Mama had another brother in her tummy. Once, when I was little, she had to go to the hospital in a hurry, but she didn't bring our other brother with her when she came home. She was very sad and ill for ages. Papa took me aside and told me it would be a long time before we got another brother or sister.

Otherwise there'd now be seven of us—no, eight counting Harald. Harald is Mama's son too, but he's much older than the rest of us and he doesn't live at home, he just comes to see us sometimes. Harald's a soldier. Is that why he's not allowed to live with us, because Papa isn't his father? Papa likes him all the same, he even gave him a motorbike once. Mama used to be married to someone else, but that was long ago, we weren't born then. We don't know Harald's father, but I'm sure Papa does.

Hedda's awake now, she's blinking at me sleepily. We cuddle up under the bedclothes with her rag doll's arm draped over my face. Hilde's far too excited to stay in bed any longer. "Let's go and see Coco," she says loudly.

FIVE CHILDREN AT table with me, still in their night clothes. Helmut munches his bread and jam in silence, Helga sits there with her shoulders hunched, and little Hedda looks as if she may burst into tears at any moment. Only Hilde and Holde, with Coco to distract them, seem relaxed. No, the housekeeper didn't bring any pastries with her, worse luck. They've hardly touched the cocoa she insisted on giving them.

They obviously don't feel at home here. I hope it won't be long before their mother's well enough to have them back.

How could I have landed them in such a situation? How could I have been rash enough to say yes when their father asked me to take care of them for a few days while his wife was having another baby? They're the children of a national figure, after all. As such, they're used to an entirely different life style. And why did he take it into his head to ask me, of all people? We haven't known each other long. It was the overpowering effect of that gigantic public address system that first drew me to his attention, because I'd supervised its installation. After that, he insisted on having me in his personal recording studio whenever he was going to record a speech for radio. That's how we got into conversation, while I was working there. Did he pick me because he sensed my approval of his views on education and upbringing? He refuses on principle to surrender his own children to the Hitler Youth. Was that the reason? I don't suppose I'll ever find out. He simply asked me, in a friendly but forceful way, if I'd be prepared to put the children up if no suitable alternative presented itself.

I must take great care not to get their names muddled up. Helga's the eldest, that's easy. Then comes Hilde, the one who kept pestering me about Coco on the way here. Then Helmut, the only boy. Then Holde, who has a slight squint. Hedda's the youngest apart from the newborn baby, Heide. Even their father seems to lose track sometimes: on one occasion, when referring to Hedda, he persisted in calling her Herta, but nobody dared to correct him. It's possible he mixes up the girls' names because so many boys' names keep flitting through his head for bestowal on imaginary sons. Horst, Hartmann, et cetera—he tries them out in his left-bank Rhenish accent to see if they would be appropriate to a male offspring of his, enunciating them with that singsong intonation betrayed by the very first phoneme that issues from his oral and pharyngeal cavity, a habit of speech that no amount of lip-pursing can eliminate when he tries to iron it out. The father's perceptible accent has rubbed off on his children. Perhaps he even experiments with Hermann, my own name, in secret.

STUCK HERE, THAT'S what we are—stuck here with a stranger who doesn't keep things tidy, whose home is an absolute mess. The kitchen's far too small to hold us all and there are only two other rooms in the apartment. Where are we supposed to play? Why didn't Mama and Papa send us to the country? Then our nursemaid could have come too. Herr Karnau's housekeeper plunks a cup of coffee down in front of him so hard it makes the skin on my cold cocoa quiver. We didn't want to come here. Mama and Papa have simply packed us off without thinking. Either they don't care if we're happy here, or they don't know it because they don't really know *us*. Only one toy each, too. Or doesn't Mama know we're here—did Papa decide it on his own? I'm sure she wouldn't have agreed.

Herr Karnau drops a piece of cheese rind for Coco. Treff isn't allowed indoors at home—it's unhygienic, Mama says. Coco snaps at the cheese rind and catches it in midair. "Really, Herr Karnau!" says the housekeeper.

But Herr Karnau acts as if he hasn't heard. He breaks off another piece for Hilde to give to Coco.

THE HOUSEKEEPER GLANCES at me over her shoulder. Do I detect a look of reproach? She reminds me a little of my colleague at the office, the one I don't get on with. We seldom exchange a word, and there are things that he and the rest of the department mustn't know about me or they'd be bound to think me insane. They mustn't get to hear about the private research I engage in, often until the small hours. The fact is, I've already made certain attempts to plumb the mystery of the human voice. Many of my experiments have become a habit, I've repeated them so often, but I still haven't found the answer or fathomed the secret. How could my colleagues be expected to understand why one of their number should so often patronize butchers' shops and abattoirs on mornings when beasts have been freshly slaughtered (I set off long before office hours, so as to get there before the anglers and dog owners) in the hope of acquiring a particularly fine severed head, preferably undamaged?

It requires a certain amount of will power not to be content to infer the function of the ear, or the operation of the tongue and larynx, from the diagrammatic illustrations common to so many textbooks. Drawings of that kind afford no real clue to the secret of living sounds, so I had no choice but to pursue my research with the aid of the real thing. Once I had familiarized myself with the basic techniques of dissection by studying a brief manual on the subject, it was time for my first visit to the slaughterhouse yard. I hesitated, possibly embarrassed by the thought of what my colleagues might have said, and my manner was awkward in the extreme. The men in line behind me grew impatient as I falteringly inquired if the horse's mouth was sure to contain a tongue. All the other customers had come equipped with buckets. I was the only one that had to ask the assistant to wrap my bloody, eyeless head in newspaper.

WE'VE GOT TO get dressed, Herr Karnau must have forgotten that, and he doesn't seem to notice that we haven't washed yet. When is he going to finish his breakfast? He hasn't eaten up his roll, and already he's smoking another cigarette. Herr

Karnau smokes almost as many cigarettes as Papa does. Mama smokes a lot too, especially when she's not feeling well. What's all that stuff Hilde's telling Herr Karnau? He's asking questions about Mama and Papa. Funny, that: if he's really such a friend of theirs, why does he know so little about them? Holde suddenly interrupts them in a loud voice: "Let's go and play."

At last Herr Karnau asks us if we want to leave the table. The housekeeper wipes her wet hands on her apron and follows us out. Then she lugs the suitcases into our room. Helmut is upset when he sees we haven't brought all the toys he wanted. He feels in his pockets. "Where's my car?" he shouts. "Where's my Meccano set? Helga, where did you put my car?"

He hurls his toy soldiers across the room and snatches one of Holde's wooden cows out of her hand. The housekeeper takes it away from him. He starts bawling and runs back into the kitchen. Crybaby. If he's running to Herr Karnau for sympathy, he's welcome.

THE STUMP OF the neck bled profusely when I emerged into the street with the horse's head under my arm. I felt sick, the bloody newspaper smelled so awful. I'm not as squeamish nowadays, and handling animal's skulls has since become a matter of course. The cloying stench of blood, too, can be almost entirely eliminated by spraying the apartment with cologne. I've long been able to dispense with my medical textbooks, those dissection manuals that used at first to lie open beside me, their pages covered with reddish-brown fingerprints from the blood on my hands.

I work on the kitchen table. Coco, who has to be shut out while I'm dissecting, waits impatiently in the hallway for me to cut up the remains and put them in his bowl. Bread knife and scissors, pincers and knitting needles—those are my instruments. And, sometimes, when a skull is particularly hard to break open, an old spade. Oh yes, and a potato peeler. I find that ideal for skinning heads.

Layer-by-layer dissection may at least be bringing me closer to the heart of the mystery, even if I never solve it by that means. The tongue, which we employ as a tool throughout our lives, we think of as a flat slab because all we ever feel of it against our teeth is the forward extremity and all we usually see of it in the mirror is the tip. Confronted by a horse's tongue, however, we can make inferences about our own tongues from that long, round muscle, and it seems inconceivable that such a crude, unshapely mass of tissue can contribute to the formation of finely differentiated sounds.

I'm familiar with the oral cavities of pigs, also horses, oxen and cows of all ages. Only last night I had to get rid of my most recent skull in a hurry and exchange it for the presence of the five children.

WHY IS HERR Karnau stroking Helmut's head? Is he going to tell me off about something?

"Helga, your nursemaid told me she'd packed your school books. Your father insists that you do a little work every day, even though it's the holidays. Hilde, will you come into the kitchen too, please?"

We're disappointed, we don't feel like doing any school work. The younger ones have to stay in the living room and play quietly, so as not to disturb us. We empty our pencil cases on the kitchen table. Herr Karnau reads out the sums we have to do, then he joins the others.

"What were you talking about at breakfast with Herr Karnau, Hilde? What were those animals he was telling you about? Those foxes?"

"Flying foxes, they're called. They're black foxes, a special kind that can really fly. But only at night, Herr Karnau says. They're very small, the size of mice. Not many people have ever seen one, but Herr Karnau knows a man who has seen them in real life, not just in pictures. A friend of his."

"Nonsense, there are no such things. What do you mean, foxes? Don't be silly, foxes run, they can't fly. You must mean bats and you've just made them up, these foxes of yours."

"No, they're flying foxes. It's true, Herr Karnau says so."

"You must have misunderstood. You weren't listening properly, so now you're lying, and you know we're not allowed to lie, not ever."

"Don't be so nasty. It's the truth, flying foxes really can fly. They only live in Africa, nowhere else."

"Rubbish. How would you know?"

"Because Herr Karnau told me. That friend of his has actually seen some."

"Herr Karnau, Herr Karnau! He doesn't even know our parents, Mama and Papa have never asked him to the house. Have *you* ever seen him at home with them?"

"You're just being stupid, Helga. Of course Herr Karnau knows our parents."

"How do you know he does?"

"You're angry because he's so nice to me, that's all."

"You and your silly foxes."

"If Herr Karnau hears..."

"Shut up and get on with your math, you little sneak."

WHAT'S GOING ON in the kitchen? Aren't Helga and Hilde working? I leave the little ones on the sofa, playing farmer, and peek into the kitchen. "What is it, finished your math already? Put your things away, then. The housekeeper will want to make lunch as soon as she's back from shopping. We can do the housework this afternoon."

The two girls give me a sheepish stare. They shut their exercise books and put away their pencils. They avoid each other's eye, I notice, probably because they've been squabbling. Then they both get up without a word and take their school things into the room next door. Did they do their math at all, I wonder. Are they frightened I'll check and be angry with them?

The housekeeper goes home after lunch. That relieves us of her presence until tomorrow morning. Hedda and Holde settle down for their afternoon nap. The others are also less lively than they were this morning. They perch on the kitchen window sill and look down at the street, talking quietly among themselves. At first I assume it's because they don't want to wake the two little ones.

I'm wrong: they're playing a game, a whispering game. Although I don't entirely follow it, I'm reluctant to ask them the rules because they're so engrossed. I notice, however, that each phase of the game ends with the same, invariable words: "Take care, or the evil whisper will get you too!"

They intone this formula in a dramatic voice, the way a malevolent magician might utter it. Apparently, the evil whisper curdles your blood and dries up your heart. It's a special kind of voice adopted for the sole purpose of paralyzing the person addressed. That shows how close they are in the imagination, the voice and the soul.

The little ones come toddling into the kitchen with sleep-crumpled faces. We've probably roused them too soon from their afternoon nap. They're thirsty, and now they'd like some rose hip tea, but not until it's cool. Suddenly I detect a strange, unpleasant smell. Has Coco made a mess in the hallway? "No," Helga says briskly. "Hedda's done it in her pants."

Don't little girls of two wear diapers? Hedda herself looks quite as taken aback as I do. Helga has already lifted her down from the chair and is pulling off her leggings and underpants. Hedda cooperates by casually raising one leg. Off balance now that she has one foot in the air, she starts to sway and violently flails her arms. Quite instinctively, I grab her hand. Equilibrium restored, she gives me such a beaming smile that I feel called upon to say something nice: "There, Hedda, it could be a lot worse. Come with me and we'll find you some clean things."

But Helga intervenes: "No, not yet, she'll have to be washed first."

Of course, I wasn't thinking. Hedda won't let go of my hand, so I'm left with no choice but to accompany her into the bathroom. I take a clean washcloth and test the water with one finger to make sure it's not too hot, but Helga intervenes once more: "What are you doing, Herr Karnau? Hedda can't stand on those tiles in her bare feet, she'll catch cold. You must put a towel down."

She soaps the washcloth and is swabbing away at Hedda before I know it. There's nothing more for me to do. I wonder if Helga looks after the younger ones as conscientiously when she's at home. She seems to handle everything with such self-assurance. "Well, Helga," I say, half-jokingly, "your own nurse-maid couldn't have done a better job."

But she doesn't respond, acts as if she hasn't heard because she's too busy drying Hedda's legs.

HOW LOUD IT crackles, how my ears are crackling. The cold makes them crackle whenever I turn my head, whenever I speak. It must be my bones, or my eardrums. How cold it is. Winter's really here already.

We're out for a walk dressed up in our warmest things, hats and all, and the little ones are wearing their mittens. Herr Karnau's walking on ahead with me, and suddenly Hilde and Helmut start chanting behind us: "Helga's got a sweetheart, Helga's got a sweetheart!"

THE CHILDREN ARE laughing behind my back. I can hear excited whispers and fits of the giggles because Helga is talking to me on her own. Odd, because earlier today I got the impression that she'd sooner not have talked to me at all. It's as if the children had only properly woken up in the open air, as if they were still bemused by their unexpected change of quarters last night. Helga has become more communicative. She's talking quite freely, pointing out leaves on the ground and naming the trees they come from, asking me about my work and telling me about her home, her parents and schoolfriends.

COCO IS TUGGING at his lead. The others crowd around Herr Karnau, they're all dying to walk Coco. Hilde runs off with him, her scarf fluttering in the air. The others dash after her, but I stay behind with Herr Karnau. I'm allowed to push Hedda's stroller by myself; she's muffled up to the neck and her cheeks are all red. She calls after the others, doesn't listen to what the two of us are saying, just watches Coco bounding across the slushy field. Herr Karnau says, "Homesick, Helga? Would you sooner have stayed at home? I often feel like that when I'm away from home. I never enjoyed staying with strangers as a child."

Maybe Herr Karnau isn't as peculiar as I thought to

begin with. He's being nicer to me, anyway, and not spending all his time with the younger ones. They're now playing tag with Coco.

HELGA'S A BRIGHT little thing. Many of the questions she asks, many of the words she uses and the remarks she makes are not at all what one would expect from a girl of eight. It's as if she were far older, as if she were already on the threshold of adult life, when a young person deliberately tries to shake off the language and conversational topics of a child. But she also keeps coming out with remarks that clearly advertise her age, as if she has involuntarily relegated herself, while speaking, to the same category as her brother and sisters. When that happens she looks up at me shyly to see if I've noticed. They're so touching, those moments, it's all I can do not to laugh. However, Helga would be bound to interpret such a laugh as a mark of grown-up arrogance.

I continually coax her to talk. I make a point of using some word she probably doesn't know yet, and, sure enough, she'll ask me what it means. Far from pretending to be omniscient, as an adult might, she's delighted when she learns something new. She'll try out the word in another context and ask if it can be used that way or if it's the equivalent of some word in her existing vocabulary. She listens intently to my explanations and statements of fact, which promptly give rise to more questions that require answers.

"WHAT IF HEIDE were a deaf-mute like the people you told me about? We don't know what they're like, because we've never seen any. We wouldn't notice a thing at first because babies can't talk anyway. Wouldn't we be able to talk together, ever? Would Heide be a cripple? That would be awful. Our mother had a crippled baby once, but it was born dead."

"Are you worried about your new sister?" Herr Karnau says. "But why say cripple, Helga? Cripple is such an unkind word. If Heide were deaf and dumb—I'm sure she isn't, but *if* she were—she would simply be a deaf-mute and not so very different from the rest of you. There is a difference, of course. Heide would have to learn sign language, and so would you and your parents. Then you could communicate with her by signs. It would mean a lot of hard work at first, because the rest of you children learned to speak without trying. Long before it utters a word, a baby that isn't deaf and dumb can hear its parents talking to it and each other, so it starts to speak by degrees—by imitating them. And even before that, what else does a baby do the whole time but try out its voice and see what effects it produces? That's what it's doing when it bellows or whimpers, chuckles or burbles happily to itself without trying to attract its mother's attention, or when it wakes up from its afternoon nap and screams because there's no one around to pick it up.

"Yes, the deaf-mute child has a hard time acquiring a language of its own. It's aware, to begin with, of every last gesture it makes to convey something, but before long its mastery of sign language is so complete that it communicates quite freely and spontaneously as long as it knows that its friends or brothers and sisters can understand it."

HOW DIFFERENT IT is, conversing with a child. I generally do my best to avoid conversations. Not because it bothers me if people address me of their own accord, but because I'm obliged to answer, to question or confirm what they say as if their sole intention were to make me conscious of my voice —as if it delighted them to make me demonstrate its unpleasant timbre.

My first encounter with my own voice goes back a long way. It was, I seem to recall, at a birthday party in my early childhood that I first heard it without speaking at the same time. Under parental supervision, my friends and I had recorded a few words on a wax cylinder and immediately played them back. Everyone present marveled at this phenomenon: all the children's voices could be heard except mine, which was manifestly missing. And then I noticed that among the sounds issuing from the horn was an unfamiliar, unnatural voice that belonged to none of my friends.

It was a while before I grasped that it could only be mine. But my internal, cranial vibrations were altogether different from that childish voice. To this day, the sounds transmitted to my ears by my bones strike me as deeper and richer than those that reach them from some external source. I was dismayed. On the one hand I felt an urge to confirm my original impression by listening to the recording once more; on the other, I was glad that my friends had already started to play a new game in which I could unobtrusively join. They had forgotten all about the wax cylinder, whereas my own thoughts were still of the quivering stylus that had relentlessly explored those grooves and converted their sinuosities into sound—into the repulsive noise I never wished to hear again.

Since then, whenever I become aware of my unpleasant vocal timbre, I break off abruptly in mid-sentence, too embarrassed to go on talking. I'm nonetheless convinced that it should be possible to remodel the voice and approximate it to the internal, cranial sound by dint of practice, by carefully adjusting the larynx and pharynx, tongue and thoracic cavity prior to speaking. It must surely be possible to master the organ that any stranger can hear, the link between oneself and the outside world, the sound that sheds more light on a person's character than any other single manifestation.

Not that Helga, who now converses with me quite naturally, seems to have noticed this vocal defect. Perhaps she takes it for granted that my voice and its owner go together because she cannot know from experience how little suited they are. Even though the other children are chattering and frolicking behind us, I feel no desire for silence.

"Herr Karnau?"

Helga brings me down to earth with another of her questions. Has she been talking the whole time?

"HERR KARNAU, DO you come from a big family like ours?"

"No, I don't have any brothers or sisters."

"So you've always been on your own?"

Herr Karnau doesn't know what to say. He's holding Hedda in his arms so the others can play with her stroller. They're pretending it's a tank and wheeling it through the puddles. I'm holding Coco's lead. Herr Karnau may be right: I mustn't worry about little Heide.

Now we're back in the warm. Coco's fur is cold, it smells of fresh air, and we've brought a cloud of coldness into the kitchen with us. Our cheeks are as red as the baby's picture on those jars of baby food, the laughing baby with the golden curls and chubby cheeks. Herr Karnau hasn't asked us about our homework again. Shall we play collecting for charity? The little ones don't like that game because they have to put make-believe money in our collecting boxes, mine and Hilde's, while the two of us pretend to be standing outside the Hotel Adlon in our fur-lined jackets. We did that with Papa last year, before

Christmas, and everyone stared at us. That's why the others are still jealous.

We play house instead, but no one volunteers to be the Mother. No one wants to be the Mother because she has to spend most of the time being ill in bed. Although she's at a health resort with lots of nice fresh air and no work to do, she's made to swallow pills whenever she has a fainting fit. Once, when they're out for a drive, the car goes around a bend and she falls out and breaks some bones and gets a concussion. We're all very worried about her, especially the Father, because he was driving too fast. Everyone wants to play the Father in spite of that, because he doesn't feel bad about it for long and he gets to order everyone around. He has his own secretaries and he's always very busy. Hilde can be the Father today. She picks Helmut and me to be her secretaries. The little ones can be the children.

The Father paces up and down his office, dictating a new speech. It's all about relentless candor, the voice of the people and ice-cold truth, and Helmut takes it down in shorthand. He can't write yet, not properly, so he only makes squiggles on the paper. Hilde speaks much faster than Helmut can write. "If things are going badly," she says, "let's admit it. Let's call a spade a spade."

The children don't have anything to do at present. The Father decides they're actors in a depressing film about a hospital, so they all have to pretend to be lying in bed and keep quiet. "That's enough medical films," he says. "Too many medical films are a bad thing." But Helmut, who's supposed to pass the order on to me, gets it wrong. "That's enough mental films," he says.

We all laugh at Helmut's mistake and call him Tran, from Tran and Helle, the two film characters invented by the Father himself. But Helmut doesn't think it's funny and he quits. He refuses to join in again until the Father is ready to censor some films. The children can now join in too, they're allowed to be present at the screening. There are mountaineering films, newsreels, and children's films, which even the Father finds amusing. Hilde tells us the story of a Mickey Mouse film. Finally the Father says, "Stop the projector. This film is banned."

I LISTEN AT the door. The children have forgotten about me, forgotten for the moment that they're staying with a stranger.

Might it be worth leaving them to play and devoting the half-hour before supper to my project? My collection of sounds is steadily growing: I've already managed to compile about a hundred examples of the strangest utterances. Some are every-day noises, vocal manifestations of which their authors are seldom aware. There's a vast range of sounds to be monitored, especially now, in the fall: throat-clearings, little coughs and sniffs that are heedlessly emitted by the sound source but mercilessly recorded on disc. My collection includes some genuine treasures, for instance this recording of a brothel behind the lines, which was given me on the sly by an acquaintance. People must be monitored even when making love. Those sounds engraved on wax are unrepeatable because the brothel was closed down soon after they were recorded, for fear of disease. According to my friend, it even employed the services of dogs trained to copulate with the aid of soiled underclothes.

Is my map of vocal nuances subject to any limitations? Is there anything I would *not* record? Yes, the voices of these children while still defenseless, as they are now, because they believe themselves to be alone and unobserved. Everything else is grist to my mill—anything and everything, the whole of the audible world. Every blank space must be filled for the sake of completeness. Every space but one: these children's voices will not be entered on my map, where they would be exposed to all and sundry and, worse still, to the children themselves. I couldn't undertake any such exposure without rendering myself guilty of distorting their childish voices into the constrained mode of speech that would inevitably result, because the five of them would find their own voices just as alien as I myself did at their age.

HEDDA HAS ALREADY fallen asleep beside me, and the others have also settled down for the night. A shame, because I'm not the least bit tired. I'd have liked to talk to them about Herr Karnau—about little Heide, too. I can't sleep, I'm too thirsty. I'll go to the kitchen and get myself something to drink. Very quietly, so as not to wake the others. I won't put the light on, I'll tiptoe out in my bare feet. Not a sound.

Somebody's talking in Herr Karnau's room, I can hear voices through the closed door. But Herr Karnau's all by himself, surely. Or did he have a visitor and we never noticed? Perhaps he's just listening to the radio. That's not German, though, I can't understand a word. Is he listening to an enemy broadcast? No, it doesn't sound like that, not loud and clear like a news-caster. Newscasters don't break off in the middle and leave long gaps—they don't keep sighing in between. It's weird. The kitchen's all dark, I'm afraid to go in there now.

The sounds are getting louder and louder. Herr Karnau must have someone in his room, he simply must—someone in pain. Now the man is screaming. Why is he making those awful noises? I want to go straight back to bed, but I can't move, I can't stop listening. No, those aren't words, it's someone being hurt. Maybe it isn't a person at all, maybe it's an animal I can hear, howling like that. My heart is really thumping. Is Herr Karnau torturing his dog? No, that's not Coco, it must be a human being. Now he's making choking noises, gasping for air, whimpering horribly. Why doesn't Herr Karnau do something, why doesn't he help the poor man?

IT'S SOMETIMES FAR easier to detect the characteristic features of a voice from its most extreme utterances—shouts, hoarse cries, whimpers—than from the spoken word, even though those sounds leave exceptionally deep scars on the vocal cords. Even though, or for that very reason? That is when the voice attains a singular clarity unsuspected by speaker and listener alike: when the organ is coping with rough treatment or contending with difficulties and striving with all its might to overcome them, for instance during a fit of coughing that threatens to stifle it and extinguish every sound. Those are the times when a person's vocal image manifests itself with unbridled freedom.

Recordings of such vocalizations get to the very heart of the sound source in question. They penetrate far deeper than monitored and recorded heartbeats, which, although they vary in rhythm from person to person, do nothing more, in the last analysis, than confirm that the engine is ticking over steadily. The heartbeat is simply evidence of life, a vegetative function common to many living creatures. But the voice, being partly subject to the will, generates sounds that all reveal the special characteristics of its resonator: the human being.

THE DOOR SUDDENLY opens, and Herr Karnau stands there looking down at me as if nothing had happened. His room is silent now. "Can't you sleep, Helga?" he says. "You haven't been crying, have you?"

I'm frightened. Herr Karnau takes my hand and leads me into his room. It's dark in there except for the light on his desk. Am I seeing something moving over there in the shadows, a visitor clutching his stomach and writhing in agony? No, it's only Coco. He comes trotting over. Herr Karnau sits me on his bed and wraps me in a blanket. Then he sits down at his desk beside the gramophone. Coco jumps up on the bed, snuffling. He wants to get under the nice warm blanket with me. Is there really nobody here but us?

LITTLE HELGA LOOKED absolutely distraught when I found her standing outside my door. She must think I'm a monster. I can't play any more of my recordings while the children are here, it's far too risky. And I thought they'd all been asleep for hours. What could the poor girl have thought when she heard those screams of agony coming from my room? I hope she'll soon feel better and forget what she heard.

She's huddled up on the bed with her bare feet protruding from under the blanket. She's still frightened. Of me? Of this gloomy room? Of the voice that has long since died away? She looks around timidly, very much a child once more. As for the adult manner she adopts toward the younger ones in imitation of her mother and the nursemaid, it seems to belong to another person altogether, not to the tongue-tied little girl who's sitting here in front of me.

I must quickly involve her again in our interplay of this afternoon, keep up a flow of words so as to steer her thoughts in another direction. The music, too, is gradually calming her down. So is the sight of the black disc on the turntable, gleaming in the semidarkness as it rotates with soothing regularity.

COCO RESTS HIS head on my lap. Herr Karnau asks me if I like Coco. "Yes," I tell him, "but what breed is he?"

"I don't know, I've never given it any thought. I suspect it would be very hard to identify."

"You mean he isn't pure-blooded?"

Herr Karnau laughs. "I'm afraid not."

"So he's a bastard?"

"Let's call him a mongrel, shall we? It sounds nicer."

Herr Karnau plays the record for me again. "I like sitting in a darkened room at night," he says, "listening to records. A lot of people find the blackout depressing on really dark nights, but I think it's lovely when the sky above the city looks dark blue, not pale the way it does in normal times—you can see the stars so much more clearly. Were you scared in the dark just now?"

"Yes, a bit, but I'm all right now. It was only out there in the hallway..."

"I know what you mean. As a child I was also scared of the dark, especially in enclosed spaces, but it didn't really bother me outdoors. I'm just the same today, come to think of it: I can only stand being inside the apartment with the lights off for a certain length of time, but I enjoy walking at night for hours on end—as long as I don't meet any shady characters."

The desk lamp is shining on Herr Karnau's hair. He's letting me stay up much later than the others. They must have been asleep for ages, but the two of us are still talking together, all by ourselves. What are shady characters, though? Not just people with shadows, because we've all got those. People who only move around in the shadows? People *made* of shadows, not flesh and blood? Herr Karnau is speaking very softly, his voice gets quieter and quieter. Are shady characters spirits that roam around at night? Or are they like the Kohlenklau, that creature on the posters Papa designed to stop people wasting fuel in wartime? Not a human being, but not an animal either, slinking around in the dark with claws instead of hands and a sack of stolen coal on its back. I'm not frightened any longer, not of the Kohlenklau's lopsided face peering out from under its cap, and not of the fact that I can't hear Herr Karnau anymore and it's gone all dark.

"Are you still awake, Helga?"

I don't say anything. Herr Karnau picks me up and carries me, blanket and all, into the room next door. Very gently, he puts me down on the sofa bed beside Hedda, who has warmed the mattress while I've been away. He tucks me in. Now he's gone.

WHAT'S THE MATTER with the dog? Why is Coco lying on my arm at this hour? Is he trying to wake me? Another weight lands on my legs. Coco isn't as heavy as that, not by far. I open my eyes a fraction: daylight already. I make out a child's smiling face. And another.

"His eyes are open!"

A chorus of giggles, a fivefold good morning. The children have crept in and are sitting on my bed. Already wide awake, they shake their little heads like dogs emerging from sleep. Their hair is thoroughly disheveled after only two nights here. The housekeeper and I have both proved incapable of plaiting it neatly. I let Holde crawl under the covers and she promptly sets to work on my hair with her doll's comb: "That's so you don't look so shaggy."

The children laugh. The rag doll dances in front of my face as Hedda sings me an aubade in a squeaky doll's voice. But after only a few bars she gets muddled, or the doll does, so she sings the first two lines again and again. Helmut is doing gymnastics at the foot of the bed. Coco, who approves of all this activity, jumps up and joins us.

Helmut collapses: he slowly buckles at the knees and lies there for a while without moving. Then he gets up again, extends one arm, takes aim at Helga with his forefinger, and loudly clicks his tongue. Helga collapses too, but much more slowly, and lies so inert that her body would be motionless but for the bedsprings' undulations. Holde watches expectantly as Hilde follows suit after Helga has aimed a forefinger at her and made the same gunshot noise. Helmut has another idea: "We won't use our fingers as pistols, we'll pretend our pillows are grenades and have a pillow fight."

Hedda and Holde emerge from under the covers and run after the others, who are fetching their pillows from across the way. Only Helga stays behind with me. "You have to be careful to do it right," she says. "It isn't so easy to fall the right way when you've been shot."

Soon they've had enough of dying and want to play something else. Helga whispers something to the others and tells me, "You've got to guess what we are."

The children line up beside my bed. Holde gives an involuntary giggle, but Hilde shushes her and tugs at her nightie, looking cross. Holde shuts up at once. The children stand there in silence. Then they wave their arms about and look at me as if to convey something, but they don't say a word. After a while they lose patience. "Well," says Helga, "haven't you guessed yet?"

"No. Swimmers? Birds?"

"Wrong."

"Windmills, maybe? Characters in a silent movie?"

"No, silly, we're deaf-mutes on parade."

They turn about, all five of them, and march silently out into the hallway.

CHAPTER

3

It's very quiet in the apartment now that the children have gone. Too quiet, for my taste, as if the floors had wall-to-wall carpeting and the walls were padded with cotton wool. They reflect no echoes of childish laughter, no childish comments or questions. The dog's snuffles, too, sound strangely unreal, like a vague reminder of louder and livelier days. My recordings are no substitute. No matter how I turn up the volume, they produce no sounds capable of soothing me. I wander restlessly from room to room as if visible traces of the children's voices may be lingering on the wallpaper or furniture. But no, nothing.

Their voices made so distinct an impression on me during the few hours we spent together that my inward ear can recall them all. Each has its own, unmistakable acoustic image. Even the piping voices of the youngest can be clearly differentiated, although they still sound ill-defined and will only develop fully as the years go by. Not that vocal development is dependent solely on physical growth. Physical mobility, too, plays its part. Children's voices develop as they romp around with their brothers and sisters, as they pit their strength against that of their peers, as they scuffle and pant and cry. They develop as the individual limbs become adjusted to each other while their owners walk, jump, and coordinate the movements of their hands. They also develop during those self-absorbed games on the floor, when the child, almost without knowing it and wholly undistracted by the extraneous noises in its vicinity, mutters a running commentary on the state of play.

At present, while their vocal cords are still supple, the children speak quite uninhibitedly. They're altogether unaware, I imagine, of the freedom with which they form words and sounds. They may even yearn to be able to speak like adults. Later on, however, their voices will inevitably lose that natural quality. It will vanish if only because they learn how to cough, to emit polite little coughs and clear their throats behind an upraised hand, grown-up fashion, instead of relieving a troublesome tickle as promptly and forcefully as possible. It will vanish if only because their voices will seldom be heard again at full strength, and because the uninhibited shouts, screams and jubilant cries of childhood will be replaced by restrained utterances delivered at room volume. Their voices will soon be subject to limitations. They will be taught to speak clearly at all times, taught not to pick up any old accent they hear, if only in passing, and temporarily substitute it for their usual mode of speech, albeit unconsciously, perhaps, when they themselves pass a remark or engage in conversation. The continual repetition of words and sentences, the persistent crying and whimpering, will disappear for ever, because every voice is monitored by the human ear.

The children may already have a secret inkling of this. Why else were they so shy when they first arrived, why else were they so reticent at first? Not a word more than necessary, and only when they couldn't avoid answering a question of mine.

Slowly, one by one, they gained confidence and ventured to address me of their own accord. But they chattered with real abandon only when playing alone in their room with the door shut so the stranger couldn't hear—or so they hoped. A diffident, inhibited manner of speaking will one day come naturally to them, and they'll be wholly unaware that their voices ever sounded any different.

Their original lack of constraint will never be satisfactorily replaced by anything they learn in the way of new vocalizations, for instance the polite, affected, swiftly subsiding laughter that greets an unfunny or unseemly joke, or the vocal fillers, the "reallys" and "you-don't-says" that dissuade people from tearing each other limb from limb at the slightest conversational tiff. The existing vocal range narrows and the voice is steadily abraded by prescribed patterns of speech until death supervenes, by which time it has become a strangled sound located at the base of the tongue. Clipped utterances are all it can produce, and any outbursts are quickly retracted.

It will dawn on the children, sooner or later, that they no longer enjoy free use of their voices. Helmut will attain this painful realization as soon as his voice starts to break. The larynx suddenly refuses to obey and becomes a sore point, an ever open wound in the throat. The vocal cords are strained and distorted, and the tongue, too, weakens because all it can articulate are fragmentary sounds that fluctuate in pitch. And Helmut will be alarmed to find that his voice is slipping from his grasp. Like everything else.

Growth alone is held responsible for all the unpleasantnesses associated with this phase: the adolescent's headaches, growing pains, and uncoordinated movements. But isn't it far more likely that changes in the voice are to blame for this feeling of disorientation, and that its gross failure has repercussions for the entire body? We know, after all, that phonation or vocalization brings many more muscles into play than are directly connected with the apparatus of speech itself. Might not the voice be far more important than is generally assumed, therefore, since it is echoed by dull aches throughout the body at the very stage when it sounds most discordant? If a breaking voice betokens adolescence, or incipient sexual maturity, must a man have slept with a woman before his voice attains its final form?

My own voice never broke, as far as I can recall, and my memory cannot be at fault or my voice would now be deeper, like those of other men. I have the impression that its pitch has never really changed, never slipped down the scale. Characterized by inflexibility, it produces a sound quite inappropriate to my age. Its melody is also false, as high-pitched as a child's and at odds with the body and movements of an adult, but devoid of a child's sincerity.

A medley of cries and hesitations, the speech of a child is colored by its upbringing.

PAPA COMES PANTING up the stairs. Helmut is screaming the house down. Papa's on the landing now, he's calling me. "What's going on, Helga?" he shouts. "What have you done to your little brother this time?"

"It's his own fault, he broke my watch."

Helmut stands there bawling, with a face like a beetroot. He runs to Papa, who picks him up in his arms and glares at me. "You're not to hit Helmut, you know that perfectly well, he's too little. He didn't mean to be naughty."

Helmut sobs in Papa's arms, looking as if butter wouldn't melt in his mouth. He unscrewed the back of my watch, the one with the red leather strap, and took out all the works.

He didn't see me coming because he was too busy rooting around in the case with a screwdriver. He was working away with all his might—so hard that his tongue was clamped between his teeth and the tip was all red and throbbing. He gave a start when he finally saw me, but by that time my lovely watch was completely ruined. The hands were bent, too—not a hope of mending it. I gave him a good slap. He started crying right away, lost his temper and swept all the bits off the table with his arm. Then he ran to the door and cried a bit louder so Papa would hear him down below.

"Did you hear what I said?" Papa says sternly.

"But he bust my watch."

"Bust? What do you mean, bust? Speak properly when you're talking to your father."

"He broke my watch."

Hilde and Heide have appeared in the doorway, wondering what all the noise is about. "Hold your tongue and go to your room at once," Papa says.

"But Helmut took it apart, he *deserved* to be slapped."

"That's enough, Helga. Don't be so damned impertinent."

And Papa gives *me* a slap. I start crying too, now. I run to my room, yelling, "You're mean and unfair, all of you!"

Papa comes after me, but I slam the door and turn the key, twice. Papa knocks, bangs on my door. "Open up at once, Helga. You know you're not allowed to lock yourself in."

But he can't come in however long he goes on shouting. He can't slap me again either, not when I'm lying on my bed with the pillows over my head. The pillows are wet with tears. Helmut doesn't shed tears as a rule because he isn't sad, just angry—angry because he isn't strong enough to hit me back. If I clamp the pillows against my ears I can hardly hear Papa banging and yelling outside.

Helmut's still so little, he doesn't realize when he's being naughty. He's far too young to know, and so are Hilde and Holde and Hedda, not to mention Heide. Mama and Papa are allowed to punish them, but not me—oh no! I'm not old enough for that, but I'm old enough to put up with those little nuisances, old enough to look after them when Mama gets one of her headaches and goes to bed, when everyone in the house has to be quiet, when Mama goes away to recuperate and Papa's not here either—when he spends the night at Lanke and doesn't come home for days on end. But I mustn't ever lose my temper with the little ones. "Helga's very understanding for her age," says Papa when he wants to butter me up in front of other people. "It's sweet, the way she looks after her little brother and sisters."

I can still hear him outside in the hallway, shouting, "No movies for you this evening. No movies, Helga, you hear?"

Then he stops banging on the door. Helmut will be playing with my watch again by now, you bet. Papa won't object, Helmut can get away with murder, being the only boy. The rest of us are just girls. Heide's lucky, she's the only one Mama really cares about. All the grown-ups rave about her blue eyes, but they'll change color soon enough. All babies have blue eyes to begin with.

I can hear Holde and Hilde laughing in the nursery—what are they playing, mothers and babies?—and Helmut is hammering and screwing away at my watch. He can't use a screwdriver properly, he's too stupid to play with his Meccano. If Papa tells Mama about our fight he'll say Helmut was playing quietly by himself. Mama won't ask if it's really true, she'll scowl at me and make her headache face. There's the nursemaid, she's saying something to the others. Now she's knocking on my door: "Helga, get tidied up and comb your hair, it'll soon be suppertime."

I'll have to unlock the door, I can't put it off any longer. I hope Papa won't be there for supper. I'll listen on the stairs first, to see if I can hear him talking.

STREET SIGNS ARE being dismantled and taken down. The men's hands are sore and callused from unscrewing so many in quick succession. Potting and glazing are in progress. Clay is being molded on the potter's wheel and fired. Now everyone will get new jugs. A summer wind is blowing across the green meadows. The blue pencil is scouring fields and ridding flower beds of thistles. Walls are being repainted, billboards white-washed over. The blue pencil bites through weeds, rips out tufts of vegetation, strips trees of foliage and lays them flat. Incredible, the extent of this clearance: threshed grain, shady hillsides, forest glades, charred signposts, barns, farms, plowland—the whole countryside is being burned off like a field of stubble. Tongues, too, are set ablaze and their last words cauterized as a prelude to extinction.

The operation is already in full swing. The entire region is being blue-penciled. Readers are combing every library. The blue pencil is inflicting deep wounds, gnawing away at the foreign vocabulary. Street names, formerly French, are being replaced with German. The blue pencil underlines, corrects, makes marginal notes, suggests appropriate German replacements. Typewriters churn out words at seventy-eight per minute. Normative regulations are being imposed, indigenous civil servants re-educated, language courses administered under the auspices of a compulsory program designed to inculcate a basic vocabulary and eliminate any pronunciation problems.

Hammers and chisels are chipping away at tombstones and excising memorial inscriptions, even the French words for BORN and DIED. Labels bearing washing instructions, too, are being ripped from the collar of every garment. The blue pencil is deleting forms of address, conventional words of farewell, verbal courtesies.

New names are being assigned to everyone and everything. The Germanizing process requires that foreign words be erased from mouths, and foreign names from passes and permits. Any inscriptions other than HEISS and KALT are disappearing from bath taps throughout Alsace. The blue pencil is prescribing financial penalties for the use of French words. All mottoes or blessings stamped on tableware, whether of silver or some other metal, are being removed.

The linguistic purge is being implemented with the utmost rigor. The authorities raid a china factory where, in contravention of a strict ban, French inscriptions are still being scratched into the soft clay of crockery ready for firing. Paint pots are tipped over, startled workers drop their brushes and are lined up facing the wall with their wrists handcuffed behind them. While the guilty parties' personal particulars are being taken down, all the crockery in the warehouse is systematically smashed, even inscribed plates adorned with floral patterns and landscapes. Fragments bearing isolated letters in cursive could have been combined into new, German words, but the blue pencil is implacably thorough: the fragments and the letters painted on them are vigorously trampled underfoot and ground to dust. Jugs for water, milk and wine are hurled through the shop window, and a trayful of salt shakers goes sailing into the street just as the prisoners are being marched away. The flying splinters cut their foreheads.

Every brow reflects the flames. A word of command, and

torchbearers standing in the fiery glow apply their brands like slow matches to a cannon's touchhole. Bonfires blaze up on all sides, conflagrations in every public square light up the night sky above the entire city. The region's linguistic heritage is being torched, a crackling, gasoline-sodden agglomeration of dictionaries and novels, cookbooks and paperbacks. It comprises every book in French, translations from German included, that could be seized in and around Strasbourg, where every household has been obliged to surrender its library. Suspects were tackled from the start by reconnaissance patrols. No one escaped their scrutiny, not even the most inconspicuous, book-engrossed figure seated on a park bench. Now, beside the crackling, blazing mounds of paper, dim figures can be seen roasting potatoes on improvised skewers, mopping their sweaty foreheads, clinking glasses of wine in the firelight. The glasses glint as they raise them to their lips and drink to the success of Germanization. In the background, flames flicker and smoke rises into the brightly illuminated sky. Afterwards, jackbooted feet aim kicks at the ashes and dying embers. The glow fades and dies.

The reorganization of instruction in all schools is a quite informal process. During excursions children are encouraged to rid the streets of all undesirable foreign words, to develop keener eyes and a keener linguistic awareness. In the classroom, suggestions are invited for Germanizing terms used in the jewelry trade, hitherto a Gallic preserve. The pupils join in with a will. Their suggestions are arranged in categories, and the author of the one deemed most appropriate is privileged to step up to the blackboard, rub out the French designation, and replace it with the German. The children have then to copy out the whole of this newly acquired vocabulary in their exercise books.

The blue pencil is neatly noting down the particulars of those who defy the linguistic ordinances. It fills out forms: date, forename, surname, address, said person to be deported to the Reich with immediate effect, signature, rubber stamp. Sharp-eared Germanizers are scouring the countryside. They round up whole gangs of intransigent French-speakers and confine them in the detention camp that has already housed well over a thousand of their number.

Having thoroughly explored the phonetic landscape at home in Germany, I realized that, in order to pursue my cartographic project further, it would be necessary to record voices from other regions. That's why I volunteered for Germanization duties here in Strasbourg.

Eavesdropping on people has landed me in some very awkward situations. My equipment not only attracts puzzled glances but has provoked physical assaults on my person and on the recording machine itself. Once, in fact, a brand-new wax disc narrowly escaped destruction. I had often noticed while passing an old folks' home at night, on my way back from work, that issuing from an open ground-floor window were the peaceful, regular snores of some aged resident asleep inside. They were so audible that on one occasion, when they ceased, I feared that the sound source had just expired. One chilly night, as I crouched beneath the window to capture these sounds, I managed to make an almost perfect recording of them. The air was still and the street deserted, so there were no other noises to spoil the faint, rhythmical snores that issued from the room as the stylus engraved them on wax. Suddenly, however, I was attacked from the rear by a woman in nurse's uniform, who had crept up behind me through the shrubbery. She set about me with a walking stick and shouted for the police. It was all I could do to defend myself, I was so startled, but I succeeded in getting away with a few bruises.

Amateur recordings demonstrate that conspiratorial gatherings still take place at which French is spoken by those present. My working conditions here in Alsace are excellent. I make a note of the most interesting recordings on file, which are very numerous, and copy them for personal use in my billet after work. In return, so to speak, I'm compelled to endure some unimaginably awful sights: third-degree interrogations, sanguinary floggings. Brutal police raids, too: complete with my recording equipment, I'm obliged to stand there surrounded by a gaggle of tearful children whose father is being hauled off by the Germanizers, and all because I myself have recorded his voice. Microphones are even installed in the confessional, where people still dare to speak French with their priest. The church is then raided.

Linguistic culling: a basic concept evolved during the Napoleonic wars by Friedrich Jahn, the father of German calisthenics and originator of the physical education program to which I was remorselessly subjected from childhood until late adolescence. Jahn held that the entire body must be toughened, including—of course—the tongue. Like the German Linguistic Association, he opposed verbal interbreeding and urged that our language divest itself of all foreign interlopers.

My supervisory officer plays me a tape. The voices are distorted and can barely be heard above the hiss of the low-volume recording, but the stresses, which differ from those of any known German accent, are clearly detectable. Now the hiss threatens to drown the voices altogether. The officer starts cursing: "What's the man blathering about? Why can't he speak more clearly? Not a single recognizable name, just isolated syllables."

There's an unusual timbre to the voice on the tape. It

reminds me of my own siren voice: "Down to the air-raid shelter," every note of it seems to say. I find the sound so distasteful I want to clap my hands over my ears. The officer turns to me. "My job is to detain French-speakers," he says, "but it's obvious that this equipment hasn't been perfected sufficiently to yield any useful information. See to it at once, Karnau. I want this tape recorder to supply all the evidence we need in order to arrest the subversive elements in question. You're the expert, use your own initiative. Copy the tape, cut it up and splice it, do all you can to improve the quality of the recording. We're in urgent need of details: names, addresses, motives for attending these clandestine get-togethers."

He looks at me helplessly, knitting his brow. I go over to the tape recorder. Perhaps if we played it slower? I switch the machine to half-speed, rewind the tape and play it again, but no deep, drawling, tortured voices issue from the loudspeaker. Silence, absolute silence. We listen a moment longer. Then, after glaring at the tape, the officer abruptly flies off the handle: "You idiot, Karnau, what have you done? That recording's a write-off. You wiped it out when you wound it back and replayed it—you pressed the wrong button. How could they have sent us an ignoramus like you? Aren't you familiar with this technology?"

Not a sound, all gone, the tape is blank. I stand there mutely while the officer continues to chew me out. He's right, of course: I should never have slipped up like that, but I hadn't allowed for an erasing function. The nature of discs, the recording medium I'm used to, is such that it's quite impossible to reabsorb voices into silence by reversing the turntable. You hear the sounds backwards as they return to their place of origin, the throat, accompanied by a distorted intake of breath.

A disc has to be melted down before the voice it bears is irrevocably silenced.

A dismal evening. Uneasily perched on the window sill in my billet, I flip a cigarette butt into the street below. Will they recall me to Berlin, now that the recording has been obliterated because of my mistake, my stupid blunder? Will the company send a replacement who's more *au fait* with Magnetophon equipment? Could this cost me my job? A pity, because I intended to devote one of my free afternoons to visiting the German University here, where they're assembling a large collection of skulls like that of Joseph Gall, who embarked on his study of comparative anatomy as a young man in this very city, Strasbourg, in 1777.

More by luck than judgment, I managed to restore some of the officer's equanimity this afternoon. My private research has evidently bred a much improved ability to distinguish between voices, because I instantly picked one out as some men were walking along the corridor past my office: it was the same siren voice, the air raid voice that had etched itself into my ear this morning. Without thinking, I blurted out, "That man out there—he's the one on the tape. It must be him, the voice is identical." I didn't at first realize what I'd done by making this remark: visibly gratified, the officer called Security and had the man arrested. A little later he told me in a genial tone that I was *some* use, at least, because I'd unmasked a local Germanizer as a member of the French Resistance. My emotions are mixed. On the one hand, I would never have thought myself capable of such a denunciation; on the other, it may tip the scales in my favor when they come to decide whether or not to report my blunder to Berlin.

The air is exceptionally warm tonight. The strains of a brass band are wafted from far away, so it seems, by a gentle breeze. The sound fluctuates, reverberating from distant streets. The music grows louder. With a sudden explosion of noise, the band emerges from a side street followed by a detachment of Brownshirts marching in step. They, in turn, are followed by a group in regional costume and some civilians who have joined the procession *en route*. Many windows are open, and the din invades the rooms behind the fluttering curtains. Across the way, curious residents are already leaning on their window sills and gazing down into the street. Many wave. The window of one darkened room is closed and the curtain drawn as if by some ghostly hand. The windowpane at my back begins to vibrate. The night air resounds to the blare of trumpets and the rattle of snare drums. They're passing the house now. The colorbearer's flag, propelled by a headwind, slaps him in the face.

The marchers break into a folk song, and the local inhabitants, their cheeks soon hot and flushed, loudly join in the first verse. An entire family sings along, clustered together in a small kitchen window. Clearly visible in their open mouths are tongues, teeth, even threads of saliva. Down below them, noisy expulsions of breath mingle, elbows collide, men jostle one another and break step, their eyelids beaded with sweat in the torchlight. Now they're out of sight. The music fades, the spectators retire into their living rooms. No sound save the agitated twittering of a bird roused from sleep as it flies across the street. A last, smoldering cigarette butt glows in the night-dark roadway.

AS A TREAT we've been picked up from school and driven into town. "Don't we have to go home and have lunch with the others?" Hilde asks.

Papa's chauffeur looks at us in the rear-view mirror. "No," he says, "the two of you are going to spend the afternoon in town with your father. The weather's so nice, he's taking an hour off work for you."

I wonder if it's only Hilde Papa wants to see because he's still angry with me, and the chauffeur is only taking me along because he doesn't dare to send me home alone. Hilde rummages around in her satchel, looking for her hairbrush. "Aren't you pleased, Helga?" she says. "We're going into town with Papa. He's bound to buy us each a present."

No, Papa doesn't look angry with me anymore. He gives me just as nice a smile as he gives Hilde when he admires our clothes. "Regular young ladies, you are. I can really take you out and about these days, you're so well-behaved and grown-up. What would you like to do first? Have lunch right away and then go shopping?

We say we'd rather go shopping first. The sun is shining, and people stare at us as they go past. They all know Papa by sight from photographs or newsreels. A lot of them actually shake his hand and say a few words. We're on our best behavior, so we say good afternoon politely. In the toy shop Papa lets us look around for as long as we like. We choose some new clothes for our favorite dolls. No, Papa definitely isn't still angry about yesterday.

Then, when we think we're going to a café, Papa takes us to a jeweler's instead. To buy something for Mama? "We're looking for a wristwatch for a young lady," he tells the shop assistant.

He smiles at me. Which of us did he mean, me or Hilde? The woman brings out some watches and puts them on the counter. I like the one with the red strap because red is our color, Papa's and mine. I'm sure it's not for me, though, it must be for someone else. Papa gives me a nod. "Let's see what it looks like on your wrist, Helga."

Carefully, he takes the watch from the velvet cushion and straps it on. He's only trying it out to see if there are enough holes in the strap. It looks nice, the kind of watch I'd like for Christmas. "Want to try another?" Papa asks.

I shake my head. Papa takes me by the chin. "Don't pout when someone wants to give you a present. You need a new watch, don't you? You're a big girl now, even if you do still act the goat sometimes, like your little brother and sisters."

"But it was Helmut who—"

Papa's eyes flash, so I stop in case he decides to take the watch back after all. Then we go to a café. We each have an ice cream sundae, but all that interests me is my watch. Hilde admires it too, she's pleased for me. The red strap is nice and shiny, and it's even got a second hand. "But take more care of this one," Papa says, "and see your little brother doesn't get his hands on it. You'd better keep it somewhere safe when you're not wearing it—don't just leave it lying around."

HOW ABSURDLY NAÏVE of me to decide against recording the children's voices and forbid myself to sit them down in front of my microphone, only to hear them on the radio soon afterwards, vigorously endorsing their father's speech in aid of the winter clothing drive. My misgivings were naïve indeed, because the children addressed their audience with total unconstraint and self-assurance. Even as I listened to the broadcast, they must have been listening to themselves at home and hearing their own recorded words. How puerile, how hypocritical of me to leave a blank space on my vocal map, when those children have grown up in daily contact with every kind of gadget—with the telephones and teleprinters, film projectors and record players, all of the latest design, which form as permanent a feature of their parental home as do armchairs and cuckoo clocks elsewhere. Their entire house is populated, not by unpredictable creatures that suddenly ring or buzz, clatter or light up, but by trusted companions.

To them, the recording studio in the basement is simply another room where their father sometimes allows them to watch the sound engineers at work as a special reward for good behavior or good grades in school, so their knowledge of certain technical matters may actually be superior to mine. The private cinema, too, is a familiar place where, on many a festive evening, their parents and guests watch home movies of them romping in the grounds or fondling pet fawns. Or even playing little parts for which they have zealously memorized the dialogue and directions, so eager are they not to be surpassed in histrionic ability by their favorite actor—an actor with whom they playfully compete, a family friend who takes the lead in these home movies and joins them in singing his latest screen hits, which every German child knows by heart.

So my misgivings—my assumption that they would be as dismayed to hear their own voices as I was as a timid child—were just another pretext for concealing my own cowardice. Although every man's voice sounds different when issuing from a loudspeaker than when coming directly from his own mouth, it doesn't necessarily follow that he finds it abhorrent, or that he will keep breaking off in mid-sentence because he involuntarily hears his voice twice over, once inside his head and once engraved on a disc. The children are thoroughly conversant with this phenomenon and think nothing of it. It doesn't inhibit them from continuing to speak freely, whereas my own voice seems to become more and more unnatural, as if the sound inside my head is coming, by degrees, to resemble its recorded counterpart.

I was too cowardly to admit that this hiatus in the relationship between me and my voice is far from being an experience common to all children, that this abhorrence does not afflict everyone, only me, and that my voice may be alone in sounding so unnatural when it comes from a loudspeaker. I was also too cowardly to concede the children's ability to live with their voices without inevitably becoming vocal cripples in the course of time. They have nice voices, that's all, and listening to them on disc will change nothing.

So my scruples have turned out to be envy, pure and simple. I was reluctant to cut a record of the children's lovely young voices, reluctant to give them the pleasure of willingly speaking into my microphone, proud and excited that a few words from their lips should be recorded on disc. So excited, perhaps, that their voices might have cracked while speaking, interrupted by laughter or protests as they elbowed each other away from the microphone, half in play, because each child wanted its voice to be the most clearly audible of all. I was unwilling to let anyone become acquainted with those young voices without knowing the children in the flesh, without having had to expose his own voice to the give-and-take of childish conversation. No one was to be allowed—in the far distant future, when death had overtaken the children themselves or their childish voices, which are anyway doomed to change in adulthood—to hear a single sound of their making.

Or was there an even deeper reason for my scruples and self-restraint? Did they betray a fear that every recording process, every modulated groove, may whittle away a child's voice? Am I wrong, and can the recording of a voice do more than explore a person's innermost being? Does it inevitably subtract something, so that, once engraved on disc, what has been recorded exists only as a sound, a timbre, on that black shellac film? Does every recording rob us of a fragment of our voices, no matter how small?

Hence, too, my instinctive fear as a child of having my voice recorded and my uneasiness on hearing it afterwards. It was as if, without my even suspecting it beforehand, something inside me had been broken off and were now at someone else's disposal.

Do I fear for this miserable voice, tinny though it sounds and useless though it may be, when it seeks, by means of a certain inflection, to convey some emotion that cannot be put into words? There's no word for that secret fear, but my clumsy voice, such as it is, may strike just the note that expresses what it means to be more afraid of voice-stealing than of anything else on earth.

So my plan to compile a map of vocalizations has sprung from an unconscious impulse to confront danger head-on. I go and stand near the recording machine, never for a moment taking my eyes off the microphone lest some insidious word, some laugh or sigh, should escape my lips and engrave itself in the wax. And I'm the person in charge of the cutting stylus.

MAMA'S HAIRDRESSER DOES us. It's awful, having our hair cut. The little ones think it hurts. Hedda always cries, she screams as soon as the hairdresser does up the cape at the back, and she only has to catch sight of the scissors to start jiggling around on the chair and jerking her head away. The hairdresser almost gives up. She tries to hold Hedda steady with one hand so the scissors don't slip and cut her or the haircut goes wrong. That would be bad, because Hedda would have to sit still all the longer. Afterwards she has a red blotch under her chin where the hairdresser's great big hand has had to hold it tight. Now it's Hilde's turn because Holde's hiding somewhere in the house, or maybe she's run out into the garden. Holde comes next as a rule, but the hairdresser won't wait any longer. She sends for Hilde because she wants to finish us off as soon as possible. She can see we're all scared and it makes her nervous.

At last she calls me in. The floor is covered with bits of hair from the others. She wraps the cape around me and shampoos my hair, taking care the foam doesn't get in my eyes and make them sting. Then she fetches her comb and scissors. I can't help clenching my teeth. The hairdresser starts at the back, where I can't see anything, just feel the scissors tweaking my hair and hear them clicking away. Some hair falls to the floor—not too much, I hope, because I don't want to stop wearing braids. I can't look, I can't move or she'll prick me. My ear—why is she snipping around my ear all this time? I feel as if I'm right inside my ear, I can feel every little puff of air, I can feel the coolness of the scissors, I can almost feel the metal on my skin. I hope she won't be much longer.

We always get a reward for having our hair cut: Mama sits with us while we're having tea on the terrace. Mama has had her hair done too, it smells nice, it's fair and wavy and shines in the sunlight. That's the hair spray. We girls aren't allowed to use hair spray, not yet. We're glad when the hairdresser finishes cutting our hair and drives off again.

She comes to do Mama's hair every other day, and Mama goes to the salon every Saturday to have it cut. I wonder when Papa gets his hair cut. It always looks so neat whenever we see him and whenever he speaks in public or gives a party, but when does he find the time? Perhaps someone comes to cut it at the office. Except that he's always so busy there. He goes from room to room, checking on things, supervising his staff and listening to their reports.

Does he have it cut while he's dictating his diary? No, he walks up and down while he's dictating. He looks at his notes, thinks of the right words, puffs at his cigarette, crumples up one piece of paper after another. Nobody's allowed to disturb him then. Papa told us once that his diaries are very important. Every word must be just right because he's going to publish them as a book later on, and they'll be a great success. The money they make will be for us children, Papa says. We'll be able to live on it, all six of us, after he's dead. Everything's settled, he says. The contracts were all signed long ago, and no publisher will be able to wriggle out of them.

While he's at the map table? No, snippets of hair would fall on the war map and alter the position of the front line. It wouldn't do during one of his radio conferences, either. How would it look if Papa criticized the broadcasters with his hair all mussed up? The hairdresser couldn't stand behind him and cut his hair then, not when he's cursing the war and calling people cretins and imbeciles. He couldn't keep his head still, not when he's doing that, and the hairdresser would have to give up. But his hair is always so neat and tidy. Perhaps that's Papa's secret.

WHERE AM I? What am I doing on this hard, creaking bed? It's just a narrow plank bed, not my own. Why is the air so strangely still, why is it so light, what's become of the darkness, is it morning already? And this acrid, penetrating smell, what is it? The stench of humanity, the tang of cheap disinfectant and surgical alcohol, that's what it is. The air in this unfamiliar room, with its two chairs, table and locker, is heavy with hospital effluvia. And no, it isn't still, the air, I can hear a muffled, intermittent rumble from far away: shellfire, it's the war, I'm behind the lines. What are those voices in the distance? What woke me? There, someone quite near me is speaking in a voice that sounds vaguely familiar: "So now describe what happened."

It's Dr. Hellbrandt, the medical director of this hospital—this field hospital, to be precise. Have I been wounded? I feel my knee, my chest and arm: no wound, no pain. Now I put a face to that cold, crisp voice: Dr. Hellbrandt, who greeted me yesterday surrounded by casualties of whom I've yet to see a single one today. Casualties...People back home say that many are horribly mutilated and scream in agony day and night. They're nothing like the war-wounded cripples who parade their gallantry medals through the streets: black leather hands, eye patches, crutches, empty sleeves in jacket pockets, baggy, pinned-up trouser legs.

Dr. Hellbrandt is speaking again. He must be quite near, right next door in his office. Now another voice joins in, faltering and hesitant as if struggling to reply. I can catch every word. The walls of the hut are so paper-thin, even the man's labored breathing is clearly audible: "So we dug in and settled down to wait in our muddy foxholes. The position was impassable, blocked by tree trunks..."

Silence once more. Where's my Magnetophon equipment? I've got to record this. A voice as distraught and exhausted as this could be heard nowhere else, it'll make an important addition to my vocal map. I jump out of bed, hurry to the table, automatically run through the routine I've learned. First I unwind the power cable. The man next door sighs and goes on in a weary monotone: "Suddenly we came under fire. The sentries out front must have been half asleep. Either that, or they bought it before they could raise the alarm..."

The cable gets tangled up. What's the matter with me? I can do this with my eyes shut as a rule. The blitzkrieg voice inside me issues the next order before I've carried out the first: Plug in microphone lead. Which is the right socket? The plug mustn't come adrift. Now thread in the tape. Thread it in so enough of it appears on the other side of the recording head: six centimeters precisely. Thread the tape in quick, up to the mark, and secure it so it doesn't slip. But it does slip as soon as the driving spindle begins to turn, and blank tape flutters from the rotating pay-off spool. I'm close to despair. In training I could do everything perfectly, ready my equipment and install the microphone in double-quick time, even in the dark. My inner voice issues a confused babble of orders while the one next door drones on: "The din was diabolical, whining bullets, screaming shells. A report came through on my walkie-talkie: "Unit wiped out after fierce firefight." Just then the flames reached the driver's cab. They ignited the camouflage netting and set it on fire. The driver was flailing away at his jacket with hands like blazing torches of flesh..."

The tape is finally secured. Last of all: Operate microphone switch. The tape is running past the head, recording is in progress: "Then I was thrown clear by the blast, found myself lying in the ditch with earth pattering down on me. A fiendish racket, intense pressure on my eardrums, a piercing whistle. Above me, comrades were running away with their hair on fire. One of them came rolling down on top of me, slammed me across the face with his limp arm. I shut his eyes, which were already caked with mud. Then silence, utter silence until I came to in the midst of another diabolical din from the men in bed around me, the bedclothes, the breathing. And the breathing turned out to be my own..."

The man emits a low, throaty sound and breaks off. I've now recorded my first front-line voice, recorded it through this thin partition wall. My hands are still trembling. Only now does it strike me that the voice must have an owner: one of Hellbrandt's patients—an exceptionally serious case, no doubt. I sneak out into the passage, eager for at least a glimpse of my sound source. The door of Hellbrandt's office is ajar: I see a pathetic, grimy figure, bare feet in boots with the laces undone, knees trembling, trousers spattered with mud. An allegory of squalor with shirt buttoned askew, lips quivering and cheeks unshaven, the patient has red-rimmed eyes and his matted hair is singed in places. He doesn't notice me. The fingers of one hand are stiffly clutching a fold of filthy trouser leg, the other hand is kneading his groin.

"What, still in your pajamas? Did we wake you? I apologize."

Hellbrandt stations himself behind me. "The MPs picked him up quite near here last night," he explains. "A malingerer? A deserter? That's what they want me to find out and certify. He can't go back into the line in any case, the war has robbed him of his eyesight. It's immaterial for the moment whether his blindness is only hysterical. He certainly acquired a good dose of shell shock at the front. He'll be going home with the next batch of wounded."

Hellbrandt turns back to the patient. "I'm sending you home," he says. A sudden thought strikes me: What if my departmental chief notices that I've misappropriated a whole reel of precious magnetic tape? Does it still matter, though? They mean me to get myself killed out here, Berlin means to see me slaughtered, that's clear as daylight. The new generation, they said, but they didn't mean young soldiers, the youngsters with contorted, steel-helmeted faces who are quitting their short lives in the cut and thrust of trench warfare, or simply in the barrages laid down by their own side; they were referring to the new generation of portable tape-recorders. Premagnetization, that's the magic word. The tape is premagnetized, so the hiss can be almost entirely eliminated while recording. A revolution in sound, that's what they call this machine. Its appreciably greater acoustic spectrum enables very faint and extremely loud sounds to be recorded for the first time in human history.

I know what happened. The children's father ran a test, as he does with every new technological development. He demanded a demonstration of this portable tape recorder and was delighted with the result: "A genuine breakthrough!" he is said to have exclaimed. And then: "If we can put this new technology into widespread front-line use quickly enough"— or words to that effect—"I foresee immense potentialities." His idea was seized upon by some ingenious desk warrior like my roommate in the firm, who promptly devised a program for testing the machine in action. Every last item of enemy radio traffic was to be recorded with crystal clarity—crystal clarity, no less—and sent back at once to the rear echelon for decoding. Why? Because it's obvious to any rational person that, unlike yours truly, cipher clerks are too valuable to be exposed to the perils of the front line.

"Harnessing science to the war effort," my head of department told me, "that's the prime requirement, Karnau, you know that yourself. Each of us must serve where he's needed most. Think of the vast, state-sponsored research projects we'll be given if we make a worthwhile contribution to final victory.

We have to compile data based on practical experience, Karnau, I'm sure you agree. And that, Karnau, as I've no need to tell you, means getting closer to the enemy."

What he omitted to say was that, by selecting me for front-line duties under the auspices of this program, he was killing two birds with one stone and ridding himself of an unwanted subordinate. He's only waiting for me to wind up like everyone else out here: felled by a hail of bullets, blown to bits by a shell, or simply crushed to death by a tank. The whole firm still laughs at my blunder in Alsace. Someone only has to say the word "Strasbourg" and my colleagues' faces light up. Then they're off: "Poor old Karnau spends his nights keeping company with horses' heads and listening to records of people panting and groaning, and he's so dozy during the day, he goes and wipes out important tape recordings. Horses' heads are hot stuff—try swapping your old lady for a horse's head some night and you'll never look back."

So now the die is cast. My first brush with the enemy is imminent and inescapable, and lying here in the wards are the wounded who have already seen everything that's in store for me. The front line: that's where inward experiences are abruptly externalized, for instance when a shell splinter or a bayonet severs your stomach muscles and your guts spill out over your genitals, thighs and feet.

Hellbrandt knocks on my door after his morning rounds: "Karnau, come with me. There's something you should see—something that ought to interest you, being a sound engineer."

He ushers me into a room off the main ward with only three beds in it. "These are my favorite patients," he says. "They don't make as much noise as the others, don't keep calling for me or the nurses. These creatures in here are always quiet. It's a positive pleasure to treat them, especially after a spell of fierce fighting, when bloody shreds of humanity are brought in and groans and screams ring out on all sides, when the corridors are jam-packed with stretchers because there's nowhere else to put them. Then it's a case of operating, operating around the clock, digging out splinters, sewing up wounds, et cetera, so that at least the severest cases give you some peace. Men with badly shattered faces have very little hope of survival. The most you can do is remove the lower jaw and patch up a hole or two. Other than that, it's just a question of keeping them quiet until the end comes. Trouble is, as soon as you've dealt with one ward, the caterwauling starts up again in another. This is the only place where silence always reigns."

The occupants of the three beds are staring at me. Slightly flustered, I say good morning. "Save your breath," Hellbrandt tells me, "but if you do speak, make sure your mouth movements are clearly visible."

He nods at the men in turn, and they all nod back. Then he produces some cigarettes from his pocket and inserts one between each patient's lips. The dry, loosely packed weeds burn down in no time, and no wonder, the way the deaf-mutes puff at them. Hellbrandt beckons me closer. "The deaf-mutes' battalion was my own idea," he says. "A special unit capable of carrying out operations to the letter, even when the noise level is extreme."

He perches on the edge of one of the beds and converses in sign language with its occupant, a man whose head is bandaged. "Most of them are also in possession of highly classified information," he tells me, without taking his eyes off the patient. "There's no danger of their divulging secrets or military objectives that could be of assistance to the enemy, even if subjected to the most rigorous interrogation methods."

The man in the next bed slowly raises his hands and begins to gesticulate in a similar fashion. Hellbrandt's eyes swivel from one man to the other. "You'll have to excuse me for a moment, Karnau. It's all I can do to follow them when they get into an argument."

He interprets their gestures in a low voice, producing a delayed translation of the visible into the audible. The picture and the sound track are out of sync: "It's days since we went into action, he says, but my stomach's still churning. It's almost like it's getting worse, becoming unendurable. You'd think the enemy had invented some ultra-special weapons designed to deal with deaf-mutes. Not shells but lethal soundwaves..."

The man puffs at his cigarette, so his next signed sentence is only fragmentary. The other patient waves to attract Hellbrandt's attention. "No need for any ultra-special weapons, he says. Crouch in a trench when a tank goes roaring over the top of you, that's good enough. Our battalion is always first in line for unpleasant assignments up front. That's because none of us can afford to dodge them..."

Such are a deaf-mute's ordeals in the audible world, and such are the audible world's assaults on the deaf-mute. The rest of us are also subjected to these assaults, but we completely fail to perceive them because we're so inattentive, so busy listening that individual sounds escape us. The death cry of a comrade may go unnoticed amid the thunder of the guns, just as the sound of a barrage may be temporarily ignored by those awaiting the order to advance. Noises are merciless assailants of us all, but whereas eyes are always required for the perception of light, tongues for tastes and noses for smells, noises are not dependent on the ears alone. They eat into every part of the body, protected or unprotected: they can set up vibrations in a steel helmet and deliver a fatal shock to the entire skull.

Now, from the bed across the room, the third patient joins in the conversation. He makes almost indecipherable signs in such quick succession that Hellbrandt is clearly at a loss to follow them and translates only scraps of what the deaf-mute's hands convey with ever-increasing vehemence. For safety's sake, he removes the smoldering cigarette butt from his patient's lips. "Far worse than all the vibration," Hellbrandt interprets, "is the lack of communication while we're operating at night. No radio, and we're in mortal danger of failing to notice when we're under fire. One of my comrades loosed off a flare because he couldn't stand the darkness any longer—because he was scared of being all alone. He was hit at once. I can see him now, all lit up with his red mouth open in a silent scream..."

Hellbrandt tries to stem the flow, but the wounded man is past stopping. His features are violently contorted, his eyes fixed and staring. Hellbrandt stops translating, he's too busy trying to calm his patient, who now, although he can hear nothing, presses his palms to his temples and, with a supreme effort, utters a series of pitiful sounds. He waggles his tongue and shuts his eyes. Oblivious of his surroundings, he begins to weep. Hellbrandt, standing over him, holds his twitching wrists together. At last the patient subsides. With a vague gesture he sinks back against the pillows and lies motionless. Anxiously, Hellbrandt prepares to give him a shot. The man's face is bluish, possibly moribund.

Although the callous way in which Hellbrandt speaks of his

patients makes my flesh crawl, no one who sees how devotedly he tends these special cases can fail to grasp, quite suddenly, that his cold-blooded tone is just a front, and that the aims he pursues here, at his place of work, are not what they seem at first glance. Superficially, his idea for a deaf-mutes' battalion was quite consistent with the attainment of final victory, but his real, underlying concern was to save lives in danger. Logically speaking, if the attribute that differentiates man from beast is speech—an ability to use the voice in such a way that the series of sounds it produces can convey extremely complex ideas—then deaf-mutes, who have no voices, are not, strictly speaking, human. It follows that, under the eugenic laws now in force, they belong to the category of living creatures unworthy of existence. And that, at the present time, means certain death. Under Hellbrandt's aegis, the poor things have at least some hope of survival.

No one will ever see through this subterfuge. Hellbrandt is an apt teacher, not an opportunist like my department chief, who's always out for himself and never averse to gambling with human lives if it helps to buttress his own position. Hellbrandt would never falter in the face of a colleague's reprimand. He doesn't care what other people think of his work or whether they laugh at him behind his back. It's all the same to him: if they want to slaughter him here, let them try. He'll stick it out to the last, here at the front, for as long as he can help his deaf-mutes. It's really worth taking a leaf out of Hellbrandt's book. Behave like a worm and you ask to get trodden on. Who cares about my snide colleagues? Who cares what they think in Berlin? All that matters here is to stand firm. All that matters here, in direst danger, is my vocal map and the opportunity to chart uncharted territory.

———

PAPA HAS JUST come home, I can hear him talking to Mama downstairs. "My new sports convertible is an absolute dream," he says.

"Not so loud, please, the children are asleep."

"But it's still broad daylight."

"Now don't go waking them up."

"I bet they aren't asleep yet, not even close. I bet the girls are lying there wide awake and bored to death."

"No, don't go up there now, it can wait till tomorrow."

"But they'll love the car. Surely you wouldn't begrudge them a trial spin?"

"Please don't disturb them."

"Why not allow them a little treat occasionally? They hardly know us, we so seldom do anything together."

"They've got school in the morning."

"They're doing so well in school, they'll manage."

Papa bustles into our bedroom. "Come on, you two, get up. Get dressed, we're going for a spin."

Hilde and I have been listening hard to see who would win in the end. We knew it would be Papa. We jump out of bed and get dressed as fast as we can. We dash past Mama. Papa's downstairs already. He spits on the windshield and wipes off some fly blood. "Hop in quick," he says. "We mustn't be too long or your mother will get some more worry lines."

We drive through the gate and out into the street, where Mama can't see us any longer. The new car is lovely, far nicer than the other ones we've got, with a top that folds down. Papa puts a cap on. He must have taken our head scarves and neckerchiefs from the drawer and stuffed them in his pocket without our noticing, because he reaches back and hands them to us. He needs a cap to stop the hair fluttering in his face while he's driving, and we mustn't catch cold. He points to the side mirror. "Look," he says, "a cobweb. It wasn't there before. Let's see if we can go fast enough to blow the spider away."

We're past the Wannsee already. It's a warm evening, but the car feels cold now that Papa's driving faster and faster. The spider's web stirs. Is the spider coming out because it knows Papa won't allow it to make its home in his new car? We're heading into the sunset. Hilde's shouting for joy. Papa isn't looking at the sunset, he keeps looking at the spider's web. Incredible how far a spider can travel when it spins its web on a car. Now it's coming out from behind the side mirror, legs first, then its big black body. The spider's ugly legs are clinging really tight to the mirror. I hope it doesn't manage to crawl back to us. Hilde shakes Papa's shoulder: "Faster, Papa, faster, we don't want to see it anymore."

Papa drives even faster to blow it away. The wind is whistling in our ears. "Just you wait," Papa shouts. "We'll get rid of the creature even if we have to drive to Magdeburg."

The spider is clinging to the driver's door with all its might. Papa isn't thinking about anything else, only the spider. His lips have gone all thin and hard, and his face doesn't move a muscle. Looking in the mirror I can see the chinks between his teeth as he stares at the spider, as he squeezes the pedal with his foot to make us go faster, as he drives straight on, on and on, overtaking one car after another. He's so set on his battle with the spider that his fur-trimmed driving cap suddenly looks silly, as if he's used to living in Siberia, or as if the soft fur is there, like an egg cozy, to prevent his head from smashing.

I'm beginning to feel sorry for the spider, it's trying so hard not to let go. It slips a little and automatically unwinds a thread, scrambles back up the thread and tries to get behind the mirror again. I don't want to watch it anymore. It'll soon be dark, but we keep on going. Are we on the way back, or are we really getting near Magdeburg? Hilde nudges me and points: the spider has disappeared at last.

By the time we get home there's nothing left on the driver's door but a few sticky threads with some little insects trapped in them. Papa is pleased he won. He's glad we like his new sports car, too.

THE SKY SHUDDERS, the fractured road surface makes the tires vibrate. The car lurches along, rumbling over stretches thinly coated with gravel and toiling through slushy mud as it steadily, inexorably follows the rutted tracks of the supply route deep into enemy territory. My head brushes the sky, the grimy, nicotine-stained sky of cloth immediately above my head, whenever the vehicle skids into a pothole. Air buffets the windows with every detonation. The earth moves too, and the gray-brown, rain-swept dusk is tremulous with gun-smoke. The explosions convulse my entire body. My hands are shaking too badly to hold the cigarette clamped between my lips—even the glowing tip quivers as the shells burst—but the driver doesn't mind the thunder of the guns. He keeps his eyes fixed on the road ahead, and all he sees is the fragmented field of vision beyond the windshield, with its smears and leopard's spots of mud.

Abruptly, the tire tracks ahead of us are effaced by a blinding flash. The driver brakes to a halt. A shellburst that has almost blown us to smithereens? No, just raindrops sparkling as they dribble down the windshield in the glare of an oncoming motorcycle's headlight. We wait for the convoy behind it to pass.

Every vehicle is adorned with a Red Cross pennant. It seems interminable, this succession of pennants so sodden with rain that not even a gale could make them flutter.

The headlights grope their way along the shoulder, and every truck that squeezes past illuminates an expanse of ditch. There among the debris and horses' carcasses, right beside the shattered remains of an armored car, I see something moving on the ground. The passing headlights continually illuminate the same spot, so recognition soon dawns: some very young puppies, probably still blind, are scrabbling around in the mire. Now the mother appears out of the darkness, bent on keeping her little together. Calmly but firmly, she grips her young by the neck, one by one, and drags them back into the lee of the armored car, whence they emerge once more and totter over to the dead horses. Little wet balls of fur, they sit there whimpering until their mother comes to round them up again. An unexpected picture so close to the front line. An indication, perhaps, that this very spot marks the war's frontier: a last symbol of peace before we enter disputed territory, the forward extremity of the rear echelon, the last stretch before the bomb and shell craters begin. Some messenger dog must have paused in the thick of the fighting to mate with a stray bitch.

What kind of war is this? Here they shoot down pigeons—blow them out of the sky. My neighbor in the dugout insists that the birds carry cameras strapped to their bodies. "They aren't just any old birds, Karnau, they're enemy artillery spotters, get that into your thick head. They're reconnoitering our positions. If they make it back to the Russian lines, it won't be long before the shells come raining down."

The soldier turns away with a shake of the head. He's frying himself something to eat amid the mud and excrement. The others make hard-boiled jokes: "Nothing like puppy meat to supplement our rations." They crouch in their trenches, war written on their faces, night glasses trained on the darkness beyond the parapet. Me, I sit beside the radio operator on my boxes of equipment, deep in the quaking ground. The steel helmet they've issued me is far too big. I have to keep pushing it back or I can't see a thing beneath the rim. "Tighten the strap, you clod." The radio operator addresses me without removing his headset. Cigarettes glow in the darkness. I'm recording enemy radio messages and conducting regular monitoring tests: yes, faint though it is, the enemy radio traffic can be heard on tape with relative clarity. Divisional headquarters sends a runner to collect the tapes three times a day. Such are my present duties as a civilian supernumerary.

I haven't left the dugout since I got here. I don't dare go outside, I'm so scared of the gunfire and the crowded trenches when an attack is in progress and the air billows sideways because a shell has landed nearby—scared above all of the earsplitting, never-ending din. I've done my utmost to conceal this fear, but my face, my set mouth and my silence, not to mention the way I screw up my eyes at every detonation, betray my state of mind to the others, many of whom are much younger than I.

The enemy transmitter has been inaudible for quite a while. I sneak outside, determined to overcome this intolerable fear, determined not to let it dissuade me from proceeding with my own work as planned. At my own risk, I intend to take advantage of a lull in the bombardment to make some recordings of a kind that has never been heard before: I propose to capture the sounds made by soldiers in battle.

A crosswind, rain. I conceal my microphones behind banks of soil, in craters and along the trench, embed their bases in damp earth, run out cables, cower and curl up whenever a shell lands in my vicinity. Then back to the dugout caked with mud. I plug in the microphone leads, don my headset and check reception, discover a loose connection in the left-hand earpiece, adjust separate access to individual microphones located in the field, and listen: a rumble of gunfire, the groans of the wounded mingled with the hiss of the evening wind and rain. I test the tape recorder, listen to a trial recording, wait impatiently for the blank section to end, and suddenly I hear it: the first voice, faint, distorted, scarred by its own violence. The tape goes taut and snaps, the voice breaks off in mid-utterance, the spool starts to race, the severed residue of tape slaps the recording head and the controls, flutters with rhythmical, electronic ferocity. A surveyor of the human landscape, as it were, I resolve to wait until the fighting abates and nocturnal peace descends.

Before long, the complete absence of background noise enables me to monitor and record sound sources that are destined to dry up in the very near future. The whole of the nocturnal landscape comes alive with these dying soldiers' swan songs, the battlefield resounds to the cries of the wounded. As feverishly eager as a child, I keep switching from one sound source to another, reaching into the box of blank tapes from where I sit and reloading the machine. Mine is a map of vowels. It will immortalize young soldiers with mangled faces long after their last postcards reach home, long after heroic words are murmured over their shattered corpses, but only, to be on the safe side, when the latter are defenseless and can no longer drown them with a spine-chilling death rattle.

I switch to the trench: heavy footsteps and a downpour. Suddenly, members of the unit come crowding into the dugout. Left ear: the voices of those around me, muffled by the headset. Right ear: cries and a patter of hailstones from the scene of the most recent fighting. I save the remains of a soldier's exhausted voice, capture the ultimate extremity of that voice and preserve it for the bereaved. Over to the position nearest the enemy: a whistling, roaring sound. It draws nearer, swells within fractions of a second to a splintering crash. Then, just as it reaches maximal volume, transmission ceases: the microphone has been buried or blown to bits.

The night song slowly fades, but the magnetized particles on the tape flicker on, steadfastly adjusting themselves to the sonic situation of the moment. Faint though they are, the noises in the headset rend my ears. I must go on listening, stay with those noises to the end. Unplug and switch over: each of the men left out there can now be clearly distinguished, chins as stubbly and voices as ravaged as the ground on which they lie dying—the ground across which I myself so recently stumbled. They're here in my ears, the men who will remain out there. Their bodies are lying beyond redemption in the lethal danger zone, but their sighs are safe in here on tape. And my tape will relinquish those sighs to no one, no enemy however strong, even if he slowly dismembers and sieves the bodies overnight, so that in the morning, when the assault is renewed, sodden corpses will scarcely be distinguishable from churned-up ground: all will have been reduced to gray slush, nothing more.

Impressive though these phenomena are, their meaning is unfathomable; they relapse into darkness. Just before the end, voices regain their naturalness and abandon all their long-acquired self-control. Out they come once more, those crude, unschooled, amorphous sounds that issue from the very marrow. Setting up a parallel connection, I hear deep sighs in a wide variety of intonations, groans, gurgles, sounds of vomiting in the mire and murk, nuances of sound in which several layers of darkness have become deposited, and which spring from the darkness of their surroundings. The moribund are returning to their origins, no longer able to restrain their voices and suppress the cries that burst forth. Animal sounds pure and simple, these are neither fashioned by the larynx nor muted by the throat; they fill the entire oral cavity. Lips, tongue and teeth are incapable of holding these involuntary sounds in check and silencing them before they leave the mouth. What an experience! What a vocal panorama!

CHAPTER

"What a view! What a vast, echoing panorama—right here, in front of us! Breathtaking, isn't it, this rugged scenery? Look at those rocky gorges on the other side of the valley, look at the snow-capped peaks of that mountain range. They hurt your eyes, don't they? See how the sunlight bounces off the glaciers, the patches of snow running down to the tree line, and the avalanche that has cut a swath through the woods. The fir trees are so dense, they seem to swallow up the light. How high are those mountains, I wonder, and how did anyone ever manage to survey them? They're so dazzling, even at this distance, they hurt your eyes. Imagine having to cross those sunlit stretches—you'd be lucky not to go snow-blind! The eye instinctively avoids them and concentrates on the level, shady expanses—there, where sunlight gives way to shadow on that alpine meadow sandwiched between the thickly wooded area on the projecting dome of rock and the peaks in the background. And what a sky! Like the clouds in a battle painting come to life. Do look, Helga."

"Yes, they're very nice, the mountains."

Mama likes this view, that's why she chose it as a

background for our family photograph. I'm trying to look at it but I can't, not properly. I force myself to look at every rock, very hard, but I can't breathe properly either. Is it the mountain air? Do you have to breathe faster up here because it's so thin, or is it this tight collar and the necklace and my new dress? It's awfully uncomfortable, the dress, not to mention these stockings and my smart new patent leather shoes. The photographer has only come here because he says there are so few opportunities to photograph all of us children together with our mother. Mama also thinks it's time we had another nice picture taken for the newspapers. We line up in a row with Mama holding Heide in her arms. "Children in front," says the photographer, "mother behind and in the middle."

We always have to stand still for so long, smiling at the camera in a friendly kind of way. It's nice to have our picture in the paper, of course. My classmates always envy me, but they don't know what a bore it is, waiting for pictures to be taken, or how good we have to be at table, sitting there quiet as mice when Papa or Mama takes us out for meals at other people's houses. My friend Conni is a lot better off from that point of view. She doesn't go to as many big parties with her parents, but in the afternoons she can always play outside till suppertime with the other girls in our class. That's why she's got so many friends. Lots more than me.

Conni lives at Nikolassee, which is too far away for me to walk or even cycle. Her parents' house is quite different from ours. It's much smaller, for a start, but Conni doesn't have any brothers or sisters to pester her and expect her to share everything with them. The photographer tells me to put my arm around Helmut's shoulder. Is he going to be much longer?

"Something's the matter with Helmut's trousers," he says. "There's a crease on the left at the top, it casts a nasty shadow. Could someone smooth it out?"

The nursemaid comes forward and tugs at Helmut's trousers, but it makes no difference. "Your pocket's bulging. Have you got something in it?" Helmut glances at Mama, looking guilty. He reaches in his pocket and brings out what he's hidden there: a toy soldier. "No tears, if you please," Mama says sternly. "You don't want to be photographed with your eyes all red, do you?"

The photographer snaps us at last.

These mountains remind me of Helmut's model Berghof, with miniature politicians standing on the balcony looking out at the view. Inside, the Berghof is like a doll's house for boys. It's where the little figures live and hold their conferences. Helmut's awfully proud of his Berghof, which is why he was so angry when someone broke a piece off the balcony railings. That boy did it, the one Helmut had to play with. He didn't want to play with him at all, but Mama insisted. "If our hosts are kind enough to make us welcome in their guesthouse," she said, "we must be equally nice to their children." It isn't as if the boy is nice to us. He acts the Führer in his Hitler Youth uniform and orders us around the whole time, and he can't even speak properly. You can't understand his Bavarian dialect, anyway, or only the odd swear word, like shit or bastard, or when he yells at us suddenly, to scare us. He's just like his fat, red-faced father, the Reichsmarschall. It's disgusting, the way he belches and grunts and snorts.

Mama's leaving tonight, she's off to Dresden for a rest cure. We thought she was going to spend the holidays with us, but she only came here to drop us. We're sad when Mama packs her bags. She says she'll telephone us. So will Papa, definitely, every evening. "Can't we come to Dresden with you?" No, it's a sanatorium. Grown-ups only.

I SCAN THE terrain, run my finger over individual areas on the map, a straightforward army-issue map with markings of the usual kind. Penciled crosses indicate tank traps. My finger roams on, tapping as it goes. These wavy lines represent corduroy roads, most of them already severed by shellfire. My forefinger traces the course of a dotted line. This area is particularly important. At this point on its outer extremity I entered the danger zone after dark, worked my way forward from an unknown position on the periphery, and then, having first consulted an expert on the terrain, a shadow specialist, set off into the blue. Searchlights were the problem, I had to avoid their roving, probing beams. Now I open my hand and spread my fingers, covering most of the map, first with shadow, then with flesh: I've sown this entire area with concealed microphones and, thus, mapped it acoustically.

That is how the unfamiliar markings on the map, the clusters of triangles and widely scattered circles, should be interpreted. Not all my recordings lend themselves to precise classification, for instance under the heading of gasps or moans, because their quality has sometimes been badly impaired by feedback resulting from their incredible, unforeseeable volume. When evaluating them, however, I have clearly detected certain invariable features in the distribution of sounds. Consonants, for example, are very seldom uttered on the battlefield at night, and then only at longish intervals, so my primary focus of attention is vowel research. This area spanned by my thumb and third finger, whose tendons briefly twitch as I spread them, contains a concentration of the vowel *a.* As for this hatching here, it denotes that certain rare sounds are uttered mainly in the immediate vicinity of the enemy line, where few words mingle with the moans and groans of the wounded, be they calling for help or scraping together the last available fragments of a prayer. Here, far out across the trenches, is where men can no longer find the words, where they hammer on the doors of their vocabulary because the enemy is launching a surprise attack on the flank; where their husks of words disintegrate, vaporized by pain and excessive exposure to the din of the enemy bombardment. Then, shortly before a sound source is finally extinguished, there are no words at all, anywhere in the monitored area, though this may also stem from loss of hearing and diminished self-control: those unable to hear their own voices refrain from speaking.

I have become a voice thief, I have left the men at the front voiceless. From now on, I can do as I please with their final utterances. By recording, I appropriate a part of any voice I choose and can play it back without its owner's knowledge, even after his death. A voice thief can play recordings of the dead and pretend—to those who know no better—that they're the voices of living persons. My tapes are vocal excerpts. I can reach into any man's depths without his knowledge. I can extract anything from those depths and take possession of it, anything and everything down to the last, intimate breath exhaled by a dying man.

How the map paper crackles under my palm, how it curls as it absorbs my sweat, producing entirely new constellations of sounds in one corner: here, where open vowels impinge on gutturals, and there, beside the mark that indicates where a youngster in his death throes lost all vocal control. I must listen to that recording again, right away. It's an unimaginable screech such as no one ever before heard issuing from a

human mouth. Mouth, did I say? It wasn't really an oral process at all. The whole throat was brought into play, outside
as well as inside. Windpipe and larynx played their part, but
the epidermis resonated too—indeed, one could imagine that
every bristle on his chin contributed to the sound.

Where is the tape? This one is a chorus of death rattles, and
this one, the label almost indecipherable because I wrote it in
the field during a hailstorm, is of silence, a whole tapeful of
silence recorded afterwards, when nothing—vocally speaking
—was stirring. Damn, the card index has fallen off the table.
Here, this must be the young man responsible for those exceptionally strident cries, if cries is what they can be called.
Not long now. Thread the tape in carefully, throw the heavy
switch, fingers trembling with expectancy, and listen. Almost
there, not another word, just listen.

That voice is all I want to hear. I play and replay it. A little
further on comes a very special sound: just that youthful
stranger's voice overlaid with my breathing, nothing but my
own hurried breathing, because there's no one else in the
room to listen with me, no one with me to look at the map
and listen to my explanations.

WE'RE BACK IN Berlin at last. Papa meets our train, he's taken
some time off specially for us. Hilde almost bursts into tears
when Papa gives her a hug. He really did telephone us every
evening on the Obersalzburg, and we wrote to him in Berlin.
Once, when he'd read one of our letters, he sent us a great
big telegram complete with a picture, and he called us just
after it arrived. He was far too impatient to know how we
liked the telegram to wait till we spoke that evening. He even
sent some presents by courier plane for Hilde's birthday.

Mama's still in Dresden. Our nursemaid and the little ones

have driven straight from the station to Schwanenwerder, but Papa takes me and Hilde to Lanke to spend a few days on our own with him. We've a lot to tell him: how we were presented with bunches of flowers, and how we could only drive very slowly, so many people were lining the village street to welcome us and Mama. By the time we got to the house the open car was full of flowers.

Hilde's grouchy. "We spent the whole day sitting in the train," she says. "It was boring."

Better than flying, though. I always feel sick when I fly.

At Lanke we have the whole house to ourselves and no little ones to bother us. They're a nuisance most of the time, always fussing, never leaving us to play in peace. Papa lets us rummage around in his bookshelves and pick out a book for him to read aloud to us.

Hilde chooses Grimm's fairy tales. We sit on the veranda, the three of us. It'll be dark soon. Mosquitoes come swarming up from the lake when it's dark. They're bound to bite us, we'll be itching all night.

"Papa, what does Germanization mean?"

"Germanization? Where did you pick that up?"

"I heard someone say it on the Obersalzburg. They were talking about Alsace. Where's Alsace?"

"Yes," Hilde says, "where is it?"

"Well," says Papa, "let's see. Alsace is over towards France, but it's really part of Germany. The French took it away from us, even though it's a hundred percent German, but now it belongs to us again."

"But what does Germanization mean?"

"It simply means that everything in Alsace has been put back into German, school lessons, newspapers, government announcements, and so on. After all, why should Alsace be any different from the rest of the Reich? Some of the people there didn't like that. They were determined to oppose everything German, so we had to put a stop to them. They try to keep their activities dark, the traitors, but the police have unmasked a lot of them."

"Shady characters, you mean?"

"Yes, you could call them that."

"Men who kidnap children, are they shady characters too?"

"Yes, but you've no need to be scared of kidnappers, no one would dare to kidnap you. Kidnapping is a capital offense, your Papa made sure of that years ago, just so that you, my darlings, could feel safe."

"But on the way home to Nikolassee, where the woods are, isn't it dangerous there?"

"No, of course not. Why do you ask?"

"Not even when it gets dark? Not even if we had to walk home in the evening, all by ourselves?"

"But you never have to do that. You're home from school long before it gets dark."

"But for instance, if Conni came over so we could play with our boats down by the lake, and if she went home too late because we forgot to look at the time?"

"Conni? The girl in your class, you mean?"

"That's right, my friend Conni."

"Her parents have moved, I'm afraid. She won't be there next term."

"But she still lives at Nikolassee, surely? Or have they moved to Schwanenwerder, near us?"

"No, not there either. Their new home is miles away. Too far away for Conni to attend your school."

"So we won't be able to see each other anymore?"

"I rather doubt it."

"Oh.... But why didn't she tell me?"

"You were down in the South for so long. How could she have told you?"

Papa lights a cigarette and opens the book of fairy tales. Soon we won't have any friends left at all, so many have already gone, evacuated from Berlin because of the air raids. "Come closer, the two of you," Papa says, "my cigarette smoke will keep the midges away." And he starts reading.

I'VE BEEN FIRMLY convinced, ever since I was a boy, that even the dead can hear. It is an established fact that although many bodily functions and processes cease abruptly after death, some do not. If a cadaver continues to be galvanized for a time by certain uncontrolled nervous impulses, why shouldn't it also be receptive to acoustic impressions, albeit possibly of a random nature? The ears, after all, are still completely intact. We close a dead person's eyes, but the ears remain exposed. The slowly cooling corpse may lie there motionless but still alert to individual sounds in its vicinity. It may not perceive them quite as clearly as it did when alive—they may be intermittent or overlaid with a hiss that steadily increases in volume as decay sets in and generates internal noises; as the bodily fluids cease to flow and the lungs are slowly eaten away, as the stomach is attacked by incipient putrefaction and gastric acids begin to digest the human frame itself.

So a dead man can still, for a while, detect the muted voices of those around him—doctors, relations, and so forth—because the latter cast caution to the winds in the belief that he has long since entered the hereafter. They debate the cause of death and discuss funeral arrangements—they may even express relief at his passing. Though incapable of joining in their conversation, the dead man can still hear all of this. And then, quite suddenly, the voices and the hiss die away.

This will form the concluding part of my lecture at the Dresden symposium. I plan to speak without notes, so plenty of rehearsals will be needed. It's a good idea, I feel, to end the lecture without a sample recording and leave the delegates to file out in sudden silence. The sample recordings . . . they're the trickiest problem, because I must select them with such care that they simply cannot fail to impress. After all, apart from my vocal maps and my daring final hypothesis, they're the high point of the entire lecture. Which items in my vast collection will be most appropriate to the occasion?

These tapes and discs are all I have left. I was fired soon after my return from the front. Several hundred meters of tape were missing, that's what did it. They refused to believe me when I said I'd lost them in the turmoil out there. That was the official explanation, but my head of department obviously guessed what really lay behind the story of the missing tapes—or, at least, he hinted as much when he said goodbye. Certain rumors had come to his ears, he said, but he couldn't bring himself to credit them. "Unsavory" was the word he used in this connection.

Had he been tipped off by colleagues of mine after one of them caught me in the cutting room one night, evaluating some death rattles? Could he even have heard, in a roundabout way, of what happened during one of my absences from home? Alarmed by a smell of putrefaction on the stairs, my neighbors summoned the police in the belief that my apartment contained a days-old, rotting corpse, but all that came to light were some half-dissected pigs' heads on the kitchen table. I had inadvertently left them lying there because my departure was so hurried that I'd had no time to feed the scraps to Coco.

My call-up papers arrived a few days later. They came as a shock. It was less the possibility of death that scared me—my sojourn at the front had already brought me face to face with that as a civilian—than the prospect of being plunged, willy-nilly, into the world of male togetherness, with its stench of sweat and coarse jokes, with all the things that made my gorge rise even as a boy.

My sole recourse was to request an interview with the children's father, who heard me out when I told him of my predicament and, in return for my having looked after his offspring, agreed to help. He kept his word: my invitation to Dresden can only have been his doing.

MAMA HAS SENT us to see Papa at his office. "He's bound to be pleased if you pay him a surprise visit," she said. Papa isn't as busy as usual, he can take us to the zoo—Hilde, Helmut and me. But we're told to wait in the outer office, it seems he's busy after all. Maybe he's on the telephone, or having a private conversation with an important visitor. It's strictly forbidden to walk into Papa's office without being asked, so we're made to sit on the sofa outside. He's in conference, the receptionist says.

At last we can go in. Papa's office is done up in red, all the chairs and his desk are covered with red leather. He's sitting at the desk, smoking. "Well, my dears, how are you? Finished your homework?"

There's no one in the office he could have been in conference with. Maybe his visitor went out through the door into the next room, and from there out into the corridor. The door isn't shut, it's only ajar. Helmut sits on Papa's lap and plays with his fountain pen. Papa stubs out his cigarette. "This *is* a nice surprise," he says. "Where shall we go, the zoo?"

He's already lit another cigarette. He isn't half as pleased to see us as he makes out, I can tell from the look in his eyes and the wrinkles around his nose. Perhaps it was a tiring conference. Helmut is jabbing the blotter with the fountain pen. "Stop that," Papa says, "you'll only make a mess."

"It's green, Papa, the ink."

"Yes, and you'll end by getting it all over your nice clean shirt."

"I like green ink."

"And look at your hands. Careful now, we'll go and wash them."

There's a sudden movement in the room next door: I see a lady through the crack, but only for a moment. She moves so quickly, her necklace catches the sunlight. Hilde says, "Papa, will we have to go straight home after the zoo?"

The door to the corridor closes quietly. What was she doing here, that lady? Did Hilde see her too? No, definitely not, she's looking at Papa, who's keeping hold of Helmut's hands to stop him making an even bigger mess. "Come on, you two," he says. "We'll wash Helmut's grubby paws and then we'll go, right away."

"Papa, when you have visitors in your office..."

"Yes, Helga, what about it?"

"Oh, nothing."

"You mean because you had to wait just now?"

"Yes."

"Were you getting bored out there?"

"Yes, a bit."

———

A HUMAN FIGURE in plastic? A tangle of electric wires? I can't make it out in the gloom, not at first. All that illuminates the big room's pale blue ceiling, high above, is some concealed lighting. A curtain at the other end, its drapery disturbed, rustles and billows out on either side. The whole wall of fabric stirs, red as an oral cavity, red as the rest of the décor. Now the thing begins to rotate on its own axis, there in the center of the room. Lights start flashing, red lines, then blue: convoluted neon tubes with a big red blob pulsating in their midst. It's clearly recognizable now: a human body in outline with its arms raised, every organ lit up in a different color. Meanwhile, in a businesslike tone, a recorded voice reads out information relating to human anatomy. Apart from that, silence. The neon tubes faintly illuminate a row of marveling faces: an entire class of schoolchildren lined up in front of the "Glass Man." Every part of him glows, the only unlit component being his larynx.

So these are the exhibition rooms of the Museum of Hygiene, but where's the lecture hall? I lose my way in the labyrinthine building, wander through a series of cellars in which pipes mounted at eye-level drip with condensation. It's chilly down here. Through an open door and into a basement storeroom. The lights are on, revealing shelves laden with boxes, and there's a woman sitting at the back—she's bound to be able to direct me. But it isn't a woman, just a plaster torso painted in true-to-life colors: smooth, pink skin, rouge, lipstick, bobbed hair. The girl who's smiling at me even has retractable eyelids and mascaraed eyelashes. The eyes are so lifelike, I failed to notice at first that her arms and legs are missing.

Suspended from the shelves are some Wagnerian heads, heroic plaster casts in *mezzo-rilievo*. Flowing locks, grimacing faces, mouths open as if hallooing or singing. What's in those black boxes? Cautiously, I take one off the shelf. Visible through the glass top is a repulsive spectacle, the head of a baby with its eyes shut, the whole nose an open wound. A freshly prepared specimen? A realistic imitation? The box bears a handwritten inscription: "Congenital Syphilis." I get the picture now: these are specimens molded in wax, pathological conditions copied from live patients for the edification of medical students. I peer into a dusty cardboard box: another head, this one swathed in bandages with only the mouth exposed and the protruding tongue a mass of blisters. And here is a head cut in half to reveal a longitudinal section of the organs of speech and the throat, life-size. I can see the bisected larynx and the vocal cords stretched taut between the flaps of flesh that have been clamped apart for better visibility.

Strange. I conduct my solitary research at home with pigs' and horses' heads, devote years of intensive study to the apparatus of speech, and all at once, in an unfamiliar setting, I'm confronted by a similar collection. Waxworks. Of human beings, though, not animals. Could it be that, without my knowing it, others have long been pursuing my own line of inquiry?

I walk on, passing hand studies, cranial casts, facial fragments, fleshy excrescences, deformities, cleft palates, pockmarked cheeks. The subterranean storeroom is bigger than I thought. Stretched out on a slab is a patient's body cast *in toto,* face contorted and mouth gaping in a silent scream as a length of bone is removed from his open thigh. Beside it lies another simulacrum: a human leg, swollen and suppurating after several days without medical treatment.

"Anyone there?"

No sign of life. At the far end of the cellar are a bust of the Führer and two genuine skeletons, one of a dwarf and the other of a fetus. Also lying there are some molds, shapeless lumps of plaster cut in half and strung together. Inside will be cavities, negative impressions of complete human heads in the round.

"Better late than never," someone says. "You're the last to arrive." It must be Professor Sievers, who's chairing this conference on speech hygiene.

AT THE ZOO we always visit the flamingos first. We like to see if they're still pink, but we can't understand how they get to be that color. I wonder who that lady was, the one who was visiting Papa. She wasn't a secretary, she must have been a girl friend. I'm sure Papa has a girl friend he meets secretly, at the office. Or at Lanke. That's why he spends the night there so often, and that's why we haven't had a new brother or sister for so long. Helmut gives a sudden squeal. "Ugh, what are those horrible worms?"

We look where he's pointing. Papa looks into the enclosure too. "Don't be silly," he says, "it's only food for the birds."

"They won't get eaten alive, will they?"

Papa laughs. "Of course they will, Hilde. Unless you'd like to rescue them and show them off in a cage of their own."

Mama doesn't want any more children from Papa, that's all. Or doesn't she know about his lady friend? Maybe she'd really like some more children but she can't have any. It's no fun today, the zoo. After the birds, the other two insist on going to see the big cats. They keep on at me till we do. I wonder if the lady in Papa's office has any children. I only saw her for a moment, with the necklace dangling between her breasts. She's got breasts like Heide's wet-nurse when Heide was still being breast-fed. The wet-nurse would unbutton her blouse and take out one breast, just one. Heide's head almost hid it, but sometimes, when she'd finished feeding Heide and didn't do up her buttons fast enough, you could just see her nipple, all red and wet and pointy. The leopards are lying in the shade, dozing. How hot it looks, the black panther's fur, and how glossy it is.

There are some steps going down to a cellar. They're dark, and Helmut is the only one brave enough to go down them, but they don't seem to lead anywhere. He rattles the door, but it's locked. I bet there aren't any animals inside.

They're feeding the lions now. The keeper throws some lumps of red meat through the bars. The lion eats first, the lioness goes on lying in the corner, but she doesn't take her eyes off the meat. I can't remember now if I really saw that lady's breasts or the tuft of dark hair between her legs, or the pale stripes on her skin where the shoulder straps go, pale like her string of pearls. The opera singer who used to visit us sometimes, she wore a string of pearls like that. The way that lion is worrying his meat! Bits of it come flying through the bars, so Papa makes us step back.

She was funny, the opera singer. She always spent ages shaking hands with Papa, and she spoke to us children in a smarmy kind of way, like: "Hello, my dears, you're far, far prettier than you look in your pictures in the paper." She smiled all the time and laughed at everything Papa said. The lion is backing away with the meat between his paws. We've seen enough for today.

SIEVERS HIMSELF DELIVERS the opening lecture. His voice is wooden rather than metallic, his subject has something to do with vowel shifts viewed in their historical context. I soon stop listening to what he's saying and concentrate on his intonation. He has a noticeable way of spinning out the vowel *e*, gulps air, speaks in jerks. Does lecturing make him so nervous that he develops an inadvertent speech defect? He's certainly no rhetorical genius. I hope the same thing doesn't happen to me this evening. Being a newcomer to this circle, I'm to speak last. Sievers is now underlining his remarks with wild gestures. No, they seem to be an integral part of his lecture, he's talking about the correct way to recite: Goethe's poems should be accompanied by clockwise movements of the hand, Schiller's by counterclockwise. He does his best to compound this absurd form of calisthenics by overemphasizing the meter with his forearm as though hammering in nails. The others hang on his every word, because he is now, with a perceptible effort, winding himself up for his peroration, a whiplash rendering of a sonnet by Weinheber. He delivers it briskly, as if short of breath, or, rather, as if vocally relieving himself of some of the air he has ingested while speaking.

His elderly listeners applaud. Next comes an ethnologist fresh from extensive field research in the Lüneburger Heide, guaranteed home of the Nordic type in its purest form. For the moment, it seems, we shall have to be content with the Lüneburger Heide, but if we manage to gain unrestricted access to the human material available in Iceland.... Negotiations to that end are now in progress. The speaker has problems with his standard German, which keeps slipping to reveal a northern accent. He reels off statistics of ear dimensions and neck circumferences, shows us slides of peasants' heads photographed in profile, like mug shots, the hair brushed back to expose the whorls of the ear. Each slide embodies a scale in centimeters.

How dare he reduce Joseph Gall's penetrating analyses to such tedium? How can character be explored with the aid of a ruler? Why was I invited to this meeting at all? What does my subject have to do with the effusions of this mutual admiration society? I'm supposed to speak about my recordings of the human voice and play some examples. That's why, for safety's sake, I've copied my fragile tapes onto discs.

I mount the platform and set up the record player beside the text of my lecture. Silence falls, all eyes turn in my direction. My voice is tremulous for the first few sentences, but it soon steadies. I begin with a brief account of my recordings and the circumstances in which they originated: close combat, trench warfare, microphones blown to pieces in no man's land. Everyone looks dumbfounded. A preliminary example: the turntable steadily revolves, the miniature loudspeaker emits a succession of groans and croaks.

"Today, gentlemen, we were told about cranial measurements compiled in the North German area and acquired a knowledge of Rilke's breathing technique. However, while we sit here in this peaceful hall, our boys at the front are dying like dogs."

I almost let slip something about the waxworks show in the cellars, I've been so bored and infuriated by the previous speakers. Another sample recording.

"When discussing what has helped to shape the German race, gentlemen, you surely don't expect any results from all this nonsense about racial materialism, with its eternal concentration on platinum blond hair?"

My voice is running away with me, I can sense it, and my manuscript is obscured by a disc—the one I've just played and put down in the wrong place. Hastily, I extemporize: "According to my esteemed predecessor on this platform, the eastern territories will soon become part of the Reich. If all the inhabitants of that vast area are to be brought into line, that process cannot confine itself to imposing certain linguistic regulations and rooting out non-German words, the way we did it in Alsace. I speak from experience, gentlemen—because I was there—and it's nonsense, the whole thing. No fundamental changes can be effected by communal singsongs and elocution exercises chanted in unison. There's simply no point in dinning a new language into people's heads at parades or over the radio until they're addicted to it. Do you really propose to bombard them, for evermore, with monotonous Brownshirt chants and marching songs?"

A murmur runs through the hall. I detect some hostile glances out of the corner of my eye. They're a sworn fraternity, these men, but there's no going back, I can't stop now. I speak over the top of my recordings, changing the discs in quick succession. "Listen to this, gentlemen, and this, and this. It's childishly simple: our first task, once we start, must be to teach people to listen carefully, because it's not just language that has to be brought into line, it's the voice itself and every sound of human origin. We must get hold of people, every last one of them, and probe their innermost being—an inner self which, as we all know, manifests itself in the voice, the link between the inner man and the outside world. Yes, we must probe the inner self by submitting their voices to close examination like good physicians capable of diagnosing a patient's condition by listening to his heartbeat and respiration. We must tackle the inner self by tackling the voice and adjusting it—indeed, we must not, in extreme cases, shrink from modifying the organs of speech by means of invasive surgery."

There's a sudden, earsplitting noise: I've inadvertently knocked the needle off the record with a sweeping gesture. Embarrassed silence, not a movement anywhere in the hall. I take a deep breath, but I've lost my thread and am utterly exhausted. "Gentlemen," I say at length, "thank you for your attention."

I step back from the lectern, oblivious of my concluding words but aware that I'm trembling in every limb. Muted applause followed by a concerted exodus for supper. I gather my discs together. When most of the delegates have left the hall, a man in SS uniform comes up to me.

"That was fantastic, Herr Karnau."

He introduces himself: his name is Stumpfecker, personal physician to SS-Reichsführer Himmler, a man of about my own age. He speaks in a clear, steely voice littered with punctuation marks: "No wonder those old fogies are suspicious of your research, Herr Karnau, they're half asleep. Anyone who adopts such a radical approach to his subject is bound to be an unwelcome visitor in such company. I've only one reservation: have you really thought it out, this vocal atlas of yours? Isn't your collection of sounds too unique to be converted into visual terms without the loss of some important nuances? Doesn't the task of mapping them on paper consume too much precious energy that might be better employed in making recordings that defy any form of graphic representation, that override all petty regulations and transcend the imagination of narrow-minded gentlemen like the delegates to this conference—recordings made in conditions of such absolute freedom that your archive could embrace every nuance of the human voice, however faint?"

WE GO ON talking in the dark when the light is switched off. "Hilde, do you remember that singer who came to dinner with Mama and Papa, the one with the beautiful necklace?"

Hilde shakes her head in the moonlight. "You mean a necklace of colored stones, like Mama's?"

"No, shiny white pearls."

"Mama's got one of those too."

"Yes, but this was a young woman. She was talking with Papa—she said hello to us before we had to go to bed."

"No, I don't remember. There are always so many people at Papa and Mama's parties, and nearly all the ladies wear necklaces. And bracelets. Or earrings, at least. It looks nice, wearing jewelry like that. Maybe we should have our ears pierced when we're older."

"I bet it hurts."

"Yes, but think of the lovely earrings we could wear."

"Mama says it's vulgar to wear earrings at our age. Only guttersnipes have their ears pierced, she says."

But Hilde isn't listening anymore. She's asleep.

"PROFESSOR STUMPFECKER DESCRIBES you as a clever man. You met him in Dresden recently, do you remember?"

"Of course."

"Well, he'll be joining us before long. Stumpfecker says your lecture embodied some very interesting ideas that might be worth putting into practice. In order to try them out—"

"Excuse me, but I don't quite understand why you sent for me. This is a hospital, an SS hospital."

"Well, assuming that Stumpfecker's report to this department is correct, the point you made was that the eastern territories cannot be Germanized in the traditional way, by teaching their inhabitants the German language and imposing German laws."

"That sounds as if—"

"We must ensure that the East is exclusively inhabited by people with truly German, Germanic blood, isn't that what you said?"

What's the man driving at? Is this an indirect way of calling me up for military service? Stumpfecker knocks and enters. The SS major turns to him.

"Something seems to be wrong here, we're not getting anywhere. Perhaps you'd better give Herr Karnau a brief account of what we have in mind."

"How far did you get?"

"The question of Germanic blood."

"Ah yes. It's like this, Karnau: you said that none of our linguistic programs and Germanization procedures, none of our attempts to din the language into people's heads by external means could ever get to the root of the matter, correct?"

"Yes, that's right."

"Didn't you also say that the German language is in one's blood from birth, so to speak, and that one can't acquire it merely by learning its grammar, vocabulary and rules of pronunciation? That language flows through the human body like a constituent of the bloodstream and permeates each individual cell? That any linguistic adjustment must logically begin with the blood itself? That one must invade a person's circulation in order to get at the thing that renders him human, namely, his voice?"

"Not exactly. What I meant was—"

"Karnau, I have an almost verbatim recollection of your closing words: 'Tackle the inner self by tackling the voice, and, in extreme cases, don't shrink from modifying the organs of speech by means of invasive surgery.'"

"Well, in theory..."

"Herr Karnau," the major chimes in, "you haven't been summoned here for interrogation. On the contrary, we're thinking of appointing you to head a special research team."

"Really? What would its terms of reference be?"

"It would develop the line of inquiry you already outlined."

Stumpfecker again: "We're thinking of a combination of theorists and technicians. You, as an acoustician, would form the link between the two groups. We, of course, would be represented by myself." He gives me an amiable nod. "This whole idea has come as a surprise to you, I know. Sleep on it and we'll meet again tomorrow."

It all sounds very fishy. Is there any chance of wriggling out of it? I must think up some pretext for regretfully declining their offer, I really must. Just as I'm on my way out the SS major calls after me, quite casually, as if the matter were of no importance:

"Oh yes, Herr Karnau, the formation of this research team will naturally exempt you from military service. As of now, you're in a reserved occupation."

WE'RE PLAYING BROWNSHIRTS and undesirable elements, the game we saw them playing in Berlin one day. "We'll give the orders," Hilde says, looking at me, "and the little ones have to obey them."

The others fetch their toothbrushes from the bathroom and hold them out for us to inspect. Then we make them get down on their knees and scrub the nursery floor. Being in charge, we're allowed to shove them around and even kick them a little. They aren't allowed to look at us while they're scrubbing the floor, they have to look down the whole time. They aren't allowed to look at each other, either. They have to keep staring at their own stretch of carpet. The two of us stand over them with our legs apart and our hands on our hips. "Go on," we tell them, "scrub harder, put your back into it."

But it's much harder to scrub a carpet than a pavement. Bits come off and get stuck in the bristles, and it isn't long before they're full of fluff. Hilde plants her foot on Helmut's shoulder. "Get a move on," she says. "Faster, cleaner!"

We yell our heads off. Hilde insists on yelling louder than me, but we both notice we're growing hoarse and get really angry with the others. They don't dare say a word, they scrub away without stopping and shuffle across the floor on their knees, faster and faster the louder we shout at them.

But suddenly someone shouts even louder than us. It's Mama. The nursemaid must have fetched her. "Have you gone completely mad?" she says. "What are you up to? Stop it at once or you'll regret it. What on earth were you thinking of? What do you imagine our guests would say if they heard you? You'll ruin our reputation. Out you go this minute."

We slink downstairs and out into the garden. There's a garden party going on, but we don't feel like saying hello to anyone, we go straight down to the lake. We don't speak, Hilde chucks stones into the water. It really wouldn't have looked good if someone had heard us playing that game. No, no one must know what we were doing with the little ones. There are things you can see but you mustn't talk about. Like that opera singer. I mustn't ever say I saw her in Papa's office. I mustn't show it if she also comes to the garden party and I have to shake hands with her. Another thing: no one in the world must know that Papa was nearly killed.

Papa tries to keep it a secret from us, in fact he seriously thinks he's managed to prevent me from finding out what I'm not supposed to know. It didn't occur to him that I might have heard about it when I asked if it was dangerous, the road home from Nikolassee. But he couldn't conceal how scared he was, the time someone planned to blow up the bridge as he was driving over it—the little bridge where there's a specially strong smell of fish and weed in hot weather. Long after the man had been arrested and put to death, no one was allowed to say the word "fisherman" when Papa was around because that was what the man had pretended to be, a fisherman.

The little ones are coming towards us through the bushes. At least they aren't angry with us, which is lucky, and maybe none of the guests heard us yelling. Most of them aren't interested in children anyway. Mama's ignoring us. We won't get any cake today, that's for sure, but I can see Herr Karnau up there on the terrace. He's peering around with his eyes screwed up. He looks sad, perhaps because no one's talking to him. Now he's looking in our direction.

I SCAN THE human terrain. The smooth, fine-pored area stands out against its rough, uneven setting, and expanses of shadow alternate with others bathed in glaring sunlight. A long curve, the softly delineated rondure of the shoulder, wrinkles radiating from the armpit, tiny shadows fanning out between the arm and the base of the breast, isolated moles and fine hairs distributed across the entire décolletage, an unpigmented streak on the upper left margin that shows off the flawless skin elsewhere to even better effect. A dark gray stripe over the shoulder, where the musculature of the neck can be discerned when the chin is raised. The central section, the source of the visual movements, is framed by a string of pearls, and it is there, on the throat, that my gaze fastens: the Adam's apple is bobbing. Every sound alters the outlines of the throat in the chiaroscuro beneath the chin. The pearls repose in her cleavage, they rise and fall with the rib cage at every breath. Tendons ripple beneath the soprano's smooth skin as soon as she speaks, which she does in a clear, incisive voice that can be heard all over the garden. The tip of her nose twitches whenever her mouth moves. Now, while speaking, the young woman scratches her neck within millimeters of the Adam's apple, that infinitely fragile, vulnerable projection of cartilage, and the glottal chink flutters as compressed air passes through the narrow vent. She continues to speak, this singer in her light summer dress, seemingly unconscious of the larynx she subjects to such rigorous training at other times. At the moment, since it produces that silvery voice on its own, it is merely a tool requiring no attention.

Dressed all in white, in a white linen suit, shoes of fine white kid and even gloves of the same color, the children's father approaches with the singer in his sights: thin mouth in a gaunt face, stern features, firm, exceptionally pronounced cheek muscles tempered like steel by countless public speeches, prominent carotid artery throbbing fiercely, prominent Adam's apple. He forbade me in advance, before the children could even learn of my request, to record their voices. Not from any fear that those voices might be distorted by their awareness that I was recording them, nor because he thought it might be indiscreet for them to speak into a microphone extempore instead of adhering to a prepared text in the usual way. He didn't refuse for any reason that commended itself to me because I myself had already thought it, but purely on grounds of copyright: "The right to exploit my children's voices is not your prerogative, Karnau. It's vested solely in the family, and that means me."

Hasn't it ever occurred to him, the great public speaker,

how dependent he is on underlings as outwardly insignificant as myself? Doesn't he realize that sound engineers have made a major contribution to his brilliant career—that without microphones, without immense loudspeakers, he would never have been blessed with such success? Didn't he often complain of poor acoustics in the Movement's early days, for instance during a speech at the Sportpalast, when the dud loudspeakers started to whistle and he had to go on speaking for nearly an hour with no amplification at all, until he was dropping with fatigue and his voice gave out entirely? Or when no one could understand him because the loudspeaker had been located behind the platform so that every word could be heard twice over, once uttered by himself and once as an amplified echo? That sort of thing went on until we disseminated his voice with the aid of as many as a hundred loudspeakers designed to hold his audiences in thrall from all directions. Does he think it's pure chance that his personal success has coincided with major improvements in the public address systems he uses at mass rallies?

Snatches of conversation: "Rubber," says someone, and "We're cut off from the plantations in South America." Perhaps they're talking about self-sufficiency in rubber, or perhaps about the modeling clay the children are playing with in the garden. You can mold it into anything—people, animals, buildings—as long as your fingers are deft enough. The children carefully knead the soft material with their fingertips. They fashion it into heads, arms and legs, then obliterate them by squeezing it hard between their palms. They indent the lumps and dig out eyes, nostrils and mouths, only to efface those features with their thumbs a moment later. It's just the same with a recording when the stylus bites into the wax: the more relentless a furrow it plows, the more accurate the result and the more clearly a recorded voice can be heard when played back.

The guests at the garden party are offered big bowls of fruit from which the stones have been carefully removed. The children's father, with the soprano on his arm, strolls down to the lake, where his offspring are romping among the trees. Blinking in the sunlight, they run up and down the bank until they can't run any more and flop down exhausted on the grass. Their light summer clothing stands out white against the greenery. They're now playing at being dogs, so engrossed in their snuffling and digging and scampering after stones that Helga's father has to yank her to her feet by the collar before she smooths down her skirt and bids the singer a polite good afternoon. The others, too, are dragged away from their game and made to shake hands in turn. But that's not enough for the singer. With the father looking on, she enfolds little Hedda in her arms and hugs her. Hedda averts her face and looks away, patently ill at ease, but her father doesn't intervene, he simply stands there smiling. Such are children's early exercises in habituation, and such is the way in which their innocent bodies go rigid when exposed to the touch of an adult. These exercises are repeated until the entire body rigidifies and the child degenerates, little by little, into adulthood: the transformation of a free-flying, aerial creature into one that is forever earthbound.

CHAPTER

Two bare feet adhere to the cold tiles. No movement, no change of position, no shift of weight from one leg to the other, not even a twitch of the toes: nothing. Either because the inevitable excretion of sweat that traces the shape of the man's soles on the tiles is gluing his feet to the floor, or because changing position would compel him to abandon a warm patch on the tiles and infuse a cold one, little by little, with body warmth. His motionless feet obscure a small area of the regular pattern of black and white tiles, which are so highly polished that his heels, and even his bony ankles, are mirrored in them. Their reflection shows up against the checkered pattern and interrupts the series of joins, the network of right-angled intersections, that runs across the room to the spot where I'm standing, though here the floor is dull and reflects nothing, neither my trousers, nor my socks, nor even a faint image of my black leather shoes.

The smooth, tiled floor is draining body warmth from the man's feet. Conversely, its chill is penetrating his soles, creeping up his legs to those parts of his anatomy that are concealed by his undershirt and drawers, and infiltrating his shoulders and his arms, which, like his feet, are motionless. They hang limp at his sides, and gooseflesh alone betrays that his body is still imbued with life as he stands there half naked in the middle of the room, exposed to the gaze of his fully clothed interrogator.

But gooseflesh is a giveaway in itself. To the observer, even distended pores and erect papillae are overly revealing. The rigidity of the man's face is intended to disguise those uncontrollable changes in his epidermis. His vacant gaze and drooping lips are an attempt to distract me from the shivers running through the exposed parts of his anatomy. They're meant to divert my attention from his bare feet, bent back, hunched shoulders and incipient paunch, from the shape beneath the front of his cotton underpants, but they fail to do so.

They even fail to disguise that faint intimation hidden from the observer's gaze: the cold sweat of fear that is trickling down the back of the body on display and very slowly tracing the line of the man's backbone on the material of his undershirt.

And we both know this. We both know that the body under inspection can conceal nothing, even though the ears pretend to be deaf and the lips mute, because my subject's eyes are still looking out from deep within him. His gaze is eloquent of the dawning realization that he has used his voice for years without paying it the slightest heed: all those countless mutilated sounds, all those crude, ill-modulated utterances have suddenly combined to create a diabolical din in his head.

That's how we stand facing each other. That's how the figure in front of me stands, like a conscript undergoing his physical—like a youngster who, for the first time in his life, sees his naked adult body exposed to thorough scrutiny by strangers. We stand there in silence for a short while only. Then it's time for me to put a stop to the man's impersonation of a deaf-mute. And, once he fills the cold room with sounds, being compelled to answer my questions, he's even more naked than before—really naked now, even though certain portions of him are concealed by the cotton that molds itself to his scrotum and limp penis. Has he already reached the stage at which tears need restraining? Can I already detect, in the corners of his eyes, slight traces of moisture with morning sunlight reflected in them? Although he hasn't been informed that he's the subject of vocal research, he clearly senses, as we talk, that I'm inexorably recording every nuance of his voice, however faint. Is that a dark spot I see on the front of his underpants? Has my subject lost control of himself and passed a drop of urine?

But he realizes that it doesn't matter whether he passes a drop that visibly moistens the material, or whether he manages to suppress this minimal efflux of urine throughout our session, because every fiber of him senses that even his muscular tension is being registered.

There it is: a twitch of the upper lip. Quite unconnected with word formation, this tic is quickly acquiring a life of its own and will persist with every sound the man utters, expressive of impending collapse and disintegration. My subject won't retain his composure for much longer, I can tell from his voice. It not only shakes but communicates its tremors to his entire body. The bare feet will soon have to move, the man in the undershirt will soon be seeking some means of support. He can't concentrate anymore, gropes desperately for answers to the simplest questions, his own voice ringing so loudly in his ears that every attempt to formulate a word misfires. Not a single clearly audible consonant emerges from his writhing lips. His throat balks, contorted by uncontrollable muscular spasms, and all that can be heard is that hideous organ, just a croak bereft of all meaning, a strangled laryngeal gurgle that drowns one misshapen sound with its immediate successor. Meanwhile, quite unhurriedly, I continue to repeat my questions in a loud, clear voice as if patiently giving my subject a second chance. I do so although we're both well aware that he's long past saving—that every renewed attempt to speak is just another step on the road to speechlessness, that every movement of the mouth, every readjustment of the vocal cords, every flutter of the tongue, is bringing him closer to ultimate and ineluctable silence.

Now to conduct an intuitive assessment of my subject's swaying figure. Should I grant him a fleeting hope of recovery, or should I push him over the edge right away? His eyes transmit no entreaty, nor does his stance convey anything of the kind, but his voice implores me to exempt it from further interrogation. A momentary pause as I prepare to ask another question—calmly, I draw breath, assume a look of inquiry, begin to shape a word—and, almost imperceptibly, a plaintive sound issues from deep within that half-naked body. Not that my subject realizes it, I've attained my objective: no need to say another word.

That last, faint sound was precisely what I had to coax from him for recording purposes. Now that silence has fallen and nothing more happens, he collapses. Is his uvula damaged? Are his gums sore? Have his vocal cords been seriously affected after only one session? I hand him over to Hellbrandt, who will check on his present condition. It's only afterwards that I become aware of an acrid smell in the room: the man spent half an eternity standing, barefoot and breathless, in a puddle of his own juices. I send for someone to mop it up.

PAPA'S GOING TO give a speech. What a lot of people, and how close together they're standing. They can't move forwards or backwards, they can't move their arms and their tummies are rubbing together. This is the first time we've been allowed to come and listen, me and Hilde. There's a smell in the air from all these people. I hope they'll let us through to our seats, all the others have been taken long ago. If we have to stand we won't be able to see a thing—we'll be crushed to death by all these grown-ups. Mama pushes a man out of the way and points to our seats, one each for her and me and Hilde, Papa reserved them for us. People wave when we sit down, and we wave back. Now they're starting to cheer. Mama nudges me. "Look," she says, "here comes Papa."

"Where?"

"Not behind us, silly, straight ahead."

Papa takes his place at the speaker's desk and looks out over the audience. He's looking in our direction. Has he seen us? Does he know exactly where we're sitting? His eyes are tired, but you can't see the shadows under them because the lights are so bright. He hardly eats a thing these days, just semolina with milk, and he smokes all the time, but now his eyes begin to shine. He's concentrating on what he's going to say. Everyone realizes this, because they all get very quiet. Now he starts speaking.

He talks about the many millions of people who are listening to him at this moment. He says something about the airwaves and how they form a link between us and everyone else on earth. Perhaps even the dead are listening to him, he says, perhaps they include the last of the Stalingrad fighters, the ones who transmitted their farewell radio message weeks ago. The people shout, "Bravo," they shout *"Heil,"* and when they clap it makes an incredible din. Papa says he intends to give us an unvarnished picture of the situation. "The storming of the steppe!" he cries. Everyone is hanging on his words. "Childish," he says, "that's a childish excuse." Papa never smiles when he says childish, it's a sign that he isn't joking.

Papa takes great care to speak clearly, so that every word can be understood. He talks about peace feelers, robots, and —there it is again—"The storming of the steppe!" How the loudspeakers rattle. Papa's really shouting now, to make himself heard above the din. The audience are so worked up, he has to keep breaking off. Now they're actually laughing, and someone in the audience calls out, "Rotten swine!" Who was it? Where is he? The voice came from quite close by, but it's too late, we can't see anyone with his mouth open. "Only the most total will be total enough!" cries Papa.

NO USE SWABBING away the blood, it tints the gums like rouge, laps around every tooth in fine skeins. A complete set? A full house, dentally speaking? The jaws are clamped apart in the usual way to avoid damaging the enamel. Slight prognathism. Several microphones are needed to investigate this remote and hitherto unexplored area. Four are focused on the test subject from different directions. A fifth, secreted in the immediate vicinity of the sound source, serves to pick up special frequencies. It is continuously modulated while recording is in progress so that certain features of the voice can be brought out on tape with precision.

The larynx, subjected to a weak and far from dangerous electric shock, gives an involuntary jerk. Will the voice go racing up the scale, into the very highest register? No, it subsides before it can do so. Murmurs uttered in a normal voice and repeated clicking sounds produce some very nice shadows. Then, slowly, barely perceptible at first, comes a dark, reddish glimmer, then pale violet, then a bright, sky-blue vocal shade. Is the light, the sound, already fading? As the larynx subsides and relaxes, so the voice becomes deeper and hoarser and displays a growing tendency to vibrate. The subject is still inclined to breathe from the thorax. Jaw movements are observable, and instinctive lingual contractions scour the gums. The more violent these movements, the more copious the flow of saliva. The subject tries to expectorate, but threads of spittle run down his chin, mingled—so far as one can tell in the gloom —with blood. Here and there the blood picks up a ray of light and carries it along. Thin, diffuse and flickering, it weaves a pattern on the darkness.

Sensors have been inserted in the folds of the ear. These provide an accurate record of how clearly the subject can hear his own voice while undergoing treatment. When the sensor is worn out after several tests and the contacts are removed from the throat, which is raw in places, I detect a shiny patch on the smooth floor: blood, or urine?

Expanses of shadow alternate with others bathed in the spotlights' glare. The smooth, fine-pored area stands out against its rough, uneven setting, where the musculature of the neck can be discerned when the chin is raised. Is that gooseflesh? No, just stubble on the edge of the ill-shaven jaw. The pink skin looks like a wound in the midst of that expanse of curly black hair, that stubborn canine fur which the razor has failed to slice off flush with the pores. The bare throat is motionless, exposed to a beam of light so dazzlingly bright that the illuminated area looks almost white. Rubber gloves squeak as the surgeon pulls them on. A final inspection of the clamps to ensure that the chin cannot suddenly sag, then the first incision. The open epidermis, the muscle texture, the blood that trickles over chin and shoulders, matting the fur. "Are you through yet?" A clamp is inserted in the throat. "More light, I can't see a thing." Next, the windpipe—a faint, rhythmical breeze plays over the surgeon's fingers. Now to insert the scalpel in the narrow aperture and tackle the larynx itself.

Is it possible to take what one removes from another's voice and add it to one's own, adopting its timbre and volume, just as a cannibal believes that he can enhance his physical strength by devouring another's flesh? Can a child's clear, youthful voice be acquired by means of surgical expropriation? Nobody knows.

Stumpfecker discards his mask, gown and gloves and lights a cigarette. The smoke rises to the brick ceiling and forms illuminated curlicues there. I survey the yellowing charts on the walls, the straps hanging down on either side of the operating table, the gown on the floor with its reddish-brown incrustations. I glance at the open door through which the patient is now being wheeled out into the gloomy corridor, feel the cool draft, and listen to the hum of the air-conditioning, which becomes noticeable only now that silence has fallen. Stumpfecker says nothing, just puffs at his cigarette from time to time, and the surgical instruments reflect its glowing tip.

PAPA'S EYES ARE shining, he's red in the face. It must be dark outside by now, he's been speaking for such a long time. "Mama, can we have something to drink?"

She shakes her head, doesn't even look around. "Mama, isn't there anything to drink here? Can we have something to drink when Papa has finished his speech?"

She looks around at last, angrily. "Don't be so impatient," she hisses.

Papa's talking about fashion houses. That interests Mama. She looks up at him, listening hard, but he says that all fashion houses are to be closed. Mama shakes her head as if to say, "No, surely not," but she's only brushing a wisp of hair out of her eyes. The people are laughing again. Papa has been talking about the pointless jobs that are done in wartime even though they've no connection with the war. It's ridiculous, Papa says. For instance, what about those experts in Berlin who've spent weeks debating whether the non-German word "accumulator" should be replaced by plain "storage cell?"

Mama laughs too. Her first husband owned a factory that made accumulators. Papa says that people who devote themselves to such absurdities in wartime aren't fully occupied and should be employed in a munitions factory or sent to the front.

There's a chapter in one of our schoolbooks where foreign words have to be replaced by German ones, but that surely doesn't mean our governess will be sent to the front. She's teaching Helmut too, these days, he's learning to read and write. I used to be the only one that could read. The others had to come to me whenever they wanted something read aloud to them.

I can't hear a lot of what Papa's saying, the people are making so much noise and shouting, "*Sieg Heil!*" He looks as if he can't decide whether their interruptions are a good thing or a nuisance. He talks about a woman with five children to look after, almost like Mama and us. Now he's going on about young men and women riding in the Tiergarten at nine o'clock in the morning. What was that word he said—graceful or disgraceful?

He gave us a pony once, Hilde and me. We were allowed to ride it, sometimes we harnessed the pony to the trap that went with it and took the others for rides. Mama rides too, but on a horse. Papa can't ride, perhaps because of the iron strapped to his leg to help him walk straight. He never wears shorts, either. Papa doesn't know we know about his iron, but we saw it once when he pulled up his socks and his trouser leg got hitched up too.

Now Papa's talking about rest cures and the people who go on them—idlers, he calls them. Everyone gets very worked up. "People who take rest cures are rumor-mongers," he says. "Shame on them," shouts the audience. Mama often has to take a rest cure. She fainted in front of us once, it scared us all to death. "Let's have no more of this bureaucratic, time-wasting, form-filling nonsense," Papa tells the audience. "Let's not fritter away our energies on countless trivialities."

A friend of Hilde, who doesn't have private lessons, told us about the nonsense she has to learn by heart in school. Like the size of an Aryan's head, so you can compare him with other races. Everything is measured down to the last detail, even the ears. Perhaps that's why Papa took us out of school. We'd sooner learn to speak English the way Mama does. She speaks a lot of languages, that's why she never needs an interpreter. Not like Papa, who can't talk to foreign visitors on his own.

THE WORLD THAT existed prior to our ability to study the recorded voice had yet to become a world worthy of the name. Until Edison invented the phonograph, the world of sound could manifest itself only in the transitory present. That apart, one was dependent solely on the fainter, vaguer recollection of sounds in the inward ear, or, less reliably, on a comparison of unreal sounds in the imagination. And then, in 1877, came the sudden breakthrough to an undreamed-of field of acoustics. Once the first words had been engraved on a wax cylinder, the speaker could hear them after the event without having to repeat them: he was the first person capable of listening to himself.

With quiet breathing and vocalizations from a single living body, that was how the process began. Since then it has been possible to recall every nuance for comparison with any other, however closely related and however almost imperceptibly different. It is impossible to conceal the fact that no two human voices are identical. Not a voice in the world can be excused by any other.

So voices set off on their journey inward, into lightlessness, gloom, darkness: Black Maria, that was what Edison christened one of his first phonographs, and that is how the leathery skin of flying foxes appears, like a dark, shadowy negative threaded with pale, barely visible lines. Wide awake, they keep their vigil in the acoustic twilight. The interplay of tonal shades that emerges from this darkness is indistinct at first. Impossible to perceive in their entirety, they are so constituted that individual parts of them light up from time to time.

All shades and nuances of the human voice must be discerned in this darkness, and every articulatory characteristic, no matter how seemingly unimportant, must be coaxed from a sound source before its tonal color lapses into inaudibility, into a soundlessness pervaded by crackles, impurities and blemishes. The darkness spanned by the flying fox's wing tips is profound, and the membrane from which its veins protrude has the dull sheen of leather. It clings to a branch upside down, its doglike snout sniffing and licking a red patch in the midst of its black fur. Its bared teeth gleam in the darkness, its ears twitch nervously as they focus on sources of sound, its muscles tense. The animal emits a squeak so shrill that it sets the eardrums vibrating and almost bursts them. Flying foxes suspended from their perch across the street hear footsteps and warn each other of an approaching figure on the pavement beneath their sleeping quarters.

PAPA WANTS EVERYONE to dismiss their household staff. Does that include our housemaids and the cook and the nursemaid? Even Mama's secretary? Is she going to have to let them all go? The audience laughs, they think Papa's idea is funny. Mama is sitting beside me, quite still. Is her hand trembling, or is she just getting something out of her handbag? Papa is shouting again: "It must flow through the German people like an electric current," he says. The veins are standing out on his neck so much, he looks as if he's going to explode. Then he quiets down again and talks about Frederick the Great. A sad figure, actually. He'd lost all his teeth, suffered from gout, and was in constant pain. A great general, but feeble and dying of disease.

Papa mentions the Führer, and they all get up off their chairs, clapping and cheering. The noise goes on for ages, it doesn't die down till they can't clap or cheer any more. Even Papa is worn out and has to take a breather.

I hope he won't be much longer, it's time we went home. The little ones won't believe us when we tell them what we've seen and heard here. But Papa's still speaking. It's so hot in here, we could do with some fresh air. There aren't any windows, either. "Seated here before me," says Papa, "are rows of German wounded from the Eastern Front, amputees without arms and legs, men with shattered limbs, men blinded in combat, men in their prime."

I try to see the men he's talking about. Hilde, too, bends forward and peers through the forest of heads in front of us. Are the amputees sitting in the front row? Are their arms and legs really missing? How did the blind men find their way here? But we can't see a thing, not even the crutches Papa mentioned. "Represented here," he says, "are the young and the very old. No class, no profession or age group has been omitted from the invitation list."

Are there babies here too? They couldn't stand the noise and the mugginess, surely? "Mama, are there babies here too?"

But Mama doesn't hear Hilde's question, Papa has just cracked a joke and they're all laughing, roaring with laughter. "No, never!" they yell, and "*Sieg Heil, Sieg Heil, Sieg Heil!*" I've had enough, I'm not enjoying this, I want to go home, I can't breathe in here. Now they're shouting again. "No!" they yell, and "Shame!" How they're sweating. Hair plastered to their foreheads, and you can see damp patches under their arms when they stick them in the air. "Fourthly," Papa says. And how their breath smells. It almost scorches the back of my neck every time they shout, "Yes, yes, yes!"

ROWS OF IRON bedsteads, their occupants bereft of speech. The click of brightly painted wooden figures rebounds from the high ceiling. The patients we've finished with are lying there like sick children. They run their fingers and palms over simple shapes, an exercise originally designed to investigate their ability to translate tactile impressions into speech. They were allowed to keep the wooden figures after we discontinued our experiments on them. All they can utter, in any case, is a series of sounds such as "track-track-track" or "crick-crack." One can't determine where their impairment lies, in the muscles of the throat or their capacity for phonic reproduction.

It's as if they've been docked like puppies of certain breeds whose tails are mutilated at birth in the same way that many babies' tongues, which have hypertrophied in the womb because of some hereditary defect, are shortened with a few neat scalpel strokes regardless of whether their sense of taste may be affected. Such infants have their tongues docked because, being orally inexperienced, they run the risk of biting them off.

Sievers shakes his head. "People strive so doggedly to prove that speech is of animal origin," he says, "as if only waiting for the collapse of all existing theories to restore their belief in its divine, inscrutable provenance. There are two possibilities: that the unintelligibly fluttering tongue is controlled by some unseen agency, projecting the voice and rendering it audible from afar, whirring like a weightless body in flight; or that speech resembles some earthbound creature whose paws adhere to the ground as though suffering from excessive gravity, aroused by instinct and born of the inadequacy of the flesh."

But what exactly happened to these tongues? An enforced return to the stage that precedes speech? Wolf children, that's what they call foundlings that are reared, not by their parents, but by wolf packs in the wilderness. Close to the beast, they know no language and never learn to use their voices in the human manner.

These ears here: gristly eavesdroppers vibrating with muscular impulses, listening intently, forever in motion; or, on another head, two rigid bell-mouths devoid of whorls and threaded with countless pulsing venules. Big earlobes, grown soft and flabby with age, alongside little, finely fashioned organs of hearing. Rays of sunlight illuminate another row of specimen jars: Stumpfecker's pickled larynxes, afflicted with ulcers, deformed by growths. The articulatory apparatus of a child born without vocal cords, though the cartilage and tendons that should have retained the cords are fully developed. Stumpfecker, as deft with the scalpel as a cook with an apple corer. A sunbeam has now irradiated a jar at the back of the shelf: shimmering floccules suspended in a murky, fermenting solution of formaldehyde—a defective brew, no doubt. It's impossible to tell what the jar contains.

PAPA IS NOW on fifthly. And sixthly. How many more questions is he going to ask? The audience keep shouting, "Yes!" at the top of their voices. I wish they'd stop making such a din. It's awfully loud, my eardrums are almost bursting.

Seventhly, eighthly, ninthly. The floor's shaking, they're stamping their feet so hard and waving their arms in the air. Hilde and I can't see anything now that some of them have climbed on their chairs. Please hurry up and finish, Papa, I can't stand it much longer. My throat's all tight and my head is throbbing. We couldn't get out of here if we tried, not yet. We couldn't get out into the street and the open air, there are too many people in the way. "Tenth and last," says Papa. He actually said it.

Thank goodness, we'll soon be able to leave. Fresh air at last. "Children," Papa says, "we're all children." Is he going to finish up with a few words about us? Hilde looks at me, but Papa means we're all children of our nation. We all need warm hearts and cool heads, he says, but my head is hot, terribly hot. I draw a deep breath, but it's no use, there's no air left in here, just smelly breath and sweat. I don't know how Papa can go on shouting in this air.

"Nation arise," he says, "and let the storm break!"

I don't know how these people can still find the breath to

sing the national anthem. Somebody touches my hand, which is all clammy. Mama takes my arm and says, "That's it, Helga, we're going home now. Papa will follow, he won't be long."

Hilde has already stood up. We go out into the air, the lovely fresh air. We're so deaf we can hardly hear Mama. "Poor Papa," she says, "he hasn't had a single cigarette for two whole hours."

Hilde's looking exhausted, as if she'd also found it hard to bear, as if Papa and the audience had scared her too. "Did you see, Helga?" she says quietly, in a bewildered sort of voice. "Papa's shirt was absolutely soaked by the end."

THE TEST SUBJECTS are slapped awake. "Shine a light there!" Just dim silhouettes, they now live in permanently nocturnal conditions. It's strange: their sense of touch is so impaired that they ought by rights to activate their voices in the darkened ward, establish vocal contact with their fellow patients and explore their surroundings with the aid of echoes, but they do nothing of the kind. Their lips have ceased to form words and are merely things to be chewed. Like the sound of silence itself: the mute tongue reposes on the lower lip. The pinkness of their skin derives solely from breathing, from the imprint of air alone. We're recording them day and night, they can sense it even though they've never seen any of our microphones. They're no longer capable of standing, and no one feels like hauling those soiled bundles to their feet and escorting them to the latrines. They now have to defecate while seated, and every change of position causes their sodden mattresses to give off such a stench that we can no longer keep the windows shut, so on many nights the mattresses end up stiff with frozen urine. They, who lead an animal existence, have finally eluded us.

Noises disturb the nocturnal hush as the acoustic twilight of dawn approaches. But this is not the rustling of some animal by the roadside, not the stirring of dry leaves; these are dry throats at work. It takes a vast amount of time and effort to master one's own voice, at least to some degree, but how quickly people can lose what they have so laboriously acquired and how little effort it takes to obliterate everything until not the smallest trace of it remains. In just the same way, dogs cast discipline and training to the winds as soon as instinct reminds them of the world that existed before the advent of man.

The rattle of parched throats... Quite young, they are, these youthful, blue-faced patients who seem to be choking on their own voices. They're becoming desiccated and drained by the endless stream that flows from every bodily orifice: not urine alone, but nasal mucus and tears. To what is it attributable, this immense loss of fluid? Clearly, people cannot cope with the sound of their own voices once they're fully exposed to them: in the long run, being compelled to listen to their naked, uncontrolled voices is more than they can endure.

THERE, ANOTHER ONE did a wee-wee, a thin jet landed on the dark floor in front of me. There's a pool of it glistening behind the bars of the cage. I couldn't see a thing at first, not a thing, but my eyes are getting used to the darkness. The flying foxes are hanging upside down with their wings wrapped around them. Now one of them has woken up. He starts licking his fur, I can even make out his little tongue as he runs it over his pitch-black tummy. I've suddenly spotted another. I didn't see him leave the place where he was sleeping, but he's fluttering around the cage. The light's very dim. That's to make the flying foxes think it's nighttime. Others have left their perches at the top of the cage. There's a whole swarm of them in the air, and the ones still hanging upside down are already unfolding their wings.

There's a flying fox sitting on the floor of the cage in front of me. Or rather, he's lying on his tummy with his wings spread out. He's sniffing around in the sand and turning his head from side to side. He crawls along a bit, but he doesn't use his short back legs, he uses his wings. He looks like a legless man strapped to a board with wheels screwed to it. He cranes his neck and listens, I can see his ears waggle. He's looking at me with his black, boot-button eyes. They're wide open and staring into the darkness.

"You see, Hilde, you didn't believe me when I said they really existed, flying foxes, and that a friend of Herr Karnau's actually kept some."

"Rubbish, that's not true. It was you that didn't believe me when Herr Karnau told me about them."

"Liar!"

"Say that again!"

"Ssh," says Herr Moreau, "not so loud, children, you'll frighten them."

Herr Moreau is stricter than Herr Karnau. Mama didn't tell us when we visited her at the sanatorium that we were going to be allowed to go and see the flying foxes with Herr Karnau. We should really have gone home again in the afternoon. It was only a short visit, because Mama isn't really well yet, she's been away in Dresden far longer than usual.

Herr Karnau told us once that he doesn't get scared in the blackout, in fact he thinks it's nice when the sky above the city is dark, really dark, so you can see it better. But this darkness here is scary. The flying foxes seem to suck up all the light—all the air, too. It's like being in an air-raid shelter when the lights go out. As if there's not enough air, as if the darkness is squeezing the air out of your lungs and every-thing's closing in and you can't breathe anymore. That's why people in air-raid shelters start singing, so they know for sure they're still breathing. The sound of their singing is just a sign that they've no need to be scared. It proves the air in the shelter hasn't given out, even though it's all dark.

"REMEMBER THOSE CIGARETTE cards I gave you when you were a child, Hermann? You never tired of looking at one in particular. It belonged to a set called *Animals of the World,* or maybe *Distant Lands,* and it showed a colony of flying foxes asleep in a tree in Madagascar. Well, here we are after all these years, watching some real, live flying foxes. I always get the strangest feeling, as if that old picture had come to life—as if the creatures, when they wake up, are emerging from that cigarette card."

Moreau whispers in my ear without taking his eyes off the flying foxes, which he brought back four years ago from a trip to Madagascar. He was my parents' friend originally, but I always felt as a child that I was the one he really came to see. Every time he turned up he had some new and exciting tale to tell—about golems, vampires and other creatures of the night. I still have a particularly vivid recollection of one of his stories: it was about a doctor who lived on a remote island inhabited by creatures midway between man and beast. Mo-reau's extensive knowledge of the animal world encouraged me to ask him innumerable questions, and it was he who later taught me to recognize animal voices and imitate them. I always thought of him as an old man, though he can't have been any older than I am now.

WE'VE BEEN LEFT in Herr Moreau's sitting room, just us children on our own. Helmut is exploring the room, looking at the pictures on the walls, the photos on the chest of drawers. He opens the top drawer, though I'm sure it's not allowed. We don't have anything to do, and we don't feel like playing a game. "Hey," Helmut says suddenly, "look what I've found."

He's opened the door of a big cupboard, and he's waving a bar of chocolate in the air. "Look," he says, "and there's lots more. Did you ever see so many bars of chocolate in your life?"

No, never. And it's real chocolate, whole slabs of it, not those little pastilles in round tins that Papa sometimes sucks although they taste so bitter. We haven't had any sweets for ages. We're fed like soldiers these days, us children, and the food we get at home tastes even worse than it did before the war. People always said our parents stinted us, even then, and a lot of our guests used to stuff themselves at home before they came to a meal at our house.

"Think we could have one of them?" Helmut says. "There'd be plenty left for Herr Moreau."

The others look at me. "Oh, please, Helga, just one."

I give Helmut a nod and we watch him unwrap the bar with our mouths watering. The silver paper makes a lovely rustling sound. It's milk chocolate. The others make a grab for it, but Helmut hangs on tight. "Don't, you'll break it. Let Helga divide it up so we all get the same."

He hands it to me. There are eight squares in the bar and six of us. One square each leaves two over—two between six.

"Here, all of you, take one. We can divide up the rest when everyone's finished theirs."

Nobody says anything, they all nibble their chocolate and look around the room. Hilde sucks hers like a lollipop, but you can also bite off little bits if you try, then it lasts longer. At home we get watery soup. When Papa comes home for a meal he sits there slurping it up without noticing how watery it is, and when we ask him something he doesn't look up from his plate, just nods and slurps even louder instead of answering. He doesn't care what he eats, so he never thinks of telling the cook to dish up something better. No wonder he stares at us sometimes, surprised, and asks Mama why we're looking so pale. When it comes to the last two squares, Helmut wants a bigger share than the rest of us because he found the chocolate. He stuffs a whole square into his mouth, which is unfair.

Helmut chews up the square and swallows it. We'll simply have to pinch another bar of chocolate from the cupboard. Herr Moreau has got so many, he'll never notice if two are missing. The only thing is, we'll have to get rid of the paper somehow. This time, to avoid arguments, we divide it up straightaway. Helmut puts a square on his tongue, talks with his mouth open, and his gooey piece of chocolate falls on the carpet. It's not so easy to talk with something balanced on your tongue. Hilde drops a piece on the carpet too, and little Heide spits hers out for fun, without even trying to say something. We unwrap the next bar. Holde puts her head back and drops a square into her mouth. She nearly chokes, which makes her laugh. There's a box of chocolates in the cupboard. We decide to try them too.

"I hope they don't have any cognac in them," Hilde says. "Cognac tastes nasty."

We open the box. The candies turn out to be nougat, and so soft they melt in your mouth even without being chewed. Hilde sits down in an armchair and Helmut holds one out. She opens her mouth, but just as she's about to close it he snatches the candy away and eats it himself. Hilde's quicker the next time, she bites his fingers, but not hard enough to hurt. Helmut goes around with the box of chocolates and pops one in everyone's mouth.

"What's going on in here?"

Herr Moreau looks at the brown smears on the sofa and the carpet, the torn wrappers on the floor. We don't say a word. The chocolate in Helmut's hand is starting to melt.

IT'S POSSIBLE, BY dint of a little will power, to become inured to the most atrocious sounds. Before long, the pathetic whimpers that once gave you a blinding headache can be taken in stride. So, indeed, can the terrible screams that fill the air day and night. You soon find them no more than a faint background noise capable of being drowned by a whisper— and this although you felt unable, in the early days, to make your own voice clearly heard above the din and had to begin each sentence several times over.

Strangely enough, however, the authors of such sounds are quick to exhibit symptoms of physical degeneration. Being of their own making, the abominable din proves too much for them and becomes life-threatening if persisted in for an appreciable length of time. Like our test subjects, they slowly but steadily go downhill. How is it that the human ear draws so sharp a distinction between its owner's voice and those of other people? Why do the staff employed in this acoustic environment remain in good health, generally speaking, whereas our test subjects react to their own phonations by developing rigors and circulatory disorders? Why do our patients shun physical contact with other members of the group but lacerate their own scalps with torn and bitten nails? Why is it that their tactile sense seems badly impaired, and that they soon become incapable of speech even when we administer stimulants?

Moreau's explanation: "Perhaps they're being eaten away inside by ultrasound. Perhaps the frequencies they produce but are incapable of hearing have a drastic effect on the subjects' bodies, causing their intestines to vibrate and inducing uncontrollable nausea. They're exposed to a sound impossible to locate, an all-pervading, ultrasonic whistle that threatens to burst their eardrums and viscera, adversely affects their blood pressure and reduces their cerebral activity. Not that they're aware of it, their voices generate ultrasonic frequencies that assail the very core of their being—the core from which those sounds derive as a side effect of the phonations they're made to utter. Strictly speaking, this is an externally induced, self-destructive process that affects every tissue in the body."

"You mean we've failed to take that possibility into account because ultrasound is, by its very nature, completely inaudible?"

"Not by its very nature. We can't hear it, admittedly, but certain species of animals can. One need only think of the conformation of a bat's head, which many people find so weird: the wrinkled snout and the outsize ears capable of rotating in any direction. Both are aids to better reception."

"One moment. Are you saying that bats' ears grant them access to a world from which we, as human beings, are excluded?"

"That's certainly true of most bats, though probably not, to the best of our present knowledge, of flying foxes. The world of sounds is very much greater than we can imagine."

"You don't seriously mean that we're at the mercy of that unknown world and at a disadvantage with respect to other species, as if we were all deaf, whereas those animals are capable of perceiving the whole realm of sounds?"

"There are degrees, of course. Dogs and cats are receptive to a considerably wider spectrum of sounds than human beings, but a bat's sense of hearing is superior by far."

"And human beings, though incapable of hearing such sounds, continually produce them without being aware of it?"

"It's more than possible. The human voice resonates with sympathetic frequencies that hold no importance for us because our ears are unable to detect them."

"Do you know what you're saying? Do you realize how greatly it affects our conception of the audible world?"

"You're an expert on acoustics. You must be familiar with the concept of ultrasound."

"Of course I am, in theory, but it's not a phenomenon that has ever been associated in my mind with sounds proper. When people say that a dog hears better than a man, I've always taken it to mean that a dog's hearing is more acute in the sense that it can recognize its master's voice and footsteps in the distance, not that it detects nuances in the human voice which a human being can never hear."

Suddenly, my vocal map is falling to pieces in my hands. The lines I've drawn lead nowhere, have always led nowhere, and the whole sheet is now blank and empty. Gone are all my entries, from the silent parade of the deaf-mutes (arms restlessly gesticulating in the misty air, feet tramping across sodden grass), to the Scharführer's barrack-square bellow (autumnal acoustic conditions, drizzle, first light), to the wounded, dying soldiers (early summer heat and nighttime), to the distraught figures in their underpants (cold tiles, gaping mouths brightly illuminated). Gone are the cries, the agitated gasps and strident whistles, gone the shouted words of command, the hopeless cripple's labored breathing and the coward's whimpers, gone the revolting moans and grunts of couples in bed, gone the fading, exhausted voices on the radio from Stalingrad. All are vanishing from my inward ear, all are being sucked back into a silent void because of those never-to-be-heard sounds in the world known only to animals.

All quiet. It's really quiet at the moment. I peep through a crack in the curtains: nothing but darkness. It's as if all the soldiers in the world were having a rest, too tired to go on fighting. It's so quiet, even a night creature mightn't be able to hear anything. And the sky's dark for once, there's no red glow over the city, not a glimmer, no shadows in the night. They've turned off all the searchlights. No bombs falling, from the looks of it. The sky is dark, the way Herr Karnau always wanted. No lines on the sky to lighten the darkness, none of those flares that look like strands of flaming seaweed, none of those jagged Christmas trees that make the night as bright as day.

It's nearly dark here too, in Mama's bedroom. Only her dressing-table light is on. Heide's talking to her quietly and watching her putting on her make-up. Mama's bedroom is the only place in the house we can escape to, nowadays. I don't know how she stays so calm—she's always so incredibly calm when she's doing her face. She was just the same in peacetime and she's never changed all through the war. When Papa gave a party in the old days, she sometimes let us stay with her while she did her face, before we had to go to bed. She would quickly remove her daytime make-up and paint her face for the evening. It only took her a minute or two. Papa would be waiting for her downstairs with the guests, but she always seemed to have lots of time. Mama's bedroom is her kingdom, and Papa never dares walk in on her uninvited. We children are the only ones allowed to come in while she's getting ready.

She still insists on being left in peace while she's making up, even though everything else has changed so much lately. "Mama," asks Heide, tugging at her sleeve, "why are there so many people in the house these days? How long will they be staying? They're strangers."

"They're refugees, Heide. We're putting them up because they've nowhere else to go. It won't be for much longer."

"They look different from us—they're dirty, a lot of them. Don't they ever wash?"

Mama has always made a point of telling us how important it is to wash properly and comb our hair. It's the same with make-up. Make-up is a kind of protection against other people, she says, and the older you get the more you feel you need it. That's why, for quite a while now, I've been allowed to have a bath on my own. I'm even allowed to lock the door so the others can't disturb me. They used to come running in when I was sitting in the bathtub—they couldn't understand that I wanted to be left in peace, no matter how often I told them. The little ones would bring their wooden boat, which is really only meant for the lake, and insist on sailing it in the bath, even though it was plastered with duckweed. And when I forbade them to get in with me they'd horse around in front of the mirror. We always had a shouting match before they finally left.

"The refugees wash quite as thoroughly as you do," Mama

says, putting on some rouge. "If they look the worse for wear, Heide, it's because they had to leave their homes before the enemy got there. They've lost everything they possessed, that's why they can't change their clothes twice a day the way we do. Right now they're simply glad to be safe here with us, a long way from the fighting. And now, leave Mama in peace for a while."

She outlines her left eyelid, concentrating hard so the little pencil doesn't slip off the edge and go in her eye. I don't suppose she realizes why Heide is asking so many questions about the refugees. She wasn't there when one of them gave Heide such a shock without meaning to—an elderly man who'd taken a fancy to her and showed her a conjuring trick. He held up a colored handkerchief and made it vanish into his hands. Heide thought she'd seen through the trick. She laughed and pointed to his sleeve, but it wasn't hidden there. Then the man produced the handkerchief from his mouth and ran it through his fingers again. Heide was looking so hard at the handkerchief she didn't notice he only had two on each hand—fingers, I mean. He looked a bit grubby, too, and his lungs made a funny rattling sound when he breathed. When Heide finally saw the stumps of his missing fingers she shrieked and ran out of the room.

Mama has finished powdering her nose. She smiles at us in the mirror, but you can tell her face still hurts. You can tell it from her mouth and the way it droops sideways when she speaks. It's that nerve on the right-hand side, even though the operation was months ago. Sometimes she spends the whole day in bed with cold compresses on her face and can't move. I doubt if it'll ever get better.

These days Heide trails around everywhere with that rag doll Hedda used to have when she was little. Mama makes another attempt to get rid of the thing. "It's all tattered and dirty," she tells Heide. "You've got some nice new dolls of your own." But Heide refuses to be parted from it. She stomps out of the bedroom sucking the doll's ear.

"Mama?"

"Yes, Helga?"

"The war, will it really be over soon?"

"Yes, this year, definitely."

"Will we being staying here at Schwanenwerder till then, or will we have to move again?"

Mama shrugs her shoulders. "That's not for us to decide. If it's safer somewhere else, we'll naturally go there."

It was awful, the journey here from Lanke. We set off in the middle of the night. The cars could hardly squeeze past the columns of refugees. They made room for us and pushed their cart to one side, the poor, ragged people, but we had to drive very slowly. Even in the darkness we could see all the things they were taking with them: suitcases, carpets, lamps—even great big wardrobes. Once I saw a horse lying beside the road. I think it was dead.

Mama ends by squirting some perfume behind her ears and under her chin. She squirts a little on my wrist as well. Then she takes one more look at her hair and stands up. "Come on, Helga, let's go down and join the others."

Everyone's in the drawing room because Papa is speaking on the radio today, something he hasn't done for a long time. It's awfully cold in February without any heating, so they're all sitting there in their overcoats. Mama gives me a rug to wrap around me. Someone turns on the radio and everyone stops talking. Then comes the announcer, and then Papa starts to speak. The situation is critical, he says, but there are hopeful signs. Our enemies rejoice too soon, as they've so often done in the past, if they think they've broken our spirit of resistance. The brutal enemy soldiers who lay slaughtered babies at their mothers' feet have taught us an object lesson. Speaking for himself, Papa says, he has an unshakeable belief that victory will be ours, otherwise the world would have lost its right to exist—in fact life on earth would be worse than hell, and he wouldn't think it worth living, neither from his own point of view nor from that of his children. He would happily cast that life aside.

"Mama, did he really mean that? Would Papa really kill himself? And his children? That's us, after all."

But Mama doesn't answer, she just stares at the loudspeaker. The others don't say anything or look at me either. They keep their heads down and concentrate with their eyes shut or stare past me at the radio. Neither for himself nor for his children . . . "Maybe it isn't Papa at all? Maybe it's just an enemy broadcaster who's imitating Papa's voice and putting words into his mouth?" But Mama doesn't hear me. All she hears is that voice.

I CAN'T HEAR a thing, not a thing, the sounds are indistinguishable, everything is drowned by this roar, this ear-numbing roar that has taken possession of the air and my trembling body. Is this the end, is this the roar in which all sounds become reduced to a final, fiendish cacophony? Is this the descent into death? No, the plane levels off once more and the stutter of its engines gives way to the whistle of the slipstream as we spiral down towards our destination, a sea of flames. No one knows exactly how far the Russians have advanced, so there's a constant threat of gunfire from the ruins below. We're coming in to land on a runway flanked by shattered buildings. Not the Kurfürstendamm, surely? But it must be, it's the only runway left. Every tree in the avenue has been felled and the tram lines are obscured by a layer of bulldozed, steamrollered rubble. As the makeshift landing strip draws steadily nearer, one detail after another flashes past at lightning speed: a burned-out tramcar, a wrecked vehicle sprawled across the pavement, mounds of debris, splintered wooden doors, bathtubs doing duty for anti-tank barriers, a legless cripple humping himself along on his hands, a string of refugees, the remnants of a family, a baby carriage piled high with household effects. I can even make out sunken cheeks, bloodshot eyes, a child's runny nose. The images vanish in a cloud of dust as we touch down with a jolt. Are my arms trembling or merely taking on the movements of our plane as it shudders to a halt?

Armed men come sprinting out of a ruined store and start unloading the aircraft almost before it comes to a halt. They stand guard, rifles at the ready, while the freight compartment is emptied of its crates of foodstuffs. The whole city is rationed. Everyone is dependent on rapeseed cakes, turnips and molasses. The inhabitants are being encouraged to gather roots and acorns, mushrooms and clover. Any living creature that can still be found among the gutted ruins is fair game—the authorities have even issued instructions on how to catch frogs. All available warm-blooded animals are to be devoured without delay. Conditions at the zoo are disastrous, I hear: two days ago, on Friday, 20 April, it was compelled to close for the first time in its history. Lack of power has immobilized the pumps and reduced the aquatic animals' pools to turbid soup, with the result that cracks have begun to appear in the dolphins' skin.

How are the flying foxes faring, I wonder. What sort of state are they in, the descendants of the creatures Moreau brought back from Madagascar and presented to the zoo? They're the last of their kind, now that the Dresden brood has been wiped out together with Moreau himself, who was buried with his charges beneath the ruins of the Chiroptera house on the morning of 14 February, when a bomb pierced the roof.

We had taken leave of each other only a few days before. I shall never forget that scene: the flying foxes' darkened enclosure, Moreau's gaunt frame, tremulous with privation, and the patient way he proffered slices of blood sausage to his debilitated bats, which ignored them, in a last attempt to keep them alive—canned blood sausage procured from who knows what secret store, canned blood sausage proffered in mute desperation, for want of anything else, because it was obvious, even when Moreau ran the cans to earth, that animals accustomed to fresh fruit would never touch blood sausage. There would be no more fighting over food, no more furious squeaks when one of them, with wildly beating wings, chased another off a peach or an apple and sank its teeth in the juicy flesh. But Moreau did not give up. He broke into the main post office at night in search of food parcels that could no longer be delivered, but the flying foxes spurned their contents too, possibly deterred by the scent of incipient, invisible mildew.

I made a resolution as soon as I learned of his death: the next time I visited Berlin my first step would be to check on the flying foxes, regardless of prevailing conditions and the risks involved. And now I've been summoned back into this sea of ruins. Clouds of smoke are drifting across the city in an easterly direction. The air trembles whenever a shell lands nearby, and shots can be heard not far away. Trees lie uprooted on the paving stones, the main gate is pockmarked with shell splinters, a bent sign on the ground reads DO NOT FEED THE SQUIRREL MONKEYS, and charred tree stumps border the path on which an injured dove is striving, with outspread wings, to drag itself in the direction of some neglected flower beds.

Dead ducks are floating in the pond. Seated motionless on a park bench, each propped up against the other, are two wounded, combat-weary soldiers, one with a cocked submachine gun across his knees. They're both staring blankly at the sky, but the latter suddenly stirs. He keels over sideways, the gun slides off his lap, and his heavy, limp-armed frame slumps to the ground. The other man, deprived of support, follows suit.

Cigarette lighter flickering, I make my way down into the cellar reserved for nocturnal creatures. This is evidently where members of the zoo staff sheltered during air raids. A flying fox flutters towards me through the gloom, skims my head and makes for the exit, where, bewildered by the bright spring sunlight, it circles in an untidy, haphazard way and quickly disappears from view. Someone has opened the cage, it seems, and as the lighter's feeble flame approaches the spot I'm overcome by a terrible presentiment. Another step, a faint splintering sound. Crouching down, I make out a tiny thorax and spinal column, both picked clean. I examine the floor round about, singe scraps of fur and surface hair with my lighter flame. A severed, membranous wing, residues of black and inedible matter. Not far away lies a peeled head with the eyes still open. Then darkness. The lighter has run out of fuel.

"ANY NEWS FOR Radio Werewolf, anyone?"

Papa smiles as he says that, but you can tell it's a strain. Radio Werewolf is his big thing nowadays. He goes out into the passage and asks someone else the same question. Papa spends the whole day collecting items of news for his radio station. "The Werewolf needs feeding," he says, and he expects all the grown-ups to submit bright ideas. Heroic deeds, that's what he collects. If Mama thinks of something, or his secretary, or even his receptionist, he makes a note of it at once. He never used to ask his receptionist for suggestions, not in the old days.

The Werewolves—yes, all our hopes are pinned on the Werewolves now. "They must gobble everything up," Papa says, meaning the power lines, the maps and street signs. They've all got to be destroyed so the invaders can't find their way around our country.

"There's plenty for the Werewolves to sink their teeth in," Papa says. "They can create as much havoc as they like. The Werewolves won't rest till they've bitten off the enemy's ears."

What does he mean? Werewolves are half animal, half human. They're something out of a horror story.

"No," Papa says, "Werewolves are partisans, guerrilla fighters. Radio Werewolf broadcasts to them from somewhere in enemy-occupied territory."

"Don't pretend to the children," Mama tells him. "The radio station isn't far from Berlin. They're figments of your imagination, these news items."

Papa looks disappointed. "I'd prefer to call them products of poetic license," he says. "They're simply the news as it *ought* to be. Don't you realize that our reports are bound to come true? Don't you realize that we broadcast them so that, somewhere out there, the Werewolves will *make* them come true? All our news items will become a reality if only we put them over in the right tone of voice. The Werewolves will act with firmness and fanaticism as long as they're worded in the pithy, punchy style I've devised to meet the requirements of this exceptional situation."

Mama shrugs her shoulders. "Besides," says Papa, "I want

every German youngster to dread being the last to join the Werewolves."

Helmut is staring at the floor. Did Papa look at him sternly as he said that? "Children," says Mama, "you'd better go to your room now."

Poor Papa, he's so proud of his Radio Werewolf. Sometimes you'd think it was all he had left. We shut the bedroom door. Mama and Papa are bound to start arguing and we don't want to hear them at it. The younger ones try desperately to think of some way of helping Papa. What Papa needs, what he needs really badly to make him feel better, they say, are stories about Werewolves performing heroic deeds. They dig out an old exercise book with plenty of room in it—we don't need our exercise books, not now we've stopped having lessons—and sit down in a corner and start making up Werewolf reports, and when every last page in the book is full they're going to give it to Papa as a present. Hilde lets herself be talked into taking down the stories even though she doesn't feel like it. So there they all sit, whispering together: "Werewolves are tearing the enemy limb from limb... Werewolves are tirelessly stalking the enemy and attacking them from the rear...."

That's Holde, with her love of horror stories, but Hilde interrupts her: "It's got to be snappy, we need really short sentences, like 'All street signs to be painted over.'"

"Radio Werewolf should broadcast marching songs and fanfares," Hedda says in a loud whisper, "with news bulletins in between."

Helmut, who has been thinking hard, says, "Papa also said you can stop American tanks by putting something in their gasoline at night."

The others rack their brains in vain. It would be nice if they really could think of something that would bring the war to an end. "We must dream up some nastier things," Hilde says. "Acid, for instance. Acid's horrible stuff, it eats away your eyes and blinds you. All right, I'll put that down: 'The Werewolves are blinding enemy soldiers.' "

"Or hacking off their hands," says Holde, but Hilde can't keep up. "Or stripping them naked and chopping them up, in that order. Or spreading fire and destruction. Or shooting all traitors on the spot. Or drinking the enemy's blood."

The others break off and look at each other as if surprised at their own thirst for blood, but they are sure they've been a great help to Papa. He'll feel much happier once they've given him their collection of news items.

BUT THIS DARKNESS affords no protection, neither from the memory of those shrill, cracked, mutilated voices, nor from the noise of the bombardment. The crash of shells exploding above ground penetrates the bunker walls, even at the very deepest level. It won't be long before the walls crack under the impact. They'll cave in and kill us—we'll be crushed to death by rubble just as Moreau's sleeping bats were crushed to death in the dark after being exposed to a momentary, blinding flash when the bomb ripped through the roof of the Chiroptera house and flooded their cage with daylight, the dazzling, agonizing light that finally destroyed the defenseless creatures' nocturnal world.

So one form of darkness has absorbed the other: black is immersed in black, in a darkness unconnected with the night-and-morning world where safety resides. Such darkness fails to act as a shield against glaring light because it does not recognize light as its counterpart: in such darkness, light is inconceivable.

Stumpfecker stands facing me in uniform. It was he that

ordered me to report to him forthwith, here in this sunless, subterranean world, in order to record the voice of his very last patient. He puts a finger to his lips. We have to be as quiet as possible in the bunker, especially here on the lowest level, because one never knows, at any time of the day or night, whether the patient is asleep, presiding over a secret meeting, or simply sitting in his quarters, saying nothing but nonetheless intolerant of any sound, however faint, in the passage outside his door.

The patient is far more sensitive to disturbances of human origin than to the thunder of the guns overhead. Stumpfecker believes that the patient's sensitivity extends to his own vocalizations: the voice that used to be so loud and clear is growing steadily fainter. "You've yet to see this for yourself, Karnau, but what really dismays me is the fact that sometimes, in the last few days, the patient has been incapable of making any sound at all. It's happening more and more often, too. He'll bid a wordless farewell to subordinates who are leaving the bunker for good, and his only response if they say something while shaking hands is a silent movement of the lips."

There's a whole set of blank wax discs on the table in my cubicle, and a portable recording machine is permanently at the ready. Stumpfecker has gone off to see how his patient is. All that mitigates the oppressive silence is the hum of the overtaxed air-conditioning system. The telephone rings. It's Stumpfecker: "Come quickly, Karnau, it's the patient, a very serious situation, he's been yelling at his subordinates in conference, hasn't strained his voice so badly for ages, it'll give out at any moment, so get your equipment down here fast."

The stairs and the narrow passage are thronged with people listening with expressions of alarm. The patient is clearly audible now, even though all the doors are closed. It's possible to hear every word he bellows in that maltreated voice, which does indeed sound on the point of giving out. I can already detect rents in his vocal cords, laryngeal lesions, but the eavesdroppers seem unaware of this: their whole attention is focused on the wording of his furious accusations and invocations of doom.

Stumpfecker, crouching outside the door from which the noise is coming, nervously fidgets with his medical bag. We continue to wait, unable as yet to enter the room but poised to do so once the tantrum has run its course. "He'll be slumped in his chair, utterly exhausted," Stumpfecker murmurs. "Stay in the background. Then, when I've checked his blood pressure and given him his medication, hold the microphone to his lips. You must start recording at once. It'll be my job to coax a few words out of him. You can't afford any slip-ups, Karnau. We don't know if he'll ever get his voice back. This could be our very last chance to record it."

But the red, raw, worn-out throat fails to emit another sound. We sit in Stumpfecker's consulting room on the lower level and listen to the recorded silence. Stumpfecker tries hard to retain his composure. "Let's hope this difficult phase will soon be over," he says. "There may be light at the end of the tunnel. After all, he's undergone several polypectomies, for instance in May 1935, on the advice of the doctors at the Charité Hospital. Having listened to one of his speeches on the radio, they inferred from his raucous voice that someone who could bellow so loudly for two solid hours must either have a larynx made of steel or be doomed to vocal paralysis. To the best of my knowledge, the last operation took place in October last year, shortly before my posting to East Prussia. It entailed the removal of another growth on the vocal cords.

"Many people regard the situation as hopeless," Stumpfecker goes on. "They think we're all condemned to look on idly at close quarters while the patient's physical condition deteriorates. There have been medical men who mistakenly believed that he was suffering from Parkinson's, but mark my words, Karnau: once the war is over—and it won't be long now—the patient's constitution will soon be restored by doses of fresh air, prolonged exposure to glorious summer sunlight, and rigorous detoxification."

It's only two days since Stumpfecker was promoted to become the patient's personal physician in succession to the man who could neatly insert cannulas into any vein he chose. Dr. Morell, renowned for his miracle pills, quit the bunker in a hurry, and no one reckoned with the possibility that Stumpfecker, of all the numerous doctors present, would replace him—least of all Stumpfecker himself. The truth is that the end of our joint research had cast a shadow over his career. Although the authorities tolerated the failure of his transplant experiments at Hohenlychen, where he attempted to graft slivers of bone taken from inmates of Ravensbrück concentration camp onto patients in the SS hospital—a procedure that resulted in the growth of proud flesh, gangrene, and, ultimately, death—they did not feel able, in the light of military developments, to fund our research any longer. Having embarked on it with the aim of exploring the foundations of a radical form of speech therapy, we had ended up with a collection of mutes.

Instead of purposefully eradicating vocal defects, we had erased whole voices. This meant, in the end, that all our efforts were expended on reversing the process, on trying to adjust and repair damaged voices—on conducting futile breathing exercises and clearing asthmatic tubes, on directing the course of these only moderately successful experiments—when there was no real hope of repairing organs already given up for lost. This fact was, of course, concealed from our guinea pigs, who would only have panicked and rent the air with countless aberrant sound waves.

Our work was finally terminated when a special SS unit herded the unresisting test subjects into a corner of their ward, doused them in surgical alcohol, and set fire to them, destroying the entire building as well. Stumpfecker felt sure he would be demoted several ranks in consequence. He owed it to his teacher and patron, Professor Gebhardt, that the opposite happened. Not long afterwards, in October of last year, he was appointed surgeon at HQ Eastern Front, where he often accompanied the patient on his daily walks.

And now, within the space of a few hours, he has had to familiarize himself with his patient's medical history by consulting the notes which Morell, in a very slapdash fashion, had kept over the years. Under present circumstances, however, the professional competence of his new personal physician matters less to the patient than his physical stature. Almost two meters tall, Stumpfecker is known here as "the Giant." Although he may not be able to administer injections as neatly and painlessly as Morell—Stumpfecker's own staff informed him of the patient's misgivings in this respect—his titanic physique would readily permit him, in the event of a dangerous bombardment, to carry the patient on his back to a safe place. Laden with a rigid figure whose straining arms threatened to squeeze the air from his lungs, he could if need be hasten from room to room, dodging the chunks of concrete and steel girders that rained down on them both. His reserves of energy would enable him to scramble over rubble for a considerable period, upturned eyes forever focused on the crumbling bunker ceiling and ears ignoring his human burden's stertorous breathing in favor of sounds indicating where the concrete would be rent asunder or the next shell would land.

At our session the next day Stumpfecker is once more filled with optimism. The patient has fully recovered from the exhaustion induced by yesterday's interminable tirade. He seems cheerful, relaxed, and in excellent voice. The needle quivers restlessly, leaving a silvery groove in the disc's matte wax surface. Every now and then the patient helps himself to a chocolate from a salver, a habit that struck me yesterday. It probably serves to lubricate his voice in a routine, unobtrusive manner.

I envy people who can fall asleep at the drop of a hat. There are some here who exemplify this ability, for instance a courier who simply nodded off in the canteen as soon as he had delivered his dispatches: he sat down at the table, slept for a mere quarter-hour in the glare of the overhead light, and then woke up in a trice, ready once more to brave the perils of a city under siege. The same phenomenon can be observed in many of the visitors who come and go in the bunker: doctors, sentries, senior army officers, Party officials. They lean against a wall somewhere for ten or fifteen minutes—indeed, often for only five—and wake up seemingly refreshed. I can't do that. I take at least half an hour to get to sleep, if not an hour, and even then it's a painful process: my head rings with past, present and future voices that refuse to be silenced. There are times when any voice is too much to bear.

This has to do with the absolute darkness that prevails in my bunker cubicle. I find it a trial, the lighting here below ground. There's no dawn light in the morning, no twilight in the evening, none of the gradual blurring of outlines that precedes the nocturnal evanescence of objects and human figures. Colors don't gradate from purple to the red of coagulated blood, from pale to dark blue, until, little by little, they're all reduced to shades of gray that eventually turn a blackish blue and envelop the whole world. There's not a glimmer now, no faint glow from the night sky, just an abrupt transition when I turn the light in my cubicle on or off. There are no light switches at all in the passages and communal rooms. The lights out there burn twenty-four hours a day. They must consume a lot of power—the generators on the lower level can barely cope. Strange that precious electricity should be wasted in this way, but I suppose it's official policy that every space apart from our sleeping quarters should be illuminated. No shadowy figures must encounter each other in the gloom and no one can be allowed to withdraw into even temporary seclusion. That may be why the sleeping courier presented such a singular picture: people are not, as a rule, illuminated while asleep; they retire into the darkness, where no one can see them. What kind of life do we lead in our ever-illuminated surroundings?

The artificial light in which we have now been living for so many days is not particularly bright. It flickers or even goes out under the effect of gunfire, thereby seeming to imitate nature, but it burns and stings the skin as soon as you turn it on. In time you perceive it less as a condition than as a substance. It diffuses an oily yellow glow over everything and defies removal, however hard you scrub. It even clings to your face, which looks cheesy, as if its original color had imperceptibly faded and been replaced by a film of artificial light. Is that skin on my milk, or is it just the light? None of us swallows his ration of boiled milk without a shudder of distaste.

Even our acoustics here are affected by the light. It suppresses natural sonic conditions: all voices sound a full tone lower, all noises muffled and indistinct. The brighter the light and the sharper the outlines, the more muffled the voices. This is an unreal acoustic environment, one in which everything loud and shrill stands out like a sore thumb. Does the wind still whistle? Do doves still coo? Do blackbirds still twitter as they hop from branch to branch? Is the air still alive with almost inaudible stirrings whose origin cannot be located? Down here, everything can be traced to its source with ease: a change of pressure simply denotes that someone has closed the heavy steel door at the end of the passage.

We no longer venture to cite the time of day or night with any certainty. When someone visits us from the outside world, he's promptly bombarded with questions about the time of day, the prevailing light:

"What are the clouds like, brilliant white against a gray background?"

"No, they're more on the hazy side."

"So the sky's overcast, is it, as if all the light and color had drained away?"

"No, not that either. It looks in places as if the sun may break through before long."

"Did you hear that? Just imagine, he says the sun may come out soon. Lucky man, to have seen it with his own eyes."

"Is there any warmth in the sun yet?"

"Are the nights getting milder?"

"What about that reddish glow the evening sky takes on in springtime? Can you tell it from the reflection of the fires in the suburbs?"

"Whenever the smoke clears, sure, no problem."

"And the gutted buildings overhead, do they reflect the light, or are they so black with soot they simply absorb it?"

It's hard on the constitution, a daily routine no longer

governed by the sun: never to bed before three in the morning, up at noon, straight off to a recording session. Still tired out, I manipulate the controls in a kind of dream, observe my movements like a stranger: my hand, the rippling tendons, the curious way my forefinger bends when I extend it, and the half-moons I've never noticed before, the pronounced half-moons at the base of my fingernails.

The bunker's entire ventilation system is on the verge of collapse. The stale air is no longer being fully extracted, so we filter the remaining oxygen from it by breathing faster than normal. Fainting fits are becoming more frequent. The ventilators themselves may be clogged with swarms of fruit flies sucked in from the kitchen. The cook can no longer hold the little insects at bay, there's too much food lying around: ration packs of rusks and crispbread, honey by the bucketful, ketchup—comestibles for which no use can be found now that most of the staff are getting their meals from a big kitchen elsewhere in the bunker.

"Look at this," says the cook. "Everything's going bad: fresh vegetables, cottage cheese, yogurt, mushrooms. It hasn't occurred to anyone to cancel them—they're still being flown in daily from Bavaria, even though the Führer won't touch them any longer. I've never known a sadder day in all my time as his personal diet cook. For years I cooked him vegetarian meals on doctor's instructions, meals that took account of his weak stomach and his digestive problems, and now what? All my good work is undone in a matter of days because he abandons his diet and refuses to eat anything but pastries and chocolates.

"On getting up he has a bowl of chocolate-flavored gruel or blancmange made from bars of bitter chocolate, but without milk. Vegetable matter only—that at least I can make sure of, being his diet cook. The Führer can't tolerate milk, unlike yogurt or cream, so I use agar instead. Regular works of art in agar, I turn out. The main thing is to make them creamy and very chocolaty. He gorges himself on chocolates and chocolate-flavored pastries all day long. The squares of nougat he mostly eats at night, during those tiring conferences of his: very sweet, good for the nerves. I'll see he goes on getting them to the last, provided our supplies hold out.

"We've just lost a whole roomful of milk chocolate—without nuts, of course. It was blown to bits, plus the sentry, off a corridor on the top floor of the Chancellery—a risky location for a secret storeroom, but ingenious. I mean, who would have dared to go looting on the top floor with all those shells falling?

"We're all fervently hoping that fresh supplies will continue to arrive from Switzerland every morning. Red Cross flights are still getting through, but the situation is critical. The members of the chocolate squad are scared of becoming embroiled in the fighting outside when they have to leave here and escort the daily chocolate consignment. As for the confectioner, who's working around the clock, he's afraid he'll be for the chop if the day ever comes when he can't produce a salverful of chocolates."

THE KILLER DOGS have been trained to attack enemy soldiers lying asleep on the ground. They know their victims are defenseless because they can hear their quiet breathing from a long way off. They can hear every snore, every breath, and when they find a man asleep they sneak up on him and nuzzle his bare throat—very gently, so as not to tickle him and wake him up. It's his Adam's apple they're after, the killer dogs. They close their teeth on it very gently, and then, without warning, they bite it as hard as they can—so quickly that their victim can't scream with pain because they've already ripped his throat out. The killer dogs make sure that anyone they attack can't utter another sound. Their eyes glow in the dark, and they've got wolf's blood in their veins.

I can't stop thinking up Werewolf stories. I don't even know whether they're nightmares, or whether they come to me when I'm awake and can't sleep. Papa was horrified when he saw the exercise book with the Werewolf stories the others had made up: it escaped him how they could have invented such grisly tales. He stopped smiling, just for a moment, and let his mouth hang open. It was as if he'd suddenly stopped believing in his Werewolves. He wasn't thinking about final victory, he was simply staring at the exercise book. He didn't care how he looked, he'd forgotten we could see him.

Papa was against the Radio Werewolf idea at first, because it meant finally admitting that the enemy had invaded our country. Then he got all enthusiastic and pushed it as hard as he could—in fact he sometimes forgets the idea wasn't his in the first place. He dreams up one imaginary act of sabotage after another, so why should he be surprised when his children do the same? He used to smack me sometimes in the old days, when he caught me lying. Grown-ups are convinced you can't tell when they're lying, but all you can't tell is how they decide whether to let you know something or lie to you instead.

Why do they tell us some things but keep us in the dark about others? Papa used to talk about his Radio Werewolf reports when we were in the room. He often bragged about other ideas of his and asked if we found them convincing. Propaganda campaigns, for instance. He'd try out an announcement about a cut in food rations, and we had to help him decide which phrases would make the situation sound less serious—in other words, hush it up. Then there were the pictures of naked women we dropped over the French soldiers' trenches to undermine their morale. Papa chose those pictures himself and thought up the captions for them. He kept wondering how best to convince the enemy soldiers that their womenfolk were having affairs with other men back home. We weren't supposed to know about that campaign, but when Papa gave it away he acted as if it didn't matter too much. He also let us in on his plan to write a book about films when it was still a secret. But there are other things we aren't supposed to know, and Papa still believes we don't have a clue about them—like how he once had Mama's telephone tapped because she kept making calls to a Norwegian gentleman.

When Papa lies he takes his time about it. He knows just how to answer a question wrongly or dodge it altogether, for instance when I overheard Mama asking him if he was having an affair with that singer. He didn't blink or turn away, didn't show how much he disliked the question, didn't hesitate before he answered. "No," he said, straight out, just "No," as if he hadn't had to decide whether to lie or tell the truth—as if there were no two ways about it.

Yes, Papa's a good liar on the whole. It's easier to tell when Mama's lying. Either she sounds as if she can't get the lie out quick enough, or she pretends she's thinking of something else and answers quite casually, as if the answer doesn't matter. But I can tell she's found it awkward, having to answer, because I've asked her an awkward question.

Grown-ups have this idea that children can't think for themselves or make up their own minds about a situation. For some strange reason they're convinced that children only ask a question once and leave it at that when they get an answer.

It never occurs to them that they aren't the only people I ask—that I hear other grown-ups talking and can see things for myself.

They smile at you with their eyes, but the eyes aren't everything. You can often tell when people are lying by their voices, by the special way they breathe. Lately I can tell for certain when Papa's lying. I can almost smell it on his breath, no matter how many pastilles he sucks to disguise it or however often he squirts himself with cologne.

TUESDAY, 24 APRIL. An absolute disaster: the patient is refusing chocolate-flavored dishes of any kind. He won't touch chocolate in adulterated form, even in pastries or gâteaus; he now insists on straight chocolate—milk chocolate, to be precise—nothing else will do. The kind of very fine chocolate that melts in your mouth without having to be chewed or sucked or rolled around your tongue: it dissolves of its own accord, diffuses itself throughout the oral cavity, and coats the teeth and gums with a thin film of creamy cocoa butter. Nougat, too, is out from now on. Stumpfecker, who has closely examined the patient's gums and tongue, diagnoses nervous irritation of the taste buds. There's no hope now, everyone can sense it: this is the beginning of the end.

Today, after all the recordings I've made that picked up virtually nothing, all the well-nigh wasted discs on which the grooves incised by the cutting stylus are almost devoid of oscillations, we're treated to another session at full volume. His nerves at breaking point, a state of affairs that may be attributable partly to the precarious chocolate situation, the patient flies into one of the notorious tantrums that can easily fill a whole set of discs. Every stirring of emotion vents itself in bellows of rage and wild, inarticulate sounds. We have just arrived for our routine recording session, and Stumpfecker signs to me to switch on the machine without the patient's noticing.

Afterwards, Stumpfecker follows me into his consulting room for a trial playback: a perfect, crystal-clear recording, its only drawback being that the patient's voice periodically swells and fades as his restless perambulations take him nearer or farther from the microphone: "Betrayed, I've been betrayed...surrounded by nothing but traitors...." Similar snatches recur on several of the discs I've cut in the last few days.

Apart from carefully eking out his stock of morphine, Stumpfecker has for some days been responsible less for his patient's health and well-being than for devising a suitable way for him to die. It was at first taken for granted—not that the patient himself was privy to such conjectures—that his bodyguard would solve this problem by assassinating him. Although the possibility of apoplexy cannot be discounted, a natural death due to chronic malnutrition and nervous exhaustion must, in view of the patient's exceptionally robust constitution, be ruled out.

Consequently, on the night of 29 April, Stumpfecker successfully tries out one possible way of causing death by external means on the patient's Alsatian bitch: he doctors her food with cyanide trickled into her bowl from an ampoule and stirred into the mush. For some unknown reason the animal spurns this offering and backs away from the bowl. She then has to be lured into the guards' washroom, where her jaws are prised apart and the contents of another ampoule, which has been crushed with a pair of pliers, emptied onto her tongue. Death supervenes within seconds.

Death by poisoning would necessitate the patient's consent,

however, because he no longer partakes of any food whose consistency would enable it to be mixed with cyanide, and one could hardly lever his jaws open and force him to swallow the ampoule.

Mouth liberally smeared with chocolate, the patient dictates his last will and testament, leafing through dictionaries and thesauruses in search of apt words and telling phrases. If one reference book fails to yield at first glance what he seeks, he hurls the heavy volume across the room and reaches for another. He dictates while lying on the sofa, cramming square after square of chocolate into his mouth. Much to the secretary's annoyance, he indicates any passages to be altered with fingers that anoint her shorthand pad with chocolate and leave greasy brown blotches in the midst of his momentous last words, which are then fair-copied on a typewriter with characters three times normal size and submitted to him for signature. The characters are uneven because the typewriter has a mechanical defect that obstructs the carriage as it glides from right to left, and the ribbon's inferior quality is such that it disfigures the paper with smudges and black fluff. The nib of the fountain pen splutters across the foot of the final sheet. The patient's signature is less neat than usual, not only because of his agitated state but also, quite possibly, because the pen is so bedaubed with chocolate that it slips through his fingers.

Meanwhile, the patient's chauffeur has been instructed to retrieve and replace the dictionaries littering the carpet. Before putting them back on the shelf, he smooths out the innumerable dog-ears that mark the places where his lord and master has discovered words and definitions of interest. Another of his allotted tasks is to stem the water trickling down the stairs into the rooms on the lower level, so much of which has already been absorbed by the carpets that every footstep is accompanied by a sound like someone smacking his lips. In this the chauffeur fails because the bunker lacks sufficient caulking material to seal the cracks in the water pipes and concrete walls occasioned by incessant detonations in the immediate vicinity.

We've been recording the patient every hour, on the hour, since the night before last. The phone rings: Stumpfecker. Surely it can't be a whole hour since the last session? One loses all sense of time down here. What's the date today? Monday, 30 April. A gramophone starts blaring in the passage. Most of the staff have gathered in the open space outside my door, which usually serves as a canteen, and are holding an impromptu dance. SS men, bodyguards and domestic staff are sitting around on the benches tapping their feet. An SS officer unbuttons his tunic, loosens his tie, and, with a bow, invites the cook to dance. She gives him her arm, and the two of them thread their way through the tables and chairs that have been pushed aside for the occasion. Once on the dance floor they traverse it with *élan* from end to end.

Down below, Stumpfecker stops me at the entrance to the patient's quarters: "No, Karnau, no more recordings, the patient's voice has given out. He can't speak anymore, not that it matters now. Fetch your things from the consulting room and get those wax discs out of here. They're the only means anyone will ever have of hearing his voice in the future, so take the utmost care of them. To be on the safe side, better make some copies right away."

I hear a familiar cough in the background just as Stumpfecker closes the door behind him and locks it from the inside. So this is the end. The water in the stairwell is now ankle-deep, and there are hand grenades, medals and peaked caps strewn everywhere. I climb the spiral stairs to the emergency exit and step out into the garden. A bright, sunny afternoon. I haven't seen the sky since my arrival. If it weren't for the infernal din, the incessant explosions, I could almost believe the war was over.

It isn't, though, so I have to take cover. Here in the lee of a ruined wall my bronchial tubes relax for the first time in ages and my lungs, having expelled the stale, subterranean air of recent days and nights, replace it with the balmy air of springtime. A sudden flicker of flame elsewhere in the garden. Are they burning the last, telltale documents? There's Stumpfecker, but he isn't carrying any folders under his arm, just holding a single sheet of paper. He bends over a body lying on the ground. More men are standing near the flames with shadows dancing across their faces. A sudden, earsplitting crash, and the figures jump back: a shell has landed nearby. They're out of sight when the gasoline-soaked uniform on the ground finally catches fire, ignited by a blazing page from a dictionary. Looking more closely, I make out the burning cadaver's gaping, blood-smeared mouth and the hole in the back of its head. A moment later it's enveloped in dense, dark smoke. Now a second corpse lands beside it and promptly catches fire too. The flames fan out from the center, upwards to the swelling bosom and downwards to the black suede shoes.

It's all settled: we're taking everyone along. Our intention is to break out of the bunker piecemeal and make our way out of the city in small, inconspicuous groups. The bunker's occupants are packing the last of their possessions, and the prevailing commotion is incredible: boots clumping along the passages, pots and pans clattering, a crash of broken china followed not by silence but by loud laughter. Not as loud as all that, though: it's the sheer contrast with the whispering and tiptoeing of the last few days that makes every noise seem so violent and protracted. None of us feels exultant, however. We're all too drained and exhausted for that.

While awaiting the breakout I sit in my cubicle and work. There are two copies to be made of our most recent recordings. One set of discs will be sent on ahead, the other Stumpfecker will take with him when he heads south. I, who intend to go west, have been entrusted with the originals.

Everyone is smoking. The whole bunker is suddenly thick with smoke after a non-smoking eternity. We all fish out the cigarettes we've been hiding for weeks in expectation of this moment, when we can at last light up again because the master of the house is no longer in a position to maintain his ban on smoking. We make up for lost time with a vengeance. Clouds of tobacco smoke fill the air, day and night. It won't be long before the walls and furniture are blotted out—indeed, I can barely see my own hand, which is in fact holding a cigarette.

Just before ten p.m. on 1 May. It must be getting dark outside, and that's how we propose to make our final exit, under cover of darkness. Where's Stumpfecker? It's time he came to collect his box of discs. Maybe he's down below in the SS guardroom. No, not here, the place is deserted. The concrete walls are covered with crudely executed pornographic murals: grinning women with massive breasts and sporrans of hair between their legs. One of the SS troopers comes hurrying along the passage with an empty jerrycan. He has just set fire to the conference room, so we'd better get out before the smoke asphyxiates us. The members of our group have already assembled in the entrance upstairs, complete with their belongings. Stumpfecker is standing guard over the two boxes of records.

He turns to me before we set off. "As long as there's any risk of our being picked up by the invaders," he says, "get this straight: your first priority is to learn to speak like a victim. Summon up a precise recollection of the words, sentence structure and intonation of your own test subjects. Recall them, imitate them, repeat them slowly, at first in your head, then in a low voice. Speak with downcast eyes, keep breaking off in midstream so as to convey that you've undergone some atrocious experiences but can't bring yourself to describe them. Say nothing of those alleged atrocities. Gloss over your doings in recent years by inserting judicious pauses. Draw a veil over your activities by stopping short just in time. Contort your face, develop a stutter, learn to make your eyes grow moist by an effort of the will, seem helpful and communicative, affect a willingness to describe the terrible things that have happened to you, coupled with heartfelt regret at your inability to do so. Break down and they'll exempt you from further questioning—in fact they'll end by commiserating with you. You'll be taken for a victim, the victim of some nameless and indescribable atrocity. In other words, you'll have changed sides. As your interrogation proceeds, you'll imperceptibly turn into one of those whose treatment at your hands formed the basis of the interrogators' original accusations. You must learn to do precisely what always revolted you in others and inspired the disgust that motivated your activities in the first place: you must stammer, dry up, pretend to be at a loss for words. For a while, alas, we're destined to play the inarticulate."

CHAPTER

7

In July 1992, during a routine inspection of Dresden's municipal orphanage, workmen removed some boards nailed over a hole in the cellar wall. Beyond it lay a secret sound archive. Despite its age and provenance, proved beyond doubt through the nature of the material stored there, no one had previously known of its existence.

The sound archive was found to be connected with the nearby Museum of Hygiene by a series of underground passages. From this it could be inferred that members of the museum staff had once had access to the premises, and that exchanges of information and personnel may even have taken place. None of the museum's current employees knew about the archive, however, so only privileged personnel could have been aware of the connecting passages, whose existence was kept strictly confidential. Very few details of the sound archive's staff had survived. The only name definitely listed in the card index, the bulk of which had been destroyed, was that of a retired security man: Hermann Karnau.

While attending a preliminary, on-the-spot inspection by a committee of inquiry, Karnau made the following statement:

"Here, gentlemen, if you can spare the time to confirm this for yourselves, you will find every conceivable aid to research into the relevant field, including, of course, a whole library of recordings representing every leading figure in politics and public life since the invention of the phonograph. It even includes that supposedly long-lost series of recordings entitled *The Führer Coughs,* shellac, seventy-eight r.p.m."

Karnau was then asked what purpose the establishment had served. His explanation:

"Weekly recordings on wax were made of the Führer's pulse rate while he was subjected to stress, in motion, or delivering a speech, so that regular comparisons could be made by playing back different weekly results in parallel. Were his blood vessels dilated? Had his blood pressure gone down? Did his heart take an appropriate time to regain its normal rhythm after a speech delivered *con brio?* Those were some of the aspects from which these cylinders, shellac discs and tapes were evaluated.

"The approaches were doubly secured by grilles and massive steel doors. Anyone working in the brick-lined vault beyond them had to crouch a little. The recording studio was more luxuriously appointed: a comfortable armchair behind the microphone, wall-to-wall carpet, and cloth-lined walls, not only for soundproofing purposes but because the important persons who frequented the studio were accustomed to a certain degree of comfort. Nothing could be heard of the children running around two floors above."

A shelf laden with tapes, some partially unwound, bore witness to sundry attempts to transfer all the recordings to the latest type of recording medium—attempts that had never progressed far because the influx of material to be evaluated and filed was far too voluminous. Although strict attention had always been paid to cleanliness (the entire archive could so easily have been destroyed by vermin), the innumerable cardboard boxes had built up a layer of fine dust over the years. This had to be brushed off with the back of the hand before the lids could be lifted and the documents inside, discs in paper sleeves, removed. Standing in one corner of the ill-lit room was a gramophone on which these discs, many of whose white labels bore no inscription, could be played. Technological developments notwithstanding, this obsolete equipment had not been discarded because of the continuing need to play historic recordings for purposes of comparison. Winding up the gramophone was a strenuous business. While doing so, a committee member knocked some 1930s sapphire needles off the table. Karnau's statement went on:

"The invention of the sound film had been eagerly awaited. Sound cameras were installed here while moviegoers were still debating whether silent films would survive, though the lenses were always kept covered because only the sound track was used. That accounts for the presence here of many kilometers of unexposed film. The sound-on-film system also enabled cutting to be carried out for the first time, an impracticable procedure in the case of sounds engraved on wax.

"Germany was far ahead of other countries in the field of sound recording. The portable tape recorders we developed for use at the front continued to be one of the enemy's favorite acquisitions until the war ended, and here at the archive only the very finest equipment and materials were employed. On one occasion our entire collection of wax discs almost melted because the heating system malfunctioned. Discs do have one advantage over tapes, however, in that contact with a magnet cannot obliterate their contents. That was another reason why security was so important. Imagine if saboteurs had installed an electromagnet here and wiped out the entire archive!

"One of our tasks was to optimize vocal conditions by technological means, for instance the public address systems used at mass rallies. Sophisticated forms of speech therapy enabled glottal stops to be suppressed, thereby avoiding overmodulation in large halls. Salivation was controlled during loud, rapid speech and glandular activity brought into balance with the aid of medication, the object being to render every last spoken word intelligible. One or two experiments were conducted into breathing under stress and its potentially disruptive effects. Amplification by loudspeakers renders such questions extremely important."

Arrayed in one corner were some tapes of which it was hard to tell whether the sound engineer had been carried away by sheer love of playing around with advanced recording equipment or whether he had made them for authentic medical purposes: for example—if the accompanying list could be trusted—noises caused by secretions of the pancreas or, greatly amplified, by eyelids opening and closing.

Another series of experiments which defied complete elucidation, but which, to judge by the medical technology employed, could not have been carried out so very long ago, included the introduction of probes into the pharynx and the bloodstream for the purpose of recording various unidentifiable bodily noises. As for the human guinea pigs from whom these data were obtained, sometimes in an extremely painful manner, the committee of inquiry could not discover where they were recruited.

Rumor had it that cleft palate patients were among those enlisted for comparative recordings. It was even said that the researchers had analyzed the potential intensity of human cries—that they had not shrunk from surgically modifying their subjects' articulatory apparatus in order to study their capacity for speech under extreme conditions—but none of this could be proved by the evidence as it stood.

"The Museum of Hygiene concerned itself with man in his visible form," Karnau explained, "whereas we dealt with his audible manifestations. We were united by our attention to detail, and pathologists of one discipline were often of service to those of the other, for instance when ascribing our clients' articulatory changes to changes of a physiological nature."

Karnau proved to be extremely talkative; more than that, he possessed a knowledge of technical matters that was wholly at odds with his status as a security guard. Apart from presenting a detailed account of the archive's division of labor, he sometimes strayed into reminiscences:

"When the morning's work was over and our clients had —in a manner of speaking—lent us their voices, staff members would often meet in the conference room during the interval between two shifts. The entire team—Professor Sievers, Dr. Hellbrandt, Professor Stumpfecker, and others— would sit there swapping ideas, and representatives of the various disciplines would exchange suggestions. Either that, or they simply sat back and relaxed in silence while the archivists went on with their work outside.

"Because they sensed that they were all on the same track and shared the same objectives, they developed close ties. They often cracked little jokes—as, for instance, when Dr. Hellbrandt said something about plastic surgery being invasive of the human body, and Professor Stumpfecker, quick as a flash, retorted, 'So is sex.' They also tried out various breathing techniques on each other, purely for amusement's sake, or indulged in theoretical discussions, for instance about whether it would ever become possible to accelerate the learning of foreign languages by effecting surgical changes in the individual student."

On examining Karnau's statements more closely, the committee members began to entertain certain doubts about them. His detailed knowledge of the archive's procedures and research projects aroused a suspicion that he had not merely been in charge of security, as he steadfastly maintained, but must have held a far more responsible position—indeed, it was not difficult to picture him hobnobbing with Hellbrandt, Sievers and the rest in one of the conference room's luxurious leather armchairs.

It also transpired that the underground complex was more extensive than Karnau, outwardly so eager to be helpful, had at first disclosed: a second recording studio came to light. Far less comfortably appointed than the first, this took the form of a tiled, neon-lit chamber whose bleak décor bespoke an operating room. A full set of surgical instruments reposed on a stainless steel trolley, and the microphone assembly overhung an operating table from which blood-encrusted straps were dangling.

Forensic analysis of the blood on the straps revealed that the most recent operation had taken place only a few weeks before. This seemed to disprove Karnau's assertion that work at the archive had ceased before the end of World War Two. On the contrary, the obvious inference was that plans had been made to continue the medical research of which the committee had gained certain intimations. Having learned by some unknown means that the orphanage was about to be inspected, the person or persons engaged in these obscure experiments had hurriedly moved out with the intention of pursuing them elsewhere. Unfortunately, no information on this subject could be gleaned from Karnau. He left the city next morning, destination unknown.

I LIE SILENT, feel no pain, just the gentle pressure of fingertips palpating my skull, hear the skin parting as the scalpel slices effortlessly through my scalp, but I feel nothing, am conscious only of the light whose beam is burning its way into my skin. Why is that spotlight focused on my head? I try to pull my head away but cannot move, the scalpel continues to cut, makes a careful incision across my forehead, but I still experience no pain. I try to speak, but I can't feel my tongue or gums, my lips are numb from the anesthetic, my mouth seems full of some unyielding, saliva-sodden mass. It's a gag: I've been gagged.

My chin is on fire, my cheeks and eyelids are twitching, my eyebrows have been singed, my eyelashes too, the rest of my face is muffled up. I try to signal, I move my arms, legs, stomach, but the straps merely tighten and fail to release me, the operating table creaks but no one notices, I strive to make a noise in my throat but hear nothing—yes, I do, a voice from behind me: "Immobilize him, please, he's struggling. Find some additional straps, a bit heavier on the anesthetic too, I can't work under these conditions." I know that crisp, clear voice, I remember it now: Stumpfecker's. "Tie off this vein for me and keep swabbing. Who was responsible for shaving him? Whoever it was, he once again did rotten job of it." My eyelids are spattered with something warm and wet: my own blood or Stumpfecker's saliva?

I hear a second voice: "Nasty mess, that. Great view, though." It must be Hellbrandt, watching the progress of the incision.

A curt response from Stumpfecker: "Peel back the perios-teum and clamp it. There it is, you see? That's the white of the cranium showing through. Get ready, Sievers. Hold the skin aside and brush on some more of that styptic solution."

Now it's Professor Sievers's turn: "Taking our cue from Dr. Gall's informative craniological measurements, gentlemen, we shall run this gramophone needle along the cranial suture. First, though, we must swab the furrow again, or the needle may become obstructed by blood."

A moment's solemn silence, a fist bears down on my gag. Sievers explains: "We should soon be able to hear the im-pulses via the electrodes, amplifier and loudspeaker." Then, in the midst of renewed silence, I hear a faint crackle. It grows steadily louder, and a current of cool air fans my face as a hand moves across my bare skull, to and fro, faster and faster, up and down the furrow. The crackle increases in volume, becoming a high-pitched hum.

"Keep going," says Hellbrandt. "Is the tape recorder on? Paraspeech, perhaps," he adds, to no one in particular.

Sievers, very excitedly: "It works, gentlemen. Our experi-ment seems to be a success."

Stumpfecker: "Keep it up, Sievers, I'm sure we'd all like to listen awhile longer. Afterwards we must evaluate the record-ing and work out some comparative figures. Then we'll be able to submit our findings to Katzenstein's archive for expe-rimental and clinical phonetics."

Cranial hum: a sound of human origin never previously heard by the human ear—the authentic headnote—yet it sounds entirely inhuman. It fades to a dull rattle and almost dies away, relapsing into the initial, metallic crackle that causes my skull to vibrate as if splinters were starting to detach them-selves from it, a frightful noise that gives me gooseflesh. Can this be the specific sound of my own cranial suture, the most primordial of all sounds?

No, it's made by the claws of a pigeon scrabbling around on the window sill, whetting them on the metal fittings outside my window because it can't decide which direction to take when gliding down into the street. But it's the middle of the night, so why isn't the creature roosting quietly? I force my eyes open: darkness. No Stumpfecker, no Hellbrandt or Sievers. I can even move my head.

Sweat has glued the hair to my scalp and soaked my pillow. It's years since I had such an exhausting nightmare. Stumpfecker has been dead for decades, I saw his body with my own eyes while escaping from Berlin. Shortly after we split up—the same night, in fact—I came upon his huge, inert carcass lying sprawled in the middle of the road bridge at Lehrter Station. As for Hellbrandt, he went abroad soon afterwards. A British contact helped him to escape in return for a consideration, as he put it. Being a collector of memorabilia, he pronounced himself satisfied with a small self-caricature scrawled on cardboard by Stumpfecker's last patient.

I'm dog-tired but I can't go back to sleep. I wander into the kitchen. It's still the dead of night, not a lighted window to be seen, only the tip of my cigarette glowing red in the darkness. Light divides day from night and governs the world's time. Periods of time are irrevocably defined by the position of the sun and the progress of the stars, whereas human time, our very own form of demarcation, is prescribed by the voice: the alternation of speech and silence, the sequence of the words, or even inarticulate sounds, that almost subliminally determine the rhythm of our footsteps while walking or the range of all our actions—even though, being scarcely noticed, they only appear to accompany our movements. The larynx imperceptibly twitches when we engage in a silent soliloquy, and internal monologues insist on venting themselves in speech once we're no longer observed. Thus the voice separates spells of solitude from the rest of time.

Why did people lose the taste for recording their own voices for so long? The dividing line came with the end of the war, which also put a temporary damper on acoustics. Yet the invention of the phonograph was soon followed by the appearance of so-called self-recorders who captured their homemade music on wax cylinders: Uncle Fritz would sing a ballad while the whole neighborhood clustered around the harmonium. Nobody needed to do any more singing after that, because a wax cylinder recital was given every Sunday. This craze, which persisted even after Emil Berliner's invention of the disc that revolved at 150 r.p.m., continued into the 1930s, the heyday when all were eager for a turn in front of the microphone and then a chance to listen to their poorly reproduced voices.

It persisted even during the war, when well-devised bulletins from the front were recorded on disc at home. The whole family would sit quietly in the living room while the cutting stylus quivered and the paterfamilias anxiously manipulated the controls with one eye on an open copy of *The Amateur Recordist's Handbook,* careful to carry out every last instruction in the manual so as not to botch the job—so as to capture the brisk effusions of the Eastern Front commentator and engrave his every tone of voice on wax: pugnacious when describing a tank attack, scathing when obliged to mention a Soviet village, dismissive on the subject of the Russian winter.

But suddenly it was over. Privately owned tape recorders were few and far between, and it was not until the audiocassette appeared at the end of the sixties that people once more began, as a matter of course, to make recordings for their personal use. Dependent at first on the poor-quality integral microphone built into every cassette recorder, they taped and played each other foolish anecdotes, long-winded accounts of their experiences on vacation, or simply dirty jokes.

Before that came the deaf, voiceless interlude. People went on taking photographs, of course, but they could no longer hear their own voices, the voices that had shouted themselves hoarse for twelve long years. Photographs can be staged and prettified to display smiles and embraces, banish medals and exchange uniforms for shabby postwar civvies. It's easy enough to shave off a moustache and alter one's appearance overnight, substituting weary amiability for martial hatred. But the human voice cannot be doctored in this way. The *Sieg Heils* and *Yes My Führer*s continue to reverberate down the years.

Many pictures are still on display. Elderly men jostle in front of the newsdealer's shelves, eager to refresh their memories of life at the front. They leaf through *Military Technology* and *Stalingrad Report,* elbow each other aside to get at the last remaining order form for the Obersalzberg video. And when tone of voice doesn't matter—when it's possible to read in silence—they also thirst for words from the lips of some old gargoyle of an SS man and stand there swiftly scanning every line rather than be seen in the street carrying a newspaper so littered with grammatical howlers that it doesn't contain a single correct German sentence.

No, nobody likes to hear the old voices anymore. It seems that one can't say, "Yes, that's how my voice sounded in the old days, but it soon changed." How everyone envied the deaf-mutes! They would all have liked to have been deaf-mutes who miraculously regained their voices in the summer of 1945. If the loudspeaker vans that toured Berlin had broadcast, not the announcement of Germany's surrender, but the last recordings of Stumpfecker's patient, his furious outbursts and strangled cries, people would never have emerged from the cellars to welcome our victorious enemies. They would have torn out each other's throats with their teeth.

Voices from the past are ever-present, strenuously though we Germans tried to introduce a rapid vocal change with the victors' active assistance. It surprised us to discover that the occupying powers had worked hard, even during the war, to compile a basic vocabulary and devise pronunciation exercises and readily intelligible grammars that would enable the vanquished to discard their old tone of voice and enjoy a brief respite from their own language. Listening to foreign languages and lip reading came as a relief to students chanting their lessons aloud in halls, gymnasiums and stadiums where parades and last-ditch rallies had been held not long before. In hopes of being able to eradicate their old tones of voice, they readily submitted to regular vocabulary assessments and checks on pronunciation. They even welcomed oral tests—in fact they positively hankered after anything that would help to rid their throats of aberrations from the norm, deviations from the group sound.

Or did they, after all, find it a trifle hard to bid their old voices farewell? Were they secretly of two minds? Did they wish, on the one hand, that the talkies had not been invented—that Party documentaries conveyed nothing but their mouth movements, their rigid stance, their regimented gestures and gesticulations? Even the sight of their contorted faces would have been easier to endure than the sound of their voices in the old days. On the other hand, each of those vocal outbursts had imprinted itself on their throats and engraved itself on their vocal cords in the form of fateful scars which no plastic surgeon, however skilled, could efface. Instead of completely replacing their old tones of voice, therefore, they resolved to overlay them with a different timbre. This has left the old voice available for use, and use it they sometimes do, even after half a century. It can unexpectedly burst forth from deep within them—as, for instance, when some old-timer catches children trespassing on his private property. Startled by his brusque, unfamiliar tone, they take to their heels as if in mortal danger.

This masterful, peremptory tone is still regarded as the embodiment of adulthood. Without being able to place it exactly, we all look back on some point in time and assume that this was the juncture at which we acquired a grown-up voice— that nothing comparable preceded it, just cute, naïve responses to grown-ups' questions and clumsy attempts to find our way around in the grown-up world, the only one that counts. This presupposes, of course, that adults cannot detect the inner voice that underlies the outward, childish voice and is sometimes in stark contrast to its hesitant, childish tone—a discrepancy that never even occurs to them because they dismiss the possibility that children have an inner voice of any kind. They will never understand that a child's audible voice has an entirely dissimilar, inaudible counterpart; that a child lives in two worlds, has two voices, and speaks two languages that may differ as completely as those of the living and the dead. It is said that, although the latter employ the same words as the former, these mean the diametrical opposite of what they did during their lifetime.

It's still dark outside. I decide to look up my old collection of voices, the recordings too precious to me to be left behind in the archive at Dresden. When we discontinued our research, and again at the end of the war, I packed the most important discs and tapes in boxes. Since then I've taken them with me wherever I go, from one apartment to another, without ever listening to them. I even possess one of the old gramophones, the same model they used for that tea dance in the bunker on the last day of the war. There's a rough patch on the lid where the death's-head emblem used to be. I erased it years ago with a kitchen knife.

I remove the deteriorated ribbon from around a packet of wax matrices and extract one from its spotty, damp-stained paper sleeve. There's no label, but it must bear some form of identification in the center: sure enough, I make out some words scratched on the matte black surface in my own handwriting. The wax resembles the high-grade material to which we in the bunker alone had access at the end of the war. Are these the recordings Stumpfecker instructed me to spirit out of Berlin?

My ears tingle unpleasantly in expectation of the first sound. To my disappointment, I realize at once that the recording isn't one of mine. A wholly unprofessional job. All I can hear, very faintly, is a youthful voice saying "clip-clap, clip-clap, clip-clap" and "hick-hack, hick-hack, hick-hack." A second wax disc, another child's voice. No, these recordings have nothing to do with me, so why do they bear my handwriting?

I've never recorded any children's voices. I don't have any children of my own and have never been around when a child is learning to speak. Those six children were the only ones I've ever been in close contact with, but I never recorded them, much as I always wanted to. I never got the chance, and besides, their father was dead against it: the thought of my possessing such recordings made him uneasy. Even at our very last meeting, shortly before his death, he was so adamantly opposed to it that I abandoned all hope. We had a heated altercation in the passage outside my bunker cubicle. By then it was far too late: I was so busy assisting Stumpfecker in his desperate endeavors to preserve his last patient's voice for posterity that I didn't have the energy for anything else.

I try a third wax disc. Can that really be Helga? Yes, despite the hiss and although the voice sounds very far away, it's unmistakably hers. Suddenly, my mind's eye summons up the images that fit the sounds: the children's arrival in the bunker on 22 April, the day on which they and their parents took refuge there. The very first evening, having renewed my acquaintance with them, I contrived while saying good night to secrete a recording machine beneath Helga's bed and surreptitiously switched it on. From then on I made more such brief recordings every night, eavesdropping on the children before they went to sleep.

8

Mama is doing Papa's hands. It's Friday today, and she always gives him a manicure on Fridays now that his secretaries don't have the time. They're working day and night. All you can hear is the snip of the little scissors and the faint, scratchy sound of the nail file. It always gives me goose pimples, that sound, like chalk squeaking on a blackboard or a spoon scraping a saucepan. Mama finishes filing Papa's nails and starts massaging his fingers. Is he nervous? Are his hands trembling, or is his blood pumping harder than usual because Mama's fingers are squeezing his as they rub the cream in? Papa's skin is blotchy these days, it looks unhealthy. It's flaking off his face, even though he still uses the sun lamp. He's run out of cologne, so he doesn't smell as nice either. Mama massages cream into Papa's fingers till the knuckles crack.

Papa will be leaving in a minute; that's why he wants his hands to look good. It's the Führer's birthday, and Papa is taking him our presents. We've all made presents for the Führer, but we can't give them to him ourselves, not this year, it's too dangerous. That's because of the shelling. There are more shells falling on Berlin than ever before. The bangs are the only thing that interrupts Papa's manicure, because they make him jump. He jerks his hands away each time, so the nail file slips and Mama gets cream on her sleeve. Papa's hands are done at last. We've wrapped our presents. Soon it'll be Hedda's birthday too, she'll be seven on 5 May. We must be sure to make her something in good time, it's only two weeks till then. Another bang, a loud one, but Papa pretends it's nothing, he doesn't even jump this time. We all stay quite still for a second, but the shell wasn't all that close to our house. Papa looks out of the window. "No," he says, "you can't even see the smoke."

Mama packs up her manicure things, Papa straightens his tie. His hands are all red and shiny now. If shells are already landing nearby, why did Papa have us brought here from Schwanenwerder two nights ago? It was much safer there. No shells or bombs, just a red glow in the sky every night, far away. The little ones thought there was a storm coming, except that you couldn't hear any thunder. They'd look across the lake and wait for the storm to break over our heads. They wanted it to rain at last, but all you could see were the beams of the searchlights and the glow in the sky.

Now we're in the city ourselves, right in the middle of the war. Mama didn't want to let on, not to any of us, but even the little ones must have taken in what she told us about the refugees: how they had to leave Berlin because it was too dangerous there. Mama once told us that the Russians would never get to Schwanenwerder, so why have we left there and gone closer to them? When Papa's ministry was bombed by Mosquitoes, why didn't anyone there say it would be too dangerous for us to move into the neighborhood? Anyone would think the Mosquitoes had gone and the war was over, but it isn't: you can tell that from all the shells landing nearby. Papa's ready to leave, he smiles and gives me a kiss, then he goes out. If it's dangerous for us to play in the garden, it must be dangerous for Papa to go to see the Führer, but he did his best to smile as if nothing could possibly happen to him.

What are Mama and Papa planning to do with us? Why did Papa insist on getting us up in the middle of the night, when we'd already gone to sleep, and make us join him here at our town house? A little while ago Mama and her secretary made a list of everything at Schwanenwerder, all the crockery, cutlery, bed linen, tablecloths, and so on. We thought we'd take them with us if we ever left Schwanenwerder, but we didn't. We also thought we'd go to some other place, not Berlin, not where there's fighting. Mama said so herself. "If things get dangerous," she told us once, "we'll leave the war behind us."

Surely she must realize that the little ones are scared, and that we older ones know she's lying. "Aren't you pleased, not having to do any more lessons?" she asks, and we all say yes, though the only one who's really happy is Helmut, who grins all over his face because he doesn't have to practice for three hours a day. Hilde and I aren't babies anymore. Mama doesn't take us in with all this stuff about no more lessons, but we can't tell her so because the little ones would be even more scared. They mustn't find out what we're in for, all of us. They mustn't find out we'll soon be dead. Dead—I can't say the word out loud because it makes my throat so tight and my mouth so dry that my tongue won't move. I can't even breathe, just thinking about it.

"Why are you looking so worried, Helga?"

"It's nothing, Mama. Will Papa be back soon?"

"Of course he will. You're afraid something may happen to him, is that it?"

Mama's face is twitching. She still gets those pains of hers; it's ages since they were as bad as they've been these last few days. When she came back from Dresden—that was the last time. The city was completely destroyed by then. Mama stayed at the Weisser Hirsch again, but not for a rest cure, just to say goodbye. She came home in a cigarette truck. Her coat looked a mess and so did her hair, but she didn't notice, she was too sad and upset. Was it something she'd heard in Dresden that made her so sad? She didn't say, she didn't even look at us properly.

The bangs are getting louder and louder, they hurt my ears. The Russians will be shooting at our house before long. Mama says something to me, but I can't understand, there's too much noise. "Helga," she shouts, "fetch the others. We'd better go down to the shelter."

There are footprints all over the carpet in the hallway. Dirt everywhere. Nobody cleans the place anymore, they're all too busy. You can hear typewriters clattering away behind every door, or meetings going on, or letters being dictated. There are people sitting working in every room now that Papa's ministry has been destroyed. The whole house is full of them, not that you'd know it on the stairs or in the hallways because nobody makes a noise there, they all talk in whispers. The rooms are getting more and more crowded. A lot of them can't be lived in because their windows have been blown out. Sheets of cardboard have been stuck in the window frames so it doesn't get too cold inside, but the wind comes whistling through the cracks and makes the candles flicker.

The younger ones are scared of all the noise, they're huddled together in the passage on the ground floor. Helmut sees me coming. "Are they firing at us, Helga?" he calls. "Have they hit the upstairs yet?"

"No, everything's fine, but we're going down to the shelter with Mama. We'll be really safe down there."

But they're too scared to move. They don't get up till Mama appears. We always went down in the elevator before, but now we use the stairs. We'd be stuck halfway down if the electricity failed, and no one would get us out, they're all too busy. Mama and us are the only ones in the shelter: the others have to stay upstairs and go on working.

Everything down here looks the way it always did. You can't hear the noises overhead. We know the pictures on the walls by heart. There isn't one we haven't looked at a hundred times while waiting for an air raid to end in the middle of the night, unable to get back to sleep even though we each have a bed of our own down here. Yes, we know every line and speck of color in these pictures. We also know the patterns on the carpets and the embroidery on the chair covers. There's no need to be so scared down here, but it's boring all the same. We don't feel like playing, we simply want the guns to stop. Mama can't think of anything for us to do. We'll just have to wait.

THE GUNS WENT on and on, but we didn't care to spend all night in the shelter. Mama didn't either. After a while we went back upstairs and slept in our own beds. We're all sleeping in one room because the others are full. It's our old nursery, but it doesn't look half as nice as it used to. All our clothes and toys are packed up in boxes. The water that's leaking from the broken pipes has left brown patches on the flowery wallpaper. That wouldn't have happened in the old days. In the old days the pipes would have been mended right away. At least we've still got our own beds. The other people in the house have to sleep on uncomfortable camp beds without any mattresses. At least we've got our own beds and bedclothes, our nice warm down blankets. It's cold in the nursery because it doesn't have any windowpanes either, just squares of cardboard. At night the cardboard looks black and the wind makes the curtains bulge. The little ones get scared when that happens, they think someone's trying to get in, but nobody did, not last night. The guns went on firing, that's all.

We see Papa at breakfast, but not for long. He shouldn't go away so often. He goes out nearly every day, makes regular trips to the front line to take the soldiers food and schnapps, but it's dangerous there.

"Papa, you won't go away so often, will you?"

"No, sweetheart."

"Let's stay together from now on."

"Mm?"

"I said let's stay together—all of us, the whole family."

"Yes, you're right."

But he isn't really listening to me, he's bolting his bread and butter and thinking about his work. It's so dismal here. Being at Schwanenwerder was much nicer. Papa used to come home in the evenings and spend some time with us, even when he was very busy or feeling ill. It was springtime at Schwanenwerder; here you wouldn't know it for the dust and filth. At Schwanenwerder we could play in the garden, almost like before the war; here we're only in the way.

"Can we watch a movie?"

"Afraid not, the theater's being used as a conference room."

"When, then?"

"Maybe tonight, if the Russians don't launch another attack."

"How much longer will they go on attacking?"

"Not much longer. It'll all be over soon."

Hedda pretends to be satisfied with Papa's answer, but he and Mama have told us the same thing lots of times, and the war isn't over yet.

IT'S ON FIRE, the whole garden's on fire. The smoke is drifting into our room. We've taken out the sheets of cardboard. The flames are on a level with our first-floor windows. Papa's staff are standing outside, pouring gasoline on the bonfires and lighting them one after another. It's paper they're burning. They go on throwing files into the flames. How easily the paper catches fire, how the flames crackle and roar! Papa isn't down there, he's in his room, recording a speech on tape. It's supposed to be broadcast this afternoon. Are there any radios left in Berlin, I wonder. Another shell bursts. Everyone forgets about the bonfires and makes a dash for the house. Now they're crouching against the wall just below us. Where's Mama? More bangs, lots of them, the guns must be getting quite close. We crawl into a corner between the beds. I wonder if Papa's somewhere safe—if he's stopped recording his speech, with all this noise. Mama comes rushing in: "Out you come, children, time to go down to the shelter."

The guns keep firing all day long. We're not allowed back into our room. We sit around, either in the shelter or the passage downstairs. Papa's staff are also down there now. It's impossible to talk, the noise is too bad, just a word or two now and then. Nobody feels like lunch. Things can't go on this way, we won't be able to stand it much longer. Papa goes out, even though he promised we'd stay together for once. The first thing he does when he comes back is have a quick word with Mama, who takes us up to our room. "Get the children ready," she tells the nursemaid. I wonder what she means. Then she says, "We're going to join the Führer."

"Will we get some cakes at the Führer's?" asks Hedda.

"The Führer is bound to have some," Holde says.

"You're talking rubbish," I tell them. "Why would he have any cakes?"

"Because he's the Führer."

"Nobody has any cakes these days. How would they get here?"

"By plane, maybe."

"Nonsense."

"Why nonsense? Planes keep landing here all the time."

"Yes, but they don't fly all the way to Berlin to deliver cakes for us."

"Not even for the Führer?" Hedda turns to Mama. "*Will* we get some cakes, Mama?"

"Anyone would think you were starving," Mama says.

The nursemaid starts packing our things. She lets me help her to get it done more quickly. Should we only take summer things or warm things as well? "Night things too?" the nursemaid asks Mama.

"No, they won't be needing them anymore."

What does she mean by that? She looks at us. "You can take some toys with you, but only one each, do you hear?"

Heide searches desperately for her rag doll, but it's nowhere to be found, neither in her bed nor in the toy box. Did she leave it behind in the shelter? Is it downstairs in the passage? No.

The nursemaid shrugs her shoulders. "Can't be helped," she says.

But Heide absolutely insists on taking her old rag doll.

Mama gets a little impatient. "Put in another doll for her," she tells the nursemaid.

Heide is almost in tears by now. Mama picks her up and

gives her a little cuddle. "What do you expect us to do?" she says. "We've got to leave here right away, and your doll has simply vanished."

Heide pretends to be happy with the other doll, but she isn't really, you can tell from the look on her face when the nursemaid puts it in the suitcase. Then we go downstairs. Papa comes downstairs too, looking very pale and walking very slowly. What will become of us now, I wonder.

There are two cars parked outside. Mama says, "Helga, you come with us in the first car. The others can go with Herr Schwägermann."

We get into the limousine the Führer gave Papa for Christmas one time. It's armored and the windows are bulletproof, so nothing can happen to us, but what about the others? Their car doesn't have bulletproof windows. Mama sits beside me, crying softly. Papa doesn't say anything, neither does the chauffeur. We haven't been outside once since we got to Berlin three nights ago. At last we can see what a mess it's in. Just ruins, walls with great big holes in them, shattered buildings on the point of collapse, mounds of rubble everywhere, shell craters in the middle of the road. "What's that over there—a dead body?" Mama doesn't answer. Is it really a dead body, that lifeless bundle of clothes? How can you tell when you've never seen one before? We've passed it already.

We turn into Voss Strasse. We always walked here in the old days, it isn't far. The cars pull up. Lucky we didn't get shot at on the way. Papa goes on ahead, the chauffeurs take our bags. The little ones come tumbling out of the car behind. They look as if they've been crying. Little Heide comes running up to me.

"What were all those holes in the road and those heaps of stones? Are they building something?"

"Could be."

"But where are all the workmen?"

"They've finished for the day. It's after five o'clock, and anyway, it's Sunday."

Heide takes my hand and won't let go of it. We follow Papa. There's rubble everywhere. We find the entrance and set off down the stairs to the cellar. The bunker, I mean.

Four little rooms, and not a window anywhere. At home we've got almost forty rooms. It was nicer in our nursery, even with cardboard over the windows. It's always dark down here unless you switch the light on. You can't see a single ray of sunlight coming through the cracks, and you can't hear any birds singing. The air never moves in spite of the air conditioning. The rooms are for Mama and us. Papa walks on down the passage, he says he's got to go downstairs. We're a long way down already, but there's an even lower level. Papa's office must be down there. I wonder how long we'll have to put up with this place. The others all start talking at once:

"Will our nursemaid be coming too?"

"What about our governess?"

"Where are they, anyway?"

"Why didn't we bring any night things?"

"Why don't we need them?"

We do need them, of course, we can see that now, but Mama doesn't answer. She puts us to bed. We're to sleep in our undershirts tonight, without cleaning our teeth. Everything's going from bad to worse. We don't even have our own beds, just air-raid shelter beds—uncomfortable double-decker bunks like little children have, the room's too small for any other kind. At Lanke we had the woods to play in, and the lake and lots of animals, though it wasn't very nice when we came across women's things there, like a lipstick in a color we'd never seen Mama wearing. That's when we realized that Papa didn't go to Lanke by himself, even though he said he did. There were other women at Schwanenwerder too, but they used to visit Papa at the guest house. Schwanenwerder was the nicest place of all, actually, because we could invite friends home from school. We went for boat rides there and learned to swim. Our rooms at the town house were lovely, too, and we often saw Papa during the day when we were staying there. We had so many toys at the town house, they wouldn't all fit into the nursery. Here we've got nothing. There weren't any cakes after all. It's been another miserable day.

Mama has just gone out. Our door is ajar and we can hear her in the passage, talking to someone. It's a man. Not Papa, but his voice sounds familiar. The first thing we see is a little black dog: Coco! He nudges the door open with his nose, and suddenly Herr Karnau comes in. We recognize him right away, even though he's covered with dust and dirt. His hair is matted and his clothes are torn. He comes straight over to our bunks and laughs because we're so pleased to see him. Why did he come? Because of us? What's he doing in the bunker? Is he here to work?

Herr Karnau says he'll have a wash first, then tell us how he got here. Coco jumps up on my bunk. Helmut and Holde, who are sharing the bunk overhead, reach down and pat him. Coco wags his tail so hard he rumples the bedclothes. He licks my face, wanting to be petted. Herr Karnau is scrubbing his neck at the washbasin.

"How did you manage to get to Berlin, Herr Karnau?"

"By plane, believe it or not."

"You mean there's still an airfield?"

"Not an airfield, no. We had to land on the Kurfürstendamm. Talk about bumpy! My tummy was full of butterflies."

"I always feel sick when I fly," I say.

"Maybe it was your plane we saw in the sky," Hedda says. "Earlier on, in the middle of the day. Was that you?"

"If it was a little plane, yes, it could have been. Why, did you see me waving?"

"Of course not, it was too far away." Hedda can't help laughing. Herr Karnau starts combing his hair.

"Why are you so dirty?" Holde asks.

"It's the dust. The air is thick with it, and you have to scramble over mountains of debris to get anywhere. No wonder I'm so dirty."

Coco goes on snuffling and licking. He recognizes us all, even though it's so long since we saw him and Herr Karnau. Hilde asks what Herr Karnau has been doing all this time.

"No, you first. How are you all, anyway?"

"Not too bad."

"Have you only just got here, like me?"

"Yes, a couple of hours ago."

"And before that you were at Schwanenwerder?"

"Yes, but we've spent the last three days here in Berlin, in Hermann Göring Strasse. It was nice at Schwanenwerder."

"But not as nice as it used to be," says Holde.

"Why not?"

Holde doesn't know how to put it. Helmut says, "There were so many people staying with us."

"And sometimes the lights went out all over the house," says Heide. "We got scared once, when Mama and Papa were out. It went all dark suddenly, but none of us had touched the light switch."

"A power cut?"

"Yes, something like that. And Papa didn't come home till late."

Herr Karnau has finished washing. Now he looks the way he used to. He gives his trousers one last flick with the clothes brush and perches on the edge of my bunk. He went to the zoo today, he tells us.

"The zoo? Wasn't it shut?"

"Of course."

"How are the animals?"

"In a pretty bad way. They could do with some peace and quiet at last, like us."

"Is there a lot of damage?"

"The staff are trying to salvage as much as possible. The keepers are still looking after their animals. Just imagine, they're combing the city for things to feed them."

"Are many of the animals sick?"

"Yes, or injured, and there's a shortage of water."

"When the war's over, let's help the poor animals."

Heide says: "The fishes first of all."

"And the lions."

The others suggest various ways of rescuing the animals. They all want to look after their favorite ones when the war's over. They must think Herr Karnau is a vet, because they ask if he'll make the animals better. It doesn't occur to them that many of them must already be dead, and Herr Karnau doesn't mention it.

Mama comes back. She says it's time we went to sleep, but Herr Karnau hasn't finished telling us his news. Heide begs him to come back in the morning.

Or is he only paying us a quick visit? Must he leave right away? A shame, when we don't have any other friends here.

He's still sitting on the edge of my bunk, he doesn't get up and go, not yet. If he does go, we may never see him again. "No," he says, "don't worry, I'm sure my work will keep me here for several days."

"So we'll see you again tomorrow?"

He laughs. "If you don't have any other plans. At lunch, maybe?"

"Yes, and in the afternoon we can do something together. We can—"

Hilde breaks in. "Herr Karnau will be busy, Hedda."

"Do you leave the bunker after work?"

Herr Karnau doesn't answer at once. He looks at us in a sad kind of way, then he smiles. "As long as you're here," he says quietly, "wild horses won't drag me away."

"Promise?"

"I promise."

He shakes my hand. His own hands are still rather dirty, even though he's scrubbed them, and the creases in his fingers are all black. He strokes Heide's cheek, tells us he's got things to do, says good night, and goes out. Our clean bedclothes are covered with Coco's little paw marks. Heide is so delighted that Herr Karnau is staying here too, she forgets all about her rag doll.

IN THE MORNING Heide wakes up cuddling her pillow tight. The first thing she says is, "This isn't my best doll."

Then she bursts into tears and wakes the others. She goes on sobbing and whining and wailing for her doll, in fact she even keeps it up at breakfast. Mama tries to console her, but it's no use. Mama isn't in a good mood either, because of Coco's paw marks. We don't have any spare bedclothes here, that's the trouble. Mama is thinking hard during breakfast, I can tell. Eventually she says, "There's no choice, we'll have to fetch some more things from the house. You children need toothbrushes and night clothes, after all."

"Will you bring my doll?" asks Heide, quick as anything.

"Of course, if I can find it."

"But won't it be too dangerous to leave the bunker now?"

"Perhaps one of the guards can come with me, then it'll be all right."

Mama tells Papa she plans to go back to the house. Papa doesn't like the idea at all and tries to talk her out of it. He uses all his powers of persuasion, but Mama's mind is made up. Finally he gives in. "At least take Schwägermann with you, he knows what's going on out there. He can help you carry things."

Mama says goodbye as if it's the last time we'll ever see her, then she leaves. I hope nothing happens to her—I hope the Russians don't capture her. It isn't until Herr Karnau pays us another visit that we all begin to feel a bit better. He does his best to cheer us up. "The diet cook will be making your lunch today, just for once. It'll be really tasty, you mark my words."

But it isn't as tasty as if Mama had cooked it. Heide isn't hungry. Is she worried about Mama or her doll?

"Remember the first time we met," says Herr Karnau, "and I let you give Coco some cheese rind?"

The others don't remember, but I do. It was at Herr Karnau's apartment. We didn't particularly like him at that stage.

"Was that where those funny animals were?" Hedda asks.

"The flying foxes, you mean?" says Hilde.

Herr Karnau laughs. "No, long before that. You were very little, Hedda. You can't have been more than two."

"That friend of yours," Hilde says, "the one who kept flying foxes, could he talk to all kinds of animals?"

"Could you teach us to talk to animals too?" Holde asks.

"But there aren't any animals here."

"Only Coco."

Herr Karnau gives in. "All right, I'll go and fetch him. He's shut up in my room. Wait for me, I won't be a minute."

As soon as he goes out we start worrying about Mama. Is she back at the house already? Is the house still standing? Hilde's as anxious as I am, but we mustn't let on to the younger ones. Fortunately, Herr Karnau soon comes back with Coco. He doesn't let him off the leash till they're inside the room. I suppose there must be people in the bunker who are scared of dogs, even little ones. Herr Karnau starts his voice lesson. We hustle Coco into Mama's room and leave the door ajar, then Herr Karnau calls his name. Coco comes trotting in at once, wagging his tail. Heide holds out her arms and gives him a cuddle. "Now," says Herr Karnau, "watch this."

Coco is made to go back into the other room, but Herr Karnau doesn't call his name this time. Instead, he calls my name: "Here, Helga!" Coco comes trotting in again, but why?

"Coco doesn't recognize words as such," says Herr Karnau. "He can tell when I'm calling him from my tone of voice."

And again. This time Herr Karnau disguises his voice, but Coco still comes out of Mama's room and trots over to us as though every call sounded the same. Herr Karnau notices how surprised we're looking.

"You see? Coco doesn't answer to his name or his master's normal tone of voice, but not because he's stupid, far from it. His ears are so sharp, he'll recognize my voice under any circumstances—better than any human being could. If you want Coco to come to you, all you have to do is to call him in a friendly tone of voice."

We take it in turns to call Coco, and Herr Karnau shows us what tone of voice to use to make sure he obeys. We only have to call him nicely and he comes and licks our faces. We're practicing growling, howling and barking when Mama reappears. What a relief. The little ones rush over to her and start rummaging in the bag of toys and cuddly animals she's brought with her. Heide hugs her beloved rag doll, dangling legs and all, but she's become very quiet. Her cheeks are flushed, and Mama sees right away she isn't well. "Come with me," Mama says, "we'd better take your temperature."

TONIGHT WE CAN hear the terrible noise of the bombing and shelling, even down here in the bunker. The explosions make our beds shake. We all wake up, and the little ones start crying.

"What's happening, Helga?"

"Have they hit the bunker?"

"Will we be blown up?"

"No, they can't hit us down here. Definitely not."

We lie in the dark and listen to the noise overhead. It never stops, one crash after another, and everything shakes: the bunks, the floor, the table. It sounds as if the shells are getting nearer. Nobody dares to get up and turn the light on. Heide's whimpering now. Why doesn't someone come? Is Mama fast asleep? Is everyone else working, or have they gone and left us all alone? It's no use calling, the explosions are too loud. We all lie staring up at the ceiling.

"Shall we all get into bed together? It'll be less scary."

The others scramble onto my bunk, complete with animals and bedclothes. It's very warm with all of us lying so close together in a tangle of arms and legs. The sleeve of my nightie is wet with Holde's tears.

"Don't be frightened, all of you. The Führer will beat our enemies in the end, that's what all the noise is about."

Heide's hot little head is resting on my chest. We both lie there staring up at the ceiling when the others have gone back to sleep. Will Herr Karnau help to get us out of here? Unless Mama and Papa do something, he's the only person left who can help us.

Papa's skin looks worse than usual when he wakes us in the morning, probably because he hasn't slept much either. He and Mama go into the room next door. They want to talk in private, but you can hear what they're saying if you listen hard. Papa asks Mama how things were at home when she went back there. Mama is absolutely furious.

"You can't imagine. Everything in chaos, every last room, and filthy footprints all over the carpets. As for finding the children's things... The servants had disappeared long ago, they simply walked out with whatever they could carry. Now the Volkssturm have taken over the house. They didn't want to let me in at first. I was stopped by a boy of fourteen or so—he was standing guard with a rocket launcher. Think of it: fourteen years old and a soldier—a child like our Helga. What was he going to do with that rocket launcher? I doubt if he knew one end from the other."

Papa doesn't say anything. Either that, or he speaks so softly I can't hear him because the noise is bad again. The others seem to have gotten used to it overnight, they're playing with their toys in the passage. All except Heide, who's being kept in bed because she's still got a temperature. Suddenly I can hear Papa quite clearly, he's almost yelling now.

"You expect me to worry about such trifles? Have you any idea of the prevailing mood down below? Morale is at rock bottom. Things can't go on like this much longer, the Führer's nerves are in shreds. Can you imagine how he takes it out on the rest of us?"

A shell bursts overhead. It drowns Papa's voice, or perhaps he breaks off because of the noise. The next word I catch is "chocolate." "Chocolate, chocolate!" he keeps shouting.

I wonder what he means. Is there some chocolate in the bunker? Would they give us a bar? We'd share it out fairly if they did. A chorus of delighted cries from the passage: "Herr Karnau's coming, Herr Karnau's coming!"

Herr Karnau looks at me. "Hello, Helga, brooding about something?"

"Not really. What's the date today?"

"It's Tuesday, isn't it? Then it must be the twenty-fourth."

"Can I ask you a favor?"

"Of course."

"It's Hedda's birthday soon—May the fifth—but we don't have any presents for her yet. Papa was talking about chocolate just now, and a bar of chocolate would make her a really nice present. Would you see if you can find one somewhere?"

"I'll certainly keep my eyes open. It might be worth taking a peek in the kitchen some time."

"Hedda mustn't find out, though, or it wouldn't be a surprise."

"My lips are sealed."

Herr Karnau smiles. He's the only person I can trust to keep a secret.

"MOSQUITOES!" SQUEALS HEDDA. "There they are, outside!"

Mama looks startled. "The Mosquitoes can't get at us down here."

"But look, Mama, there they are, flying around outside the door."

Sure enough, the passage is full of little black insects. Mama says, "Oh, you mean fruit flies."

"No, mosquitoes."

"Those aren't mosquitoes. Mosquitoes sting, fruit flies don't."

"But there are so many of them."

"They come from the kitchen, Hedda. They won't hurt you."

Mama must have thought she meant those enemy airplanes. She looks relieved. "How about some lunch? Hungry already?"

"Yes, a bit."

Holde says, "Will there be strawberries for lunch, Mama?"

"No, I'm afraid we don't have any strawberries. Anyway, it isn't summertime yet."

"Strawberries would be nice, though."

"Yes, sweetheart, very nice. Later on, maybe, when we get out of here. Never mind, we'll cook ourselves something good."

We have to stay in our room whenever Mama goes to the kitchen to prepare our meals—she says the cook isn't too keen on having children in the kitchen. Sometimes, when we have lunch, they're only just clearing away the grown-ups' breakfast things. That's because they get up so late. They work till late at night, Mama says, so they sleep till midday. We have to keep quiet until they wake up, just as we have to keep quiet when they take their afternoon nap, which is really their night's sleep. It's crazy. We're only allowed down on the lowest floor when they're awake, not otherwise, and at night, when everyone else is up, we're asleep.

You can't think straight when you're always having to scurry to and fro because you're scared. It makes everyone stupid. You can't talk properly when you're scared, either, or not much. It's the same with everyone, not just us children. The things we say get shorter and shorter. Mama's and Papa's sentences often consist of single words like "What?" or "Yes?" as if they've only just noticed that one of us has said something—as if the air's like treacle and our words have to fight their way through it, one by one, and take a while to reach their ears. Anyone who can still think straight and put long sentences together must be really thick. We're done for, and they haven't realized it yet.

Everyone sounds odd down here. Papa's voice never sounded like this before, nor did Mama's. Even when she smiles you know there's something wrong. There are some weird-looking people in the bunker, and even the ones who used to be quite normal are behaving in a funny way. You'd think they'd all gone crazy. There's one man whose eyes keep twitching all the time, and not long ago someone else suddenly shouted out, "The bunker is a fountain of youth!"—whatever he meant by that.

Everyone was startled—they stared at him with their mouths open. People don't raise their voices here as a rule. Visitors keep arriving. They go downstairs to the lower level, but they never stay long, then they leave. Sometimes we see them walking past, but they usually look grim and say nothing. What news do they hear down there that's so terrible? We're allowed downstairs too—every day, if the Führer feels like seeing us—but nobody tells us anything. They just make friendly noises and say things are fine. Won't anyone tell us how we're really doing? The Führer's mouth keeps twitching, his lips tremble all the time we're with him. Then his doctor,

Herr Stumpfecker, comes in and tells us it's time to go back upstairs.

LET'S PLAY DIGGING. We'll pretend the teaspoon's a little shovel and the sugar's sand. There's a heap of it in the sugar bowl, and we've got to dig a hole. The hole keeps filling up with sugar. If you hold the sugar back with another spoon so it doesn't trickle into the hole, you can see a little bare patch on the bottom. It's shiny, the bottom of the sugar bowl, but grains of sugar are starting to cover it again.

"Hedda, take your fingers out of the sugar bowl."

A fork. A fork makes a good rake. You can flatten the sugar with a spoon and then rake it with the fork.

"What shall we play now?"

"Can we have some strawberries?"

"There aren't any strawberries, so don't keep asking. How many more times do I have to tell you?"

"But at Lanke you said, 'Look, there are strawberries growing in the garden.' Why can't we have some now? Aren't they ripe yet?"

"No, they aren't."

"Can we go outside, outside the bunker, when the strawberries are ripe? Then we can pick some ourselves."

Mama starts to cry behind her hand. She gets up from the table and goes into her room. She slams the door, but we can still hear her crying. It's quiet for a little while. We can hear her crying through the steel door, through the thick bunker wall.

"Why do you have to keep getting on Mama's nerves, all of you?" I say. "She does everything for us. She darns the holes in our clothes and sews on our buttons and cooks our meals every day. Where do you expect her to get strawberries from?

Do you want her to get shot out there, just for the sake of your silly strawberries?"

No one wants that. They all stare at the floor and say nothing. Mama is still crying in her room. It's so dreary here. Dreary sugar, dreary sugar bowl, dreary spoon and fork—everything's dreary. You have to live inside yourself down here, there's no room anywhere else. Dreary table, dreary floor. There's nowhere to go. The rooms are dreary too, and so is the lighting. You can't go anywhere, you can only roam around inside yourself, to and fro, back and forth. The dogs are the only ones you could call cheerful. Coco roams around too. He always thinks you've got something in your hand he might like to eat. We'll never get out of here.

Mama comes out of her room. Her eyes are red. "Well," she says, "do you plan to spend the rest of the day sitting here like statues?"

"Could we go and see the garage?" Helmut asks. "When we got here, Papa's chauffeur said he was going to take the cars to the garage."

"It's much too far, Helmut, we'd have to walk along miles of passages. Why not ask Herr Schwägermann what the garage looks like, I'm sure he'd be happy to tell you. Listen: the guns have stopped. Perhaps we could go for a stroll in the Chancellery garden. Shall we ask one of the guards if it's all right for you to go and play in the fresh air?"

We all put our jackets on. Hilde and I help the younger ones with them while Mama goes looking for a guard. As soon as she comes back she says, "Well, are you ready? The sentry says things are quiet at the moment."

Everything looks quite different outside, we notice that at once. Before, there was just a stretch of grass; now there's a deep, sandy hole where a tree has been blown out of the ground. The little ones dash over to it and start digging. We can shelter from the Russians and the shells behind the root ball, which is huge. Hilde tugs my sleeve.

"Look over there, Helga. You see all that rubble? That's where we walked a few days ago, when we got here."

"Yes, and the pillars have gone too."

"They're still lying there, smashed to bits."

"Look at the holes in the roof."

"It's bound to collapse before long."

Mama also sees how much damage the bombs have done. We don't dare look across at our house—we don't even look in that direction. The soldiers defending us are hidden in the buildings all around. Are they really just children, or was Mama exaggerating? The air is still. The sentry sitting up there in the tower will warn us if things get dangerous. We can walk around for a bit, in between the heaps of rubble and debris. How will they ever rebuild this place? The street is completely blocked. Heide, Hedda and Helmut are playing tag. It's wonderful to be able to breathe some fresh air and swing our arms, the bunker's far too cramped for that. Holde looks up at the sky.

"There's a plane up there, see?"

Helmut stops running around and points at the clouds. "Yes, it'll soon be overhead."

"Mama, why can't we get in a plane and fly away?"

HERR KARNAU'S THE only grown-up here who isn't crazy. The others are nice to us too, but they all act strange in some way. He's the only one you don't feel is hiding something. He even tells me about his secret chocolate hunt.

"Helga," he says, "can we have a quick word in private?"

I follow him into our room. What does he want to tell me?

Is the war over? Has something happened to Mama or Papa? No, he wouldn't be looking so cheerful if something was wrong. He shuts the door behind us and produces a bar of chocolate from his pocket.

"That's terrific. Where did you get it?"

"I can't tell you that. Just between the two of us, there'll be hell to pay if someone notices it's gone."

"You mean you pinched it?"

"Can you really call it that, when it's a question of finding Hedda a birthday present?"

"Maybe not . . ."

"You see? We won't talk about it any more, but you must promise to hide it somewhere safe. No one but you must know where it is. Not your mother, not the others—no one. And please don't bring it out until Hedda's birthday. Nobody must know about this bar of chocolate. If you leave the bunker before May the fifth you must leave it behind, understand? That's so no one finds it on the journey. Promise?"

"Yes, I promise. The best place to hide it would be—"

"No, don't tell me. No one must know that but you."

Herr Karnau kept his word, even if he did steal the chocolate from somewhere. He turns his back so as not to see where I hide it. Under my pillow? No, if the others crawl into my bunk again they may notice it. But here, under the mattress, that's a good place, no one will look there. Herr Karnau still has his back turned. Since he trusts me so much, he won't pass on that awful thing Mama said today.

"Herr Karnau? You know that man whose name sounds like a wild animal—Leopard, or something . . ."

"Professor Gebhardt, you mean?"

"That's right, Herr Gebhardt. He paid a visit to the bunker last night, and he asked Mama—I could overhear her and Papa talking beforehand without meaning to, I know it's wrong to eavesdrop, but they were talking so loudly I couldn't help hearing every word—anyway, Herr Gebhardt suggested taking us all out of here. He wanted to save us, he wanted us to leave with him right away, with the Red Cross, but Mama...Instead of saying yes, she said we didn't want to go at all, she said we'd much rather stay. But it simply isn't true, we'd give anything to get out of this place!"

"Don't cry, Helga. Come here, that's right. You must have misheard. Why should your mother have said such a thing? She only wants what's best for you all."

"No, she doesn't."

"You mustn't talk like that, Helga."

"We're all going to die."

"What on earth gives you that idea?"

"We're all going to die very soon."

"Stop it, Helga."

"Mama and Papa want us all to die. Mama didn't want us to bring any night things, she didn't even think we'd be alive in the morning."

"She was confused, that's all. She doesn't want her six darling children to die, Helga, you don't believe that yourself."

"So why does she act this way?"

"Things aren't going too well at present, as you know, but you can rest assured that everyone in this place will do their utmost to prevent anything bad from happening to you children. They'd lay down their lives for you, every last one of them."

"Really?"

"Really and truly."

Herr Karnau looks straight at me, and his eyelids don't twitch. If Herr Karnau says something, you can believe it. Even if no one else was prepared to help us, Herr Karnau would. Hilde knocks on the door.

"Are you in there, Helga?"

THE BATHROOM DOOR IS locked. There must be someone inside. There always is, when you're in a hurry.

"Hello? Is that you, Mama?"

No answer. I bang on the door, but that doesn't do any good either. How much longer?

Mama still doesn't answer. Perhaps she's feeling ill again. Is there another toilet somewhere? Not on this floor, but there must be one downstairs. There must be, because they don't all come up here when they need to go. I'll have to go down there on my own, that's all. It's forbidden, really, but I'm the eldest, I can't do it in my underpants. Mama would be angry, she'd have to wash them. We've brought so few things with us.

I don't meet anyone on the stairs, but I can hear people working down below, they're talking in a room along the passage. Maybe this is the toilet, this door at the foot of the stairs. There's no one to ask, but who cares? If there's no one around, no one will mind.

It *is* a toilet. It smells awful, but I can't wait. I wouldn't have time to run back upstairs and try our own toilet again. What a disgusting place. I need to pee, badly. I can't sit down, the seat's too dirty. You have to hold your breath in here, there's such a stench. Perhaps it's only a men's toilet.

Someone's been scribbling on the tiles. We're never allowed to draw on bathroom walls, not at home and not upstairs. There's a girl's face, very rough, just a few lines. She's smiling with her arms behind her head so you can't see her hands under her long hair. She's naked, with huge breasts and big nipples. Her legs are apart, and there are lots of black squiggles between them. They're meant to be hair, I suppose. What sort of person would draw a picture like that?

Any toilet paper? Yes, just a little bit left on the roll. Now out of here, quick. Thank goodness, it doesn't smell out here. I can still hear someone talking in the room along the passage, only one man's voice, though he's talking to someone else. The door is ajar. When he sees me peering through the crack he beckons me in and points to a chair and goes on speaking into his mouthpiece. It's the telephone operator.

He puts through one call after another, quickly plugging the cables into the switchboard. An urgent call comes through from outside. The operator takes off his headset and goes into the room next door. A soldier hurries in and speaks into the mouthpiece, the operator comes over to me.

"Lost your way, Helga?"

"No, there was someone in the bathroom upstairs."

"Well, so now you've seen our switchboard."

"Is it fun, telephoning all the time?"

"The calls aren't for me, but I overhear a lot of interesting stuff."

"Could we make a phone call some time?"

"Not today, there are too many urgent calls coming in. Maybe tomorrow will be a bit quieter. Who did you want to call?"

"I don't know, really..."

The switchboard buzzes, so he has to put his headset on again. He smiles at me and shrugs his shoulders. "Back to work," he says.

THE RUSSIANS ARE coming, we can hear their boots on the stairs. We get into the kennel and hide at the very back. The dogs don't move, they know they've got to protect us. We crouch down so the Russians won't see us. Coco's fur is tickling my face. Are we crouching down low enough, so the Russians won't even see the tops of our heads? They're quite close now, we'd better hold our breath. Will they shoot us? Is it time for us to die? The footsteps come nearer. The dogs start to fidget, but they stay where they are. The kennel smells, they must have done it on the floor where we're hiding. My hand is all wet, but it doesn't matter, not now. If we hold our breath we can't smell the dog dirt. A man's voice in the passage: "Come out of there."

Is he a Russian? Does he know we're in here? Is he going to take us away with him? Where are Mama and Papa? Where are all the others? Why is it so quiet? Don't breathe, whatever you do. Only a little longer. I hope the others manage to hold their breath too.

"Come out of there at once."

The footsteps are really close. We can hear someone breathing outside. The dogs are getting restless, shifting from paw to paw. He's right in front of the bars, he's bound to notice that the door isn't shut properly. Now we're in for it. The kennel door creaks open, the dogs back away, pushing us up against the wall. We don't look, we don't look at the door. The dogs move aside. He's coming in, we can see his black boots. "Come on out," he says. "What are you doing in there?"

I catch a glimpse of his hair. He's so huge, he can see us over the top of the dogs. "Why are you hiding in there?" he says. "It's far too dirty."

It's Herr Stumpfecker. He holds out his arms. Is he going to strangle us? "Come on, children," he says, "this is no place for you. Your mother's looking for you upstairs."

We can't stand up, we're too scared. Will he really not hurt us? He's found us now, so we'd better come out. "Come upstairs with me," Herr Stumpfecker says. "You can wash your hands up there. Everything's all right, what on earth's the matter with you? Imagine getting in with the dogs. It never occurred to us..."

He shakes his head and smiles at us in a funny way. There's a big scar over his left eye, it twitches now and then. We scurry past him and run up the stairs to Mama, who's waiting in the passage. We've shaken off Herr Stumpfecker, thank goodness. Mama looks relieved to see us.

"You're all out of breath. Why were you running like that?"

"We were frightened. We wanted to get back to you as fast as we could."

"Where have you been hiding?"

"Down in the dog kennel."

"But you're not supposed to go down there by yourselves."

"We only wanted to telephone."

"Telephone?"

"Yes. The man said we could make a phone call today, but it's no good now, all the lines are cut."

"Sit down, all of you, and let me comb your hair nicely. We're going for a walk along the underground passages. Papa's coming too. He only just got up. They were working all night down there."

"Where are we going?"

"To another air-raid shelter, for a party with some city folk."

"Will there be children there too?"

"Of course."

"What kind of party?"

"We're going there to say good—" Mama stops short. Papa has just appeared in the doorway.

He must have heard us, because he says, "It's just a little treat for the people in the air-raid shelter, that's all."

He's carrying a basket filled with presents for them. The shells are landing right above our heads now, everything's shaking. We haven't been allowed outside for days. I hope we don't have to walk very far. The lights in the long passageway flicker suddenly. They'd better not go out or we'd get lost in this labyrinth, but they keep on flickering. We walk quite slowly, so it takes ages to get there. At last we come to a room where a nurse is waiting for us. There must be an underground hospital here, because doctors walk past in gowns with bloodstains on them. Some wounded men are led in, hardly able to stand. One has his whole head bandaged. His head is so flat at the sides, I can tell he doesn't have any ears. "Why is he done up like that, Mama?" Heide asks.

Mama doesn't answer. More and more people come in, women and children too. They look exhausted. We stand aside, Hilde and me. What we'd really like to do is hide behind Mama and Papa. Hilde feels the same as I do. She's a bit embarrassed to be wearing such nice clothes, as if there isn't a war on at all, but we can't stand back against the wall, we have to sit with Mama and Papa at the table in the middle. The people are staring at us. They stand there, packed together like sardines, and stare as if they're planning to do something nasty to us at any moment. "You see," Mama whispers, "they're glad we came."

Papa says a few words before he hands out the things he brought with him. The children get sweets. We don't feel like helping Papa to hand them out. We used to enjoy doing that in the old days, but here we feel a bit scared. Suddenly a boy steps out of the crowd and walks up to the table. What does he want?

Nothing, he only wants to sing with us. There's an accordion on a strap around his neck, and he can play it even though his left arm is bandaged. When he opens his mouth you can see that most of his front teeth are missing. The people all join in as soon as the boy with the accordion starts playing. Their voices are awfully loud. Shells are bursting all around us now, even beneath our feet, or so it seems, though the noise can't really be coming from there. The explosions go on forever, and so does the singing. A terrible din, but it doesn't stop the people singing. You can't hear them anymore, all you can see is their mouths opening and closing.

MAMA'S HAIRPIECE HAS slipped, the blond plait she pins on at the back with hairpins. She's lying in bed and refuses to leave her room. Her eyes are all red, we saw them, even though she told us earlier that we'd soon be leaving the bunker. "There's no point in staying here any longer," she said, "so we're going to escape by air. The plane will fly us out of the city and take us somewhere far away, somewhere where the fighting stopped long ago." Herr Karnau must have given her a serious talking-to. He must have convinced her it's time we got out.

Even so, she's been crying all day long. We're not feeling too cheerful ourselves. Hilde and Helmut start fighting—why, heaven knows. Helmut lashes out with his fists, Hilde scratches back, Helmut kicks Hilde in self-defense but she grabs him by the hair and yanks it so hard he falls down. He goes on lashing out, but she sits on him and holds his wrists. Helmut yells and spits, but he misses Hilde's face. He hisses at her through his brace. Just then Mama appears in the doorway. "Stop that," she shouts, "stop it, both of you. How could you, today of all days?"

The room suddenly goes quiet, no one moves. Hilde is still sitting on Helmut's tummy, but he isn't trying to fight her off any longer. They both lower their arms and stare at Mama. The rest of us stare at her too. Not a sound. We were watching Hilde and Helmut fighting, but now all we look at is Mama. We see her eyes, which are red from weeping. We see the way she's clinging to the doorpost, the way she's trembling all over, the way she's breathing and her bosom is rising and falling. None of us says a word. We all go on staring at her for what seems like hours.

I don't know who broke the silence. Was it Mama who spoke first, or was it Helmut, because he couldn't stand Hilde's weight on his tummy any longer? And which of them made the first move? I can't remember, but they don't make up till suppertime. Herr Karnau sees we're feeling low as soon as he comes in. He's being allowed to put us to bed tonight because Mama says she doesn't have the energy. He stands at the washbasin and squeezes toothpaste onto our brushes. "What's the matter with you all tonight?" he asks.

"Mama was acting strange just now, even though we'll soon be leaving here by plane."

"Leaving, eh? What did I tell you? You won't have to stay down here in the dark much longer, you'll be seeing the sky again. It's sure to be nice and sunny outside. Maybe you'll fly south to the mountains. It'll soon be peacetime, too. Just imagine, the war will be over."

"When we were in the mountains," Hilde says, "we heard people yodeling. Can you yodel?"

"No, Hilde, I'm afraid not."

"We can, a bit. The people in the mountains showed us how."

Holde makes a funny noise. Hilde laughs. "That's not yodeling, Holde. Listen, this is how it goes."

Hilde can yodel properly. Not for long, but she sounds just like those people in the Tyrol.

"You're really good, Hilde," Herr Karnau says. "Show us how you do it."

We all watch Hilde's mouth in the mirror. Toothpaste froth runs down her chin.

"More, Hilde, more!"

"Slower, so we can really see."

Hilde gives a little shriek. "Ouch, that's cold!"

The froth has dripped onto her tummy. She can't concentrate on yodeling anymore, we're laughing so much, but she does her best to keep a straight face. Herr Karnau backs her up. "You'll never learn if you fool around," he tells the rest of us. "Watch her mouth closely. The tongue, that's the most important thing."

We all try to imitate her. "No, Helmut," Herr Karnau says, "you're opening your mouth too wide. You must form a hollow for your tongue to vibrate in."

But it isn't so easy to do that with braces like Helmut's. Hedda can't help laughing, she chokes on some spit. Herr Karnau thumps her on the back. We all yodel at once. Then it's time for bed. Heide has to sleep next door because she's still got a cold and Mama doesn't want us to catch it. She's sad at not being allowed to sleep with the rest of us. Mama comes in to say good night. We beg her to let Herr Karnau tell us a story before lights out, and she says yes. Then she goes off to play patience and Herr Karnau sits down on the edge of my bunk. Herr Karnau's good at telling stories. He has to keep stopping every two minutes so we can take turns running to tell Heide what happens next.

THE BAR OF chocolate is still there. Still in one piece, too, though it could easily get broken every night when Herr Karnau sits down on the edge of my bunk. It's the first of May today, only four days to go to Hedda's birthday. If we leave before then the bar of chocolate will stay here forever, which would be a waste. Maybe it would be better to eat it up right away. Or some of it, at least—just a little bit. Except that the others would smell it. They haven't had any chocolate for so long, they'd be bound to notice the smell as soon as I opened my mouth to speak. Herr Karnau stole the bar, and my chocolaty breath would give him away.

Herr Karnau's eyebrows are all bunched together. "Is something wrong?" I ask him.

"Yes, everything. The last few days have been a strain. Everyone's very tired."

"Will you also be leaving the bunker soon?"

"Yes. Once you're safely out of here, the rest of the grown-ups will go too."

"Where to?"

"No idea. As far away as possible, I hope."

"Abroad?"

"Perhaps."

"Does that mean we'll never see each other again?"

"Of course not, Helga. We'll still be seeing each other long after you and the others are grown up. I'll be an old codger by then, and so deaf you'll all have to shout to make your-selves understood."

He smiles at me. He must be just as happy as we are to be

getting out of here at last. We both picture aloud how lovely it is outside. It's been ages since we smelled a flower, or saw any animals apart from the dogs, or breathed fresh air, or felt rain on our faces.

"It's springtime, Helga. Imagine standing in the rain without an umbrella. It could rain and rain till the clothes clung to your body, but you wouldn't feel cold. Think how good the air smells after a spring shower. Think of sea air and waves breaking, think of the sound of the sea."

"We used to go to the Baltic for holidays sometimes. We made sand castles and sunbathed and swam. We got ever so brown."

Mama comes in with the others and Herr Karnau leaves us alone. Mama says we must all have a good wash before we catch the plane. Papa comes in too. He plays with Heide and her rag doll. As soon as we've finished washing, Papa is going to read to us. Mama has ironed our night things, and my blue nightie is nice and soft. Helmut puts on his white pajamas, the ones with the little red and turquoise flowers. The younger ones lie on the bed and listen to Papa reading, but there are too many thoughts going around in my head for me to listen properly. Papa reads slowly, stroking Heide's hair all the time.

It's too early to go to bed, so we're allowed downstairs for a while. Herr Karnau isn't there, and we don't see Coco either. It doesn't smell the same as usual, people must have been smoking down there. We all go into Papa's office. He's sitting under the sun lamp with his goggles on, which always looks dangerous, and he's actually smoking a cigarette, something he hasn't done since we arrived here. Mama combs our hair very thoroughly, one after the other.

"Will we really be taking off soon?"

"Yes, Hedda, really."

"Tonight? Tomorrow morning?"

"We don't exactly know yet. The sky must be really clear of enemy planes first, so nothing happens to us. A few hours more or less don't matter, though, do they?"

The sun lamp bell rings. Papa takes off his goggles. His face always looks a bit red at first, but later you can see how brown the skin has gotten. He puts the sun lamp back on the shelf with his books and goes out into the passage. The downstairs floor is sopping wet, which isn't a good sign. Something must be wrong. I wonder where the dogs are. Why aren't they in their kennel? We didn't pass them on the stairs. Have they been taken outside some other way? Something's wrong, something must have happened to Coco. Papa and Mama are looking terribly depressed. All of a sudden, I can't do anything but cry, just cry. Mama puts her arms around me, but I go on crying. It's all so sad and dreary here. Hilde starts crying too.

Mama takes us back upstairs and says we must go to bed. "Why so early?" I ask. Mama can hardly stop herself from crying either, and her voice is trembling. "You want to get plenty of sleep in, don't you, before we catch the plane?"

Mama lets Heide get into my bunk although she still hasn't gotten rid of her cold, not completely.

"Mama, will Herr Karnau come and say good night to us?"

She promises to go and look for him. "No need to settle down right away," she says. "A doctor will be coming to give you all an injection to stop you feeling sick in the plane."

Then she switches off the light and goes out. To fetch Herr Karnau? We can hear her talking to someone outside. The door is opening.

"Is that you, Herr Karnau?"

CHAPTER

"Is that you, Herr Karnau?"

Yes, that must be Helga, the eldest child. And just before that, on the same disc: "Mama, will Herr Karnau come and say good night to us?"

That's little Heide, there's no mistaking her voice, even though she sounds rather hoarse. And that's their mother's voice, in the interval between the two children's questions: "No need to settle down right away."

I can distinguish all the voices if I listen closely enough. But on what night was this recording made? It should be possible to arrange the discs in chronological order by consulting the dates scratched on the wax. The inscription beside the inner-most groove on the first disc I played reads: Monday, 30 April 1945. That's the one with "clip-clap" on it. So it isn't a defective recording after all. The children are really saying that, but in heavily disguised voices, and the same is true of "hick-hack, hick-hack." But what do the words mean? Did the children speak a kind of secret language among themselves when no one could overhear them? They definitely used private code words from time to time, I noticed that soon after we met, but why did they disguise their voices on this occasion?

I play the passage again, and suddenly I understand: they're not speaking some private language, they're repeating made-up words from a fairy tale. It's true, they once asked me to tell them a bedtime story before they went to sleep. They're imitating my voice, my fairy tale voice, and recalling incidents from the story. It must have made such an impression on them that a few key words sufficed to conjure it up in every detail. And to think they're imitating my voice as well.... Although it sounds unfamiliar to me, they're reproducing certain features of my diction too accurately to leave me in any further doubt. It never occurred to me how closely they were listening to my voice and taking note of its peculiarities.

Once more from the beginning. Here's the very first disc: Sunday, 22 April. The children are talking about me. They're happy to have seen Coco again and are discussing the zoo. The poor little things didn't know how badly the animals were faring at this stage, or that many of them had long been dead. But their voices also convey a certain unease. Perhaps they were scared because this was their first night in the unfamiliar bunker.

Here, on the second disc, they're imitating dogs barking and howling. Their yapping is punctuated by peals of laughter. How carefree their vocal experiments sound! The first shells began to land in the grounds of the Chancellery only a few hours later, but by then they were probably too sound asleep to notice.

The six voices have passed into my possession. They ring out in the darkness. Their sound fills the kitchen, unheard by anyone but me. The rest of the world is asleep. Unbeknown to the children, I am their only audience.

Wednesday, 25 April. A lively conversation about twitching faces, strawberries, sunken cheeks. I can't make head or tail of it, though all six voices are quite distinct. Helmut is the only one who sounds odd, as if his mouth is too full of saliva—as if his teeth aren't helping his tongue to form sounds in the normal way and the words are having to overcome some additional obstacle.

I listen to the voices on another disc. At the beginning of the recording the children are calling after me from their beds: "Will you be sure to come back tomorrow?"

My reply is inaudible, I'm already too far away from the concealed microphone. Then the children's tone changes. They no longer sound as childish as they do in the presence of adults. They speak falteringly, earnestly, about the fear they feel whenever a bomb or a shell bursts overhead. About their fear of never being able to leave the bunker again. About the sneaking fear of their parents that has overcome them in the last few days, because their father and mother, clearly unable to disguise their own alarm, have been acting more and more strangely under the pressure of events. The children's tone conveys a vague presentiment that they will never see daylight again.

At this point the nocturnal conversation is interrupted by a loud rustle, a disturbance emanating from somewhere near the microphone beneath the bed. What can it be? As soon as it ceases I hear the children talking normally. Then the inexplicable sound is repeated. I stop the turntable and decipher the inscription on the disc: Friday, 27 April. Not a date that affords any clue to the origin of the rustling sound.

I can't bring myself to listen to any more, not for the moment. It's still dark, but a light has now come on in a window across the way. Behind the glowing curtain I can make out the shape of a man slowly, sleepily getting dressed in time to leave before daybreak for the early shift. Silence still reigns, but my head is filled with the six children's voices.

A terrifying possession, these very last recordings of them, for all six died soon afterwards. Not in an air raid, not while escaping, not of debility or malnutrition in the aftermath of war. Before any such fate could befall them, they were killed in the bunker itself. It must have happened at a time when their murderer could feel sure that I wouldn't catch him in the act. Someone must have timed their murder with care to guard against interruptions, because I hovered in the vicinity of the children's room on the upper level whenever I could spare a moment from my work. Quite instinctively, I felt it essential to keep an eye on them.

The children themselves could not have known about their impending murder, but why didn't I, an adult in regular contact with the other occupants of the bunker and well placed to overhear them talking together, get wind of those lethal preparations? Although no one betrayed them to me, why didn't I, the sound expert, detect some sign in the voices around me, be it only a faint undertone, a brief hesitation, or a sudden silence—the curtailment of a remark uttered in passing? Hadn't Helga, in the course of a private conversation during those last days in the bunker, extracted an assurance from me that all present would do their utmost to ensure her own and the others' survival? Who would deliberately have broken such a promise?

A certain Dr. Kunz was interrogated on 7 May 1945. Kunz, who had a habit of opening his mouth with a jerk and exposing both rows of teeth as if biting the air, testified that the children's mother had asked him on 27 April to help her kill them, and that he had agreed to do so. Between four and five p.m. on Tuesday, 1 May, she called him on the internal phone—all links with the outside world had been cut for some time—and asked him to come to the bunker. He took no medicines with him, he insisted, fixing his eyes on the interrogation room's ceiling as if air raids still presented a danger: his medical case contained no painkillers, not even a sticking plaster. The children's mother then informed him that the time had come. Their father, who appeared some twenty minutes later, said that he would be very grateful if Kunz would help to put the children to sleep. At that moment, said Kunz, whose tie did not hang inert on his chest but swung to and fro in time to the vehement gestures that accompanied his testimony, the bunker lights began to flicker. For some unaccountable reason this reminded him of early mornings in his childhood, when he would sit at the kitchen table and run his hand over the oilcloth.

The children's father had then disappeared and their mother spent approximately an hour playing patience. Then she took Kunz to her living quarters, where she produced a hypodermic syringe filled with morphine from a cupboard in the outer room and handed it to him. The syringe and its contents had been given to her by Stumpfecker, said Kunz, keeping both feet flat on the floor as if afraid of losing contact with it. Together, they then entered the children's bedroom, where the six were already in bed but not yet asleep. Their mother addressed them in a low voice: "Don't be frightened. The doctor here is going to give you a little jab, the kind that all other children and soldiers are getting."

On that note she left the darkened room and Kunz proceeded to administer the injections in descending order of age. Helga, Hilde, Helmut, Holde, Hedda, Heide—all received a 0.5 cc shot in the lower arm to make them drowsy. Kunz particularly recalled the softness of their skin. After completing this task, which took him between eight and ten minutes, he rejoined the children's mother and waited with her for another ten minutes to allow them to go to sleep undisturbed. He looked at his watch: eight forty p.m. They then re-entered the bedroom, where the mother took some five minutes to insert a crushed ampoule of cyanide in the mouth of each sleeping child. "There," Kunz recalled her saying, "all over."

Again the record makes that rustling sound. Of course! It's paper, wrapping paper—the bar of chocolate Helga was going to give Hedda for her birthday on 5 May. Helga had asked me to get her some chocolate, and I'd managed, behind the diet cook's back, to purloin a bar from her well-stocked store cupboard—a perilous undertaking, given that stealing food was an offense punishable by summary execution: no trial, just a bullet in the head. Would that have applied to a child, too, I wonder. Helga needed a hiding place, so she must have concealed the present under her mattress and checked on it at night, when the lights were out and the others couldn't see. By feeling for the chocolate, she would unwittingly have put her hand near the microphone.

The switchboard operator, whose name was Mischa, testified that Dr. Naumann had come to the telephone exchange and told him that Stumpfecker was going to give the children some "bonbon water," in other words, that they were to be killed. He could not, however, be precise about the time he received this information. He only knew that all the outside lines were dead.

But what was "bonbon water?" Now that the rustling sound has ceased, I'm able to follow the children's conversation without further interruption. They recall their visit to Moreau. Never having been told of Moreau's death, they refer to him as if he's still alive.

Hilde: "Do you think Herr Karnau's friend is still angry with us for getting chocolate all over his furniture?"

Holde: "If only we had some chocolate now..."

Helga, in answer to Hilde's question: "No, I'm sure Herr Moreau isn't angry anymore, Herr Karnau calmed him down. Remember how we went outside with them that night?"

Helmut: "Yes, looking for bats."

Heide, disappointedly: "But they never came."

"Yes, they did."

"No, they didn't. Not one."

"You'd probably fallen asleep by then, sleepyhead."

"Did not."

"Anyway, we saw some."

Holde: "Those were birds."

Helmut, impatiently: "No, they weren't. Bats flap their wings quite differently, Herr Moreau showed us."

"But it was dark by then."

"It was prickly, hiding in those bushes."

Helga's voice again, very near: "No, later on, when we were standing under that light. We threw stones in the air, and the bats darted after them."

Hedda, from above: "They flew down, right past our heads. They ruffled our hair."

"Well, almost."

"But they came very close, the horrid black things."

Helga: "Herr Karnau said the bats mistook the stones for gnats."

Heide again: "Yes, gnats. And mosquitoes."

At this point on the night of 27 April the recording breaks off. Earlier that day the children's mother had called Dr. Kunz for the first time. Who was Kunz, and why should he have acceded to her request? Why did our paths never cross at that time? Someone should have restrained the man, if necessary by force. At a second interrogation on Thursday, 19 May 1945, Kunz retracted his previous statements in the light of suspicions that another doctor was also involved in the murder of the six children. Continually stroking his hair, fiddling with his ears, and wiping his eyes as if plagued by swarms of little black flies, Kunz conceded that his earlier account of the circumstances of the killing had been inaccurate: it was true that Stumpfecker had helped him.

But what was "bonbon water?" Was it a pleasant-tasting drink consisting of water in which bonbons had been dissolved with an admixture of morphine, or was the sweet, strong-tasting beverage doctored not with sedative but with the lethal poison itself? Or should bonbon water be construed as an imprecise description of chocolates with a poisonous liquid center that were given to the children to suck, no resistance being anticipated because it was so long since the six of them had had any sweets that their tongues would swiftly have licked away enough of the outer crust to let the cyanide seep through into the oral cavity? Were the doctors apprehensive because they could not be absolutely certain that the dominant sugary taste would so desensitize the children's gustatory nerves to other stimuli that they would fail to notice the poison and unsuspectingly swallow it, mingled with saliva and sugar?

Having injected the children with morphine, Kunz left them and joined their mother in the room next door, where they waited for them to go to sleep. She then asked him to help her administer the poison itself, but he refused, so she sent him to fetch Stumpfecker, whom he found in the bunker canteen. She had already disappeared into the children's bedroom by the time Stumpfecker got there, so he went straight in. When the two of them emerged four or five minutes later, Stumpfecker walked off without so much as a word to Kunz.

Stumpfecker was a man who had shattered children's legs at Ravensbrück and adorned his office with jars containing pickled fetal speech organs. I would have thought him capable of anything, but not of that, not of ending those six young lives. He sent me off to make copies of our recordings. Why? To get me out of the way while he dealt with the children. "Copy them all very carefully," he told me, meaning those wholly unimportant recordings of a crippled voice. And to think how insistent he was, once the deed had been done, that those discs should be preserved intact...

Saturday, 28 April. Helga recounts a distasteful experience: "And the whole place was awash with wee-wee."

The others giggle. "It wasn't funny," Helga says indignantly, "it was awful. You've no idea how it stank in there, not to mention the revolting pictures on the walls."

"What sort of pictures?"

"Naked, grinning women with big breasts and their legs apart so you could see the hair between them—even the slit. Make sure you never end up in that bathroom, even when there's somebody in the one up here. Better to do it in your pants than have to go down there."

A BELATED NIGHT owl pedals along the street below my window, bicycle tires whirring over the asphalt.

The Führer's driver, Kempka, one false witness among many, testified that Stumpfecker told him that the children's father had requested him to end their lives by injecting them with some fast-acting poison, but that he, Stumpfecker, had refused on the grounds that he would be too mindful of his own young family to do such a thing. The children's father had been at his wits' end, he said.

Kempka kept inquiring after the dogs and sniffing his fingers. He was sorry, he said, but he hadn't managed to wash off the smell of gasoline even now. The couple had eventually found a sympathetic doctor among the refugees in the other bunker, and it was he who put the six children to death. Who was this doctor? Not Kunz, it seemed, and no other candidate presented himself. Had Stumpfecker been so anxious to conceal his tracks that he lied to the others in the bunker before anyone could question him about his involvement?

" 'We're going there to say good—' What did Mama mean?"

"When?"

"Earlier on, before we went to that party in the other bunker."

"Yes, Papa interrupted her."

" 'Goodbye'—was that what she meant to say?"

The others sound agitated. Helga tries to soothe them: "Goodbye? Why? Who would we have said goodbye to? The wounded haven't left, they're still in that underground hospital."

Heide: "And the children?"

"Yes."

Hilde: "It's funny, there aren't any children left in Berlin apart from them."

Helmut: "We're still here, aren't we?"

Holde: "They looked awful."

"Who, the children?"

"No, the wounded. There was one hidden right at the back because he hadn't got a mouth."

Helga: "You're making that up to scare us."

"No, honestly. No mouth at all, just a sort of hole."

"That's enough."

Helga's tone is so peremptory that silence reigns for a while on the disc marked Sunday, 29 April. It's as though each child is trying to stem the flood of images conjured up by Holde's reference to the wounded. Or as if they're doubtful of Helga's dismissal of their mother's truncated remark. Or as if Helga herself is aware that she's desperately trying to reassure the others by saying things she doesn't believe herself.

The father's aide, Günther Schwägermann, testified that he had seen the children's mother go into their bedroom at about seven p.m. She emerged a few minutes later, ashen-faced. On seeing Schwägermann she threw her arms around him, sobbing and mumbling incoherently. Schwägermann, who, while being questioned, continually fiddled with the loose threads marking the spot where his SS collar patches had been ripped off, gradually took in what she was saying: she had just killed all six children. In a state of total collapse, she allowed Schwägermann to help her to the conference room, where her husband, looking very pale, was awaiting her. Realizing what had happened without a word being said, he remained silent for a considerable time.

Mischa, the operator, stated that the children's mother, her face devoid of expression, had walked past the switchboard room and gone into her husband's office, where she sat down at the table and played patience, weeping as she did so. After about twenty minutes she went upstairs again. There was no sign of her husband during this time. Mischa could not refrain from mentioning that Schwägermann had once indignantly confided that Helga had made indecent advances to him.

Schwägermann's assertion that the children's mother had nearly fainted and was utterly distraught is at odds with other accounts to the effect that she first made herself some coffee and then, as one witness put it, chatted briskly about old times with her husband, Artur Axmann, and Martin Bormann. Kempka, too, reported that the couple were looking quite calm and composed at eight forty-five p.m., when he went back into the bunker to say goodbye to them. He kept pausing to listen while being interrogated, as if receiving instructions from some unseen third party. The children's mother had ended by asking him to convey her affectionate regards to Harald, her son by her first marriage, if ever their paths should cross.

According to one reconstruction, she put her six children to bed at about five thirty p.m. and then gave them a sleeping potion, probably Veronal. Later, when they were asleep or at least stupefied, she poured cyanide into their mouths from glass ampoules. This laborious method would, it seems, have obliged her to lean across the nearest children in order to get at the ones beyond. They could not, after all, have assisted her by craning forward and opening their mouths to take the deadly poison. Dosing the occupants of the upper bunks presented a special problem to someone ill-attired for such an activity in the brown dress, trimmed with white, which she had donned in readiness for her own death, because it must have taken considerable dexterity not to spill the cyanide while raising a child's head with her free hand.

All the children passively submitted to this treatment—all, it is alleged, except Helga, who refused to take her "medicine." When all attempts at persuasion failed, her mother had no alternative but to introduce the poison into her mouth by force.

Whose account of the affair is this? The details sound quite incredible, because the woman could not have done all this unaided. The source of the account, who refuses to divulge his name, is concealing something. Who else was in the children's room on that last, fatal night?

I play the 30 April disc once more. Before the children start imitating my fairy tale voice, I can also hear my own voice in the background. We're singing a bedtime song together: "If I should die before I wake, I pray the Lord my soul to take." Fatigue notwithstanding, the youthful, high-pitched voices are doing their best to sing in unison.

But the song is overlaid by muffled grunts and moans from the next apartment: my neighbors making love before dawn.

THE GIRL IS naked. That much is obvious, though all that suggests it are her bare, slender shoulders. The pale oilskin sheet covering the body from the chest down has slipped a little, revealing the left breast, because the head has been raised to show off the slightly pointed chin, the full, loosely compressed lips, the delicate nose, the closed eyes beneath the broad ridges of the brow, the long lashes, the arching eyebrows, the smooth, unlined forehead. The skin is flawless, and the complexion would be healthy but for some bluish flecks and the greenish tinge that discolors the whole face, all the more noticeable because the hair has been swept back off the forehead. Unnaturally taut in appearance, the hair is, in a sense, supporting the weight of the entire body: a whole hank of it is clutched in the gloved hand of the uniformed mortuary attendant, who has turned the dead twelve-year-old's head towards the camera and is holding it in front of his black rubber apron to ensure an even more effective contrast between pale face and dark background.

The six children, all wearing light night attire, were discovered in their bunks in a separate room in the bunker of the

Reich Chancellery, which has since been razed to the ground. Also buried there, crushed by shattered concrete and mingled with the soil, are the remains of a bar of chocolate. All six children exhibited signs of poisoning. To enable them to be identified by persons closely acquainted with them, their bodies were removed to the Berlin-Buch headquarters of the Smersh Section of the Red Army's 79th Rifle Corps.

The following report was compiled during the autopsy performed on Helga's corpse:

"External examination: The body is that of a girl about fifteen years old in appearance, well-nourished and wearing a pale blue nightgown trimmed with lace. Height: one meter fifty-eight. Circumference of chest at nipple level: sixty-five centimeters. Color of skin and visible mucous membranes: pink to cherry-red. Back of the body mottled with red postmortem lividities that can no longer be dispersed. Fingernails bluish. Skin in the region of the shoulder blades and buttocks noticeably pale owing to pressure. Abdominal skin dull green, discolored by putrefaction. Head macrocephalous with flat temples. Hair long, pale brown, plaited. Face oval, tapering towards the chin. Eyebrows pale brown, eyelashes long, irises blue. Nose straight, regular, small. Eyes and mouth closed. Tip of tongue loosely gripped between the teeth. When the body was turned over and pressure applied to the thorax, serous fluid seeped from the mouth and nose and a very faint smell of bitter almonds could be detected. Rib cage normally developed, nipples small, no hair visible in the armpits, abdomen flat. External sexual organs normally developed. Labia majora and mons veneris hirsute as far as the pubic symphysis. "Internal examination: Mucous membrane somewhat bluish. Intestinal contents unexceptional. Womb firm, four centimeters long, three centimeters wide and two centimeters thick at the oviduct. Vagina slit-shaped, hymen intact."

Although the autopsy report speaks of plaits, the photograph shows Helga with her hair loose. Who undid the corpse's plaits? The pathologist's assistant in his rubber gloves?

AN EARLY BIRD is stirring. Awake now, it starts to sing and promptly evokes a chorus of twitters from other trees round about: the night is over at last. How much can I really reconstruct from these recordings? I've listened to every disc with care, more than once, and managed to recognize every voice including my own and that of the children's mother. Would it be better to destroy these wax matrices? No, I can't bring myself to render the children's final days on earth inaudible. I can't consign them to silence, those children who listened to me telling them a bedtime story the night before their murder.

That was on 30 April: the last recording, made on the night we saw each other for the last time. At noon the next day all the recording materials and machines were rounded up and destroyed, some of them in the bunker itself. Nine nights from 22 April onwards: nine wax matrices. I arrange the discs in their correct order and check the dates. But there are ten discs here on the kitchen table, not nine. Did I start the sequence on 21 April? Or cut two discs the same night? Impossible, I could never have changed the discs after lights out. Besides, Stumpfecker sent me off to make copies late on the afternoon of 1 May. Did we ever make a recording during the day? In my cubicle, on another machine? The children knew about my work, so did they make me a recording by themselves? No, they would never have done so in defiance of their father's wishes. No date, no serial number. There's something wrong here, I didn't record this.

"Is that you, Herr Karnau?"

I've already listened to this disc, with its brief exchange between Helga and Heide and their mother.

"Is that you, Herr Karnau?"

Those are the last words I can make out. No, this isn't one of my recordings, definitely not. It doesn't display the tonal quality of the others, nor does it convey any idea of the children's animated conversations after lights out. This one must have been made by someone inexperienced. Helga's unanswered question is followed at first by some unidentifiable sounds, nothing more. On the other hand, I was the only person who knew about the microphone and recording machine concealed beneath the bed. Now an adult's voice breaks the silence. Man or woman? I can't decide which, the sound is too fragmentary. All I can make out, very faintly, is: "Yes, yes, oh yes..."

Nothing more from this point on, just a liquid gurgle repeated six times over. Was that a muffled cry? A little sob? Nothing now but breathing, the superimposed breathing of six young children with different respiratory rhythms. The sound decreases in volume and intensity until, in the end, nothing more can be heard. Although the disc continues to revolve with the needle in the groove, absolute silence reigns.

ALTHOUGH CERTAIN CHARACTERS in the foregoing narrative bear the names of actual persons, they are as fictitious as those that do not.

THE INTRODUCTORY QUOTATION is taken from an entry, dated 20 April 1941, in the diaries of Joseph Goebbels.